FRAMED

Ellie Hohenstein

Copyright © 2023 by Ellie Hohenstein
www.EllieHohensteinAuthor.com
All Rights Reserved.

No part of this publication may be reproduced, stored in
or introduced into a retrieval system, or transmitted in
any form or by any means, electronic, mechanical,
printing, recording, or otherwise, without the prior
permission of the author, except for use of brief
quotations in a book review.

Please purchase only authorized electronic editions and
do not participate in, or encourage, the electronic piracy
of copyrighted materials. Your support of the author's
rights is appreciated.

For permissions contact:
EllieHohensteinAuthor@gmail.com
Cover design by GetCovers
Editing by Denver Murphy Editorial

ISBN – 979-8-9882478-0-7 (eBook), 979-8-9882478-1-4
(Paperback), 979-8-9882478-2-1 (Hardcover)

This is a work of fiction. Names, characters, places, and
incidents either are the product of the author's
imagination or are used fictitiously, and any resemblance
to actual persons, living or dead, businesses, companies,
events, or locales is entirely coincidental.

Dedication

To my husband who is my greatest supporter, to my parents who inspired my passion for books, and to my children that I hope to inspire in turn.

Chapter 1

Jake

R ed and blue flashed upon the house in the distance. The sirens had long since stopped and the crime scene team was now collecting evidence. The chief had called me in at two this morning, waking me out of a dead sleep. My T-shirt and jeans looked a bit out of place against the uniformed officers on duty tonight, but being a detective had its perks. Besides, my jacket covered the casual clothes well enough for me to look presentable, if not exactly professional. That was the best they were going to get during one of these middle-of-the-night calls.

I took in the scene as I stepped out of my car. The estate's large driveway was full of squad cruisers, but there were no ambulances or a coroner's van, so we were most likely not dealing with a murder. There were officers and crime scene technicians all over searching for evidence or

FRAMED

taking pictures for the reports. With this kind of turn-out we either had a very important missing item, or very important victims.

I spotted my partner talking to one of the techs and headed over. Junior Detective Ryan Mason was an up-and-comer within the department. I had noticed him as a uniformed officer, fresh out of the academy, and took him under my wing. He had a passion for upholding the law, was wicked smart, and technically savvy to boot. His potential was endless, if I could just get him to be a little more relaxed.

"Hey, Ryan," I said through a yawn.

He excused himself from his conversation as I approached. "Good morning, Jake! I've got you a cup of coffee in my car. We can chat while we grab it." We headed back toward the driveway. Ryan was young enough to bounce right up with only a few hours of sleep and still be peppy, no matter the hour. We had been working together long enough for him to know that I often forgot to make coffee in my early morning haze.

"What are we looking at here?" I asked, knowing that Ryan had a knack for organizing the techs and gathering preliminary information. He flitted around a crime scene like a butterfly, talking to everyone he could, and his mind was like a steel trap. By the time he left, he would practically be able to recreate the entire scene.

"Our victims, the Schwartz family, called in a robbery around midnight. Mr. Schwartz reported that a prominent piece in their art collection was missing and that someone must have broken in, but no alarm was triggered. Very little evidence has been identified so far, but they are still searching to be sure."

We had reached his car, and he paused as he reached in to grab the liquid gold that would wake me up enough to function until I could get my blood properly flowing. "I've talked with all of our people on the scene; that was the last tech I was chatting with when you got here. I'm about to head back to the station to call the security company for the camera footage and to start pulling names and putting together the bios for our case board. I've got enough to get started. Later today we should be able to go out and start conducting interviews."

I nodded, gazing around the yard, trying to decide where to start. "Alright, I'm going to take my own look around and talk to the family, find out what they saw. When I get to the station, we can compare notes and see where we need to go from there. The first officers on the scene should have taken down everything, but those initial statements aren't always the most reliable, so we'll probably be back here before the day is done."

We said our goodbyes and Ryan promised to have everything ready for me to review by the time I got to the station. I was headed back toward the house when I saw Chief Douglas raise his hand and beckon me over.

"Griffin, get over here!" the chief called out from where he was talking to an older couple and teenage boy. I walked over to the group and shook his hand.

"Mornin', Chief," I grunted out. Despite the many times it's happened in my years on the force, getting interrupted in the middle of a good night's sleep was

FRAMED

something I did not handle well. My coffee would need to kick in before I could be much more pleasant.

"This is Gerald and Joyce Schwartz, and their son, Daniel. Sometime during the night their centerpiece went missing. Mr. and Mrs. Schwartz, this is my head detective, Jake Griffin. He will be handling the investigation of your case."

Mr. Schwartz puffed himself up proudly, taking the lead. "Centerpiece? You uneducated fool..." It was an effort for me not to roll my eyes. It seemed we had one of *those* types on our hands. The kind who thought they were more important and better than everyone else. From looks alone, it was a fair bet that the couple fit that category.

Gerald was a larger man, his body shape implying he enjoyed the finer things in life, but not a good exercise routine. His curly, light brown hair was mussed from sleep, or possibly from yanking on it in frustration or panic. Joyce was the opposite, an extremely thin woman with straight, blonde hair, pulled into a bun so tight it was straining the skin on her face. Her expression was a stern, no-nonsense frown, and the lines around her eyes and mouth indicated that was her normal look. The couple appeared to be in their mid-forties and were dressed in monogrammed pajama sets, their hair and skin beginning to show signs of aging despite their clear efforts to keep it at bay.

Their son looked to be sixteen or seventeen, hiding behind his parents with his arms crossed, looking like he would rather be anywhere but here. His T-shirt was baggy and his sweatpants hung low on his hips, possibly a normal comfy sleep attire or could just be the style he chose to wear. He resembled his mother closely, with lighter hair and an athletic body, but his father was evident in his eye and nose shape.

Mr. Schwartz continued brusquely, "It is not *just* a centerpiece! That bust is an antique sculpture worth millions. And it didn't 'go missing', it was stolen! Our idiot son forgot to set the alarm when he came in last night, leaving us susceptible to all sorts of hooligans and thieves, like the scum he calls his friends."

Daniel popped out around his parents, speaking up to defend himself. "Dad, stop. I told you I set the alarm when I got in. I don't know how this happened, I always—"

"Hush, Daniel!" Mrs. Schwartz shoved her son back behind them, dismissing him. "You'll be lucky if we don't move you out to the pool house, so this kind of thing doesn't happen again. It's bad enough that you come home at ungodly hours after doing who knows what all night," his mother scolded. Daniel brushed her off and stormed back to the house mumbling to himself.

"As I was saying," Mr. Schwartz continued, recomposing himself after his son's outburst, "my wife and I went to bed around ten, and everything was as it should be. We don't set the alarm when we retire since Daniel is never home by that time. When he comes in, he is supposed to set the alarm. When we went upstairs, the bust was on the table in the foyer, where we proudly display it.

"I woke up around twelve-thirty, and something felt off. I tossed and turned but I just couldn't shake the feeling that something was wrong. So, I went downstairs

FRAMED

to get a glass of water. When I got to the bottom of the stairs the bust was gone! I checked the alarm, and it was not active. I immediately called the police. Now then, the chief has assured me that you're the best detective he has, and we absolutely won't settle for anything less. You *must* recover our sculpture."

The nerve of this guy, I swear… We were obviously going to do everything we could, but his attitude rubbed me the wrong way. The upper echelon of our town was always like this, treating everyone like they worked for them and expecting everything in life to go their way. They were most likely more upset about the act of the theft and the interruption to their perfect life than the actual loss of the bust.

I channeled my most gentlemanly voice, knowing these folks responded best when you sounded posh and educated, like them. "Well, we will certainly do our best to recover the bust, Mr. Schwartz. I know you gave a statement to other officers, but can you please tell me if there is a place where we can review security cameras on site?"

"No, the security company manages the cameras, and if we want copies of the footage then we have to contact them. They have a call center during off hours in case alarms are triggered, but the people with access to the footage won't be in until their office opens in the morning." It didn't sound like Gerald even called them. Whether the alarm was set or not, contacting the security company would have been my first step if I had been robbed.

ELLIE HOHENSTEIN

"And what about the alarm codes? Did you provide the officers with a list of people who might know them?"

"There was no need for a list, it is only our family who have codes, no staff. We each have a unique code that is exclusively known to us. I don't know my wife's code, and she doesn't know mine. Neither of us know Daniel's either. I disable the alarm every morning before the staff arrives."

"And is your son forgetting to set the alarm a normal occurrence?"

"Well, no. I don't think he's actually forgotten before..." Gerald looked a bit sheepish admitting that, despite his vehemence that his son was guilty this time, it was replaced quickly by his anger. "But of course, the first time he does is when something happens."

"Thank you, Mr. Schwartz. If you all will pardon me, I'm going to go check in with the team and take a look at the scene. I promise, we will go over everything with a fine-toothed comb to ensure we don't have to disrupt your schedule any more than absolutely necessary."

I looked to the chief, giving him a chance to stop me if I needed to rub elbows with the victims some more, but he simply nodded and turned back toward the family. He was better at schmoozing than I was, used to it after so many years of fundraising events. I didn't mind interacting with people, but I had a hard time keeping my cool with people who acted like they were better than me.

I stepped away and walked across the perfectly manicured lawn into the house. The estate featured a three-story mansion, made of gray bricks with stone accents. The driveway looped around the front with a

FRAMED

shoot-off on the right toward the three-car garage. The front entryway had a large, covered porch supporting a widow's walk above the front door. Inside, the foyer was wide and open. Polished white tiles lined the floor and a curved staircase sat against the far wall leading up to a second-floor balcony. The stairs, railing, and balusters were all made of a rich solid wood. A glistening crystal chandelier hung down and lit the room.

The forensics team was scattered around, taking pictures of everything from the lock on the door to the alarm system keypad on the wall beside the base of the staircase. In the middle of the foyer sat a mahogany table that I assume was previously used to feature the bust.

I spoke quickly with the forensics lead, but it looked like they had come up short. No physical evidence and no sign of a break-in, which supported the theory that the kid had possibly forgotten to lock the door and set the alarm. According to him, there didn't seem to be much evidence to go on at this point, but he was hopeful that everything would turn out to paint a good picture once we were able to look at everything together.

For the next two hours I walked around the rest of the main floor, taking in the layout of the house, looking for any missed evidence, and checking the other possible entrances. Nothing looked amiss, but I found it interesting that there did not appear to be any staff on site. The pool house in the distance behind the house was dark, telling me that no one lived out there, at least not full time.

Deciding I had gotten as much from the scene as I could at this point, I headed back to the station to see what my partner had uncovered.

ELLIE HOHENSTEIN

The sun was starting to rise as I made my way into town. Willow Springs was a medium-sized city, sporting a few high-rises in the growing business district, while maintaining a bit of small-town charm with some local mom-and-pop shops and preserved historic buildings. The police station was strategically placed next to the courthouse in the town center, but we didn't have much space for records and evidence storage on-site, so we also had a few remote offices around the city.

Thanks to some charitable donations from a few of the city's elite, the station was a gorgeous building, with two stories above ground and a basement below. The front featured tall marble pillars framing the glossy oak double doors. The building itself was made of bricks of the deepest red that were pressure-washed at least monthly to keep the appearance pristine. The waiting area inside the station was similarly opulent with a two-story foyer, wooden benches with velvet cushions for seating, and beautiful artwork on the walls.

One would think that with all the money spent on decor, we would have a decent operating budget. However, the city's focus when allocating funds seemed to be more on *looking* good rather than *doing* good. Once you stepped on the other side of that security door, the posh benches and artwork were traded for folding chairs, broken down desks, cubicle walls, and rows upon rows of filing cabinets.

I entered through the back door, accessible only from the officer parking deck. This door came out in the basement, which contained a few holding cells, a

FRAMED

processing area, and evidence storage. There were stairs and an elevator to access the rest of the building.

The main floor was mostly a large open area for the uniformed officers, many of whom shared a desk between the different shifts. There were a few interrogation rooms, and it also contained the break room, where I stopped to top off my coffee before continuing up. The second floor held the offices for the chief and detectives, as well as some conference rooms.

As partners, I shared an office with Ryan. The room was sized to accommodate our two desks, a few file cabinets, and the two white boards we used to display pertinent information about our active cases. We also had a few recreational items, such as a small basketball hoop above our trash can and a mini fridge to hold energy drinks, bottled waters, and snacks.

Ryan was pinning items up on the case boards when I walked in. I shrugged off my jacket as I greeted him, grabbed a power bar, and settled down into my chair. On the board he had posted a printed picture of the bust that was stolen, a few photos from the scene, and headshots of the Schwartz family along with a few personal details and known associates. He had also written out the names and occupations of a handful of people to be interviewed so we could cross them off as we went.

"You've sure been busy," I laughed. Ryan was an over-achiever, but I loved the organization he brought to the team. I was more of a fly-by-the-seat-of-my-pants kind of guy, so we balanced each other out well.

Ryan had been my partner for around three years now, having been promoted to detective after only a few years in uniform, just missing my record for youngest detective by a few short months. He was twenty-five and had a passion for the law that was almost unparalleled around here. He held himself to a rigorous standard, keeping neat and orderly in both his appearance and his workspace.

His black hair was buzzed short and his face was kept clean-shaven, making him look closer to eighteen than his actual age. His brown eyes seemed to peer into your soul, trying to pull out all of your wrongdoings so he could deliver justice. He had a similar body style to me, an athletic build, but with more muscle mass. I kept my body toned with a little muscle built in, but Ryan more closely fit a "shredded" description thanks to his strict diet and copious amount of time spent at the gym in his off hours.

Where I tended to dress down for work, maintaining a casual appearance to blend into a crowd at a moment's notice, Ryan was always wearing at least a dress shirt and tie, slacks, and fine dress shoes, and often preferred a full suit when it wasn't too hot out. I figured part of it was personality, but another part might be him feeling some pressure to prove himself.

"There wasn't much evidence, so it didn't take long to put all that up. I haven't been able to get in touch with anyone at the security company who can actually provide me with the footage or alarm records, so I was able to focus my time on the family. I'm hoping you can see something in their bios to give us a better direction."

That had been my assessment of the scene as well— not much physical evidence to go on. The bulk of our investigation would be hearsay. Ryan's experience with the security company lined up with what Schwartz had

FRAMED

mentioned, as well. Not the best way to start an investigation, but usually the statements pointed us in the general direction of where to find the physical evidence.

"Alright then, let's jump right in. Tell me about our victims," I started.

Ryan stood up straight, preparing to launch into what I called *report-mode*. He was almost robotic in citing all the details—the kid had an exceptionally impressive memory.

"Okay, first up we have Mr. Gerald Schwartz, Owner and CEO of Schwartz and Son, a local antiquities dealer."

Antiquities, that was ironic considering what was stolen.

"His kid is a little young to be involved in the family business. He's what, sixteen? Seventeen?" Their relationship seemed strained, not at all conducive to working well together at the office. At best, the kid seemed to try to stay under his parent's radar.

Ryan confirmed my suspicion. "No, Gerald is actually the son referenced; he inherited the company when his father passed away about five years ago."

"Five years, you say?" I started to get excited. "And an antiquities dealer?"

For the last five years our town had been experiencing a string of thefts that left virtually no physical evidence. We had come up on dead ends in all cases, without any obvious links between the different victims, the types of items taken, and their levels of value. The lack of evidence was really the only common thread between the cases.

However, we had been playing with the idea of a wide-spread insurance fraud ring, where the "victims" were taking their own property and having it fenced—sold in

12

an underground, illegal market—then collecting the insurance payouts. There were a few outliers where the items were not insured, but most had policies. Theoretically, the outliers could be unrelated. The only question was how they were making contact with the fences, the middle-men selling their items. As an antiquities dealer, Schwartz could be the leader of the whole operation who just got sloppy or cocky. This case could be the luckiest break for us.

Ryan shook his head. "I know what you're thinking... From a quick glance at the books everything looks clean, but I've requested permission for a forensic accountant. At the very least, it's worth looking into Schwartz's employees over the last few years to see if there are any connections."

Damn, for a fleeting moment it had seemed so promising. A struggling business would have been the perfect motivation for Schwartz to panic, fence his own items, and inadvertently tip us off. Unfortunately, it didn't look like it would be that easy.

"Smart plan." I sighed. "Best to follow all theories. Alright, let's move on to Mrs. Schwartz."

"Right, not much to tell here. Joyce Schwartz is mostly your typical housewife, but she also works loosely with the company, liaising between them and some of the local charitable foundations. Her main associates are other housewives and the local upper class, but only one or two out of her large circle have been impacted by recent thefts. There's none with a close enough association to be a trusted confidant in terms of financial weakness, much less to spur setting up some kind of scam."

FRAMED

That was no surprise. In those groups, the only thing worse than not having any money was *appearing* like you didn't have money. Every move was calculated. considering how it would look to others, so there would have to be either no connection or a very close friendship for someone in those circles to be willing to admit they were having any kind of issues, financial or otherwise.

"And how about the son? The parents seemed quite sure he didn't set the alarm. He insisted that he did, but he could have been just trying to cover up his mistake."

Ryan grabbed a file off his desk and handed it to me. I opened it up and saw a rap sheet for Daniel. Nothing major yet, just some petty theft, breaking and entering, and he had been spoken with more than once on suspicion of other crimes. No convictions had stuck, so my guess was his parents had paid off a lot of folks to keep him out of juvie—likely out of the papers as well.

On the next page was a list of known associates. There were many names I recognized as being low-level members of one of the local gangs. It looked like his parents weren't too far off base in calling his friends "hooligans". The theory that he had taken the bust, or that one of his friends had, might hold water after all.

"It's hard to say," Ryan began. He ran his hand through his short hair, a nervous tick he did when things weren't adding up in his head. "On paper it definitely looks bad. But Daniel has been loosely involved in the gang's activities for a while now, and everything so far has been low-dollar stuff. It doesn't make sense to jump up to such a high-profile piece, and from his own home no less. It could have been acting out against his parents, but that doesn't feel quite right either.

"If he did do this, take the bust and give it to the gang, where would they even have the connections to sell it? They can't pawn it for fast cash, and the people he's been seen with are all the bottom rung in the hierarchy.

"That's the gang's MO—target the rich kids, milk them dry, and either leave them to deal with Mommy and Daddy or in jail. There is always an exit strategy since these rich kids don't make good gang-bangers. This level of theft just doesn't make sense."

I leaned back in my chair, pondering for a few moments. "Hmm… Let's think through Daniel's motive. When I spoke to the family, it seemed like the parents were very dismissive of Daniel. This rap sheet speaks to me as a kid crying for help, or trying to get his parent's attention. He might have taken the bust to take those antics to the next level."

I knew from personal experience that it wouldn't work, wouldn't end well. My parents had struggled with addiction, choosing drugs over me time and time again. As a young child, I'd taken a similar route to try and make them care, but it never worked. Getting away from them was the best thing I'd ever done.

"I want to be the one to interview Daniel again," I continued. "Maybe I can get through to him before it's too late. Even convince him to give the bust back if he did take it. Did the team do a thorough sweep of the house, or did they focus on just the main level?"

Ryan reviewed his notes. "When I left, the focus was on the main level, but I think some of the officers walked

FRAMED

through the rest of the house just taking a quick look for the bust. I assume Mr. and Mrs. Schwartz would have searched Daniel's room before calling the police, if they think it's his fault. It would be pretty embarrassing for them if they called the police out there and it was in his room the whole time."

I nodded, but was unsure whether they would have even known where to look. "I'll take a look when I go talk to him, to be safe. The cleaning staff might be the better ones to ask about hiding places. We also need that camera footage to make sure he didn't hand it off to someone waiting outside, along with looking for any other suspects. But aside from attention-seeking, why would he take the bust? Do you think it was for the money?"

Ryan shuffled through a few papers on his desk and handed me a financial report. "These are Daniel's accounts," he said. "He has a trust fund set up from his grandfather that should last most, if not all, of his life, but he doesn't get access to that until he turns twenty-five. He's also got a lot of stocks and other liquid assets that he can use now, though, so I don't think it would be financially motivated if he did this."

I shook my head. "I don't believe so either. If it was just about the money, he could have taken any number of items that probably wouldn't have been noticed. No, this piece was taken to make a statement. It was taken *because* it was high-profile. It was the pride and joy of the Schwartz's collection, known to everyone who entered the house. Who else might have felt the need to make that statement?"

16

We were silent for a few moments, considering. The house was far enough away from other properties, and the city in general, that there was no chance this was a random break-in. They had been targeted. This piece was carefully selected, which begged the question of which target came first? The item or its owners?

My gut was telling me it wasn't the kid, and while I was relieved that Ryan and I were on the same page, we still had to follow the evidence trail before we could officially cross Daniel off the suspect list.

We discussed the staff members that might have had access and made a plan of who we needed to interview. Ryan prepared a folder for me with all the bios, as well as information on a few of the gang members that Daniel had been seen or arrested with.

I checked my watch. The last of the officers had been doing a final pass of the Schwartz house when I left, so they should have released the scene by now. I was hopeful that the family would continue their day like nothing had happened, so I could get a chance to speak with Daniel and the staff without Mr. and Mrs. Schwartz there to influence the interviews.

"While you're out, I'm going to try to contact the security company again, as well as do some more digging into Schwartz and Son. I'll see if I can find anything from a high-level, to point the forensic accountant at first. I want to make the most out of his time. Just call if there's anything you need."

Chapter 2

Jake

The drive back out to the Schwartz house was pleasant in the light of day. On my way, I tried to look for spots that could either be used to hide a vehicle or be a good pick-up location for a getaway car.

Nothing jumped out at me, but the thief could have easily taken some kind of motorcycle and still been able to transport the bust. All signs so far pointed to this being a targeted theft, not a random break-in with no clue what kind of loot they might find. A motorcycle could have easily been hidden anywhere in the woods and not leave much of a trace.

I pulled into the long drive and looked around the grounds. Trees started around fifteen feet back from the side of the driveway, thick enough to provide cover to someone hiding, especially during the dark of the night. I walked over to take a look at the woods.

There were clear signs of a disturbance in the trees, but I couldn't tell if it was from our crime scene techs, the thief, or possibly just the wildlife living there. We were far enough removed from the city that I wouldn't be surprised to find deer wandering around.

I could hear the faint buzz of a trimmer in the distance, telling me that the gardener was here this morning. We had given the family the green light to continue business as usual around the property, having collected all the evidence we anticipated earlier. I followed the sounds and waved to the gardener once I spotted him, attempting to get his attention over the noise of his equipment.

"Good mornin', may I help you?" his thick southern accent trawled.

"Hi there, I'm Detective Jake Griffin." I mimicked his tones, an old trick I had picked up over the years to make people more cooperative. "Do you mind terribly if I borrow you for just a few minutes, sir?"

"Sure, detective. Let me put this down and we can sit, if it's not too much of a bother." The gardener appeared to be around fifty to sixty years old, with a deep tan thanks to spending his days outdoors, but was in fantastic shape for his age.

Looking around, it appeared he was a master of his craft; the hedges and bushes were perfectly shaped and there were even a few topiaries within the grounds. There was a large garden to the rear of the house, with a table and chairs set up next to a fountain in a clearing. Flowers of all types bloomed despite it being early spring, and I would bet that the gardener had organized the space so that something was in bloom all year long.

FRAMED

I followed him to the table and we sat. He leaned back in his chair, happy to take a break, and I leaned forward to rest my arms on the table.

"Whew, I sure am glad you stopped by! Gave me the perfect excuse to take myself a break," the gardener said, laughing. "The name's Leroy. Now what can I do for you, detective?"

"Nice to meet you, Leroy. I'm not sure how much you've heard but there was a break-in here last night. A very expensive sculpture was taken, and we're looking for any information you might have to point us in the right direction. Have you seen anything out of the ordinary lately?"

He thought for a moment, fingers stroking his chin. "Not off'n the top of my head. I'm not allowed inside the main house, so I've never even seen the sculpture to know what to look for. Mrs. Finch would have my hide if I tracked dirt in there. She brings me lunch or drinks out to the covered patio when it's time for my break. Gotta' love a woman who takes pride in her work, though.

"I wouldn't say it's out of the ordinary, per se, but that youngin' Daniel's been runnin' with an awful rough crowd lately. All covered in tattoos and piercings, pants sagging down to their ankles. Might've even seen a gun or two, but that could've been my old eyes playin' tricks on me. Not sure what them boys would be doin' with some fancy sculpture though."

I agreed, doubtful that the gang would have the connections to fence such a prominent piece.

"And what do you think about the Schwartzes? Are they good to work for? Any financial issues like your paychecks bouncing?"

"Naw, none of that." He waved off the idea. "They pay better than most, and that Mrs. Schwartz knows what she wants out of her garden, I'll give her that. Some folks think they know what they want, or don't give clear directions, and by the time you get the flowers all grown they're changin' it up all over again. The Schwartzes are strict, but they treat the staff all fine."

"And what about their son? Do they treat him fine as well?"

Leroy frowned at my question, shaking his head slightly. "Now, that's not for me to say. I don't see much, most o' my work is done in the mornin' before the boy usually gets up. But sometimes I see Mrs. Schwartz scolding him when he's out by the pool. Ain't much more than a momma tryin'a set her boy right though, if you ask me."

"Thanks so much, Leroy. You've been a big help."

"Anytime, detective."

I pulled out my business card and handed it over to him. "If you think of anything else, don't hesitate to call."

"Will-do, sir."

I excused myself and walked back around to the front of the house. I wasn't quite sure what to make of the conversation with Leroy. He definitely sounded like he thought Daniel could have done it, but like me he didn't seem to have a clear understanding of how or why.

I approached the front door and rang the bell. There were a few cars in the driveway, but I was hoping I was lucky enough that Mr. and Mrs. Schwartz would be out, and I'd be able to get some honest answers from their staff. While lying during the course of an investigation was a crime, some folks held back anything negative when their bosses were around. And unfortunately, that's usually the type of stuff we need to hear to solve the crimes.

My luck held true when a tall, thin woman dressed in simple, professional attire, answered the door. I introduced myself and asked if I could come in.

"Oh of course, detective! Please, right this way." She led me through the foyer, under the stairs and to the sitting room. "I'm Melanie Finch, the house manager. Please, have a seat! Can I get you a glass of water, or a light snack?"

"That won't be necessary but thank you. I was hoping to be able to chat with a few of the staff members today, and if Daniel is home, I would like to check in with him as well."

She bristled as I mentioned Daniel. "That boy probably isn't even awake yet," she said angrily, then she appeared to soften and continued, "but I do suppose he had a late night. Let's get you in with some of the staff first, then we'll see if we can get Daniel up. Who would you like to speak with?"

"I've got you on my list as well as the chef. I've already talked with Leroy outside. But if there's anyone else who you think might have seen something, or who you think I should talk to, I'm happy to be here as long as it takes to get to the bottom of this."

Melanie checked her watch then shook her head. "Ben's the chef, I think he's starting to get things pulled together for lunch, but there's still some time before he needs to start cooking, so he should have time to talk. I've got time now, then I'll send in a few of the maids to give their statements. Not sure how much help we'll all be, but we will do what we can."

"I appreciate you taking the time." I said as we settled down on the couch. "Now, do you or any of the staff live on the grounds? It's a mighty big house for just the Schwartz family."

"No, none of the staff are permitted quarters in the manor. The Schwartzes like their privacy and, in fact, most of the staff are gone by the time Mr. Schwartz gets home. So, I'm afraid none of us will be able to shed any light on what actually happened during the night. I am usually the last to leave, and nothing seemed out of the ordinary when I left yesterday."

"That's alright, any information you can give me would really help. How would you describe the interactions between the members of the Schwartz family?"

"Oh, they're cordial enough when we're around. Daniel's got a bit of a mouth on him though—all that teen angst and rebellion." Her disapproval was clear in her tone. "It's a wonder Mr. Schwartz hasn't kicked him out or cut him off yet with all the trouble he's been getting into. Mr. and Mrs. Schwartz seem happy enough, they both thrive on their status and wealth, so not much to complain about from either of them.

"Mrs. Schwartz goes out a lot, she's involved in many of the local charities. They try to give back to the

FRAMED

community. Although their donations haven't been as big in the last few years…"

"And why is that?"

"Oh… Well…" She twisted her hands, her discomfort evident as she appeared torn between her duty to her employer and her need to comply with my questions. "My guess is they've got their funds too tied up in giving *other* types of donations… covering up for Daniel's shenanigans."

Melanie definitely had a biased opinion against Daniel, but I still needed to be sure if she thought he had done this. "And do you believe Daniel is responsible for this theft? Do you think he took the sculpture?"

She spoke with more confidence now, having no problem talking down about Daniel. "Without a doubt. I'd be willing to wager that he handed it off to one of his buddies. Who else would have been able to get in here so easily? Check the security cameras, I'm sure you'll see something."

"One last question for you, if you don't mind, Mrs. Finch. Do you know if anyone has been into Daniel's room to search for the sculpture? I'm sure the crime scene team took some pictures, but I doubt they'd know precisely where to look, not in the same way your staff might."

"Hmm, I don't believe anyone has been in to clean today, but there aren't many places in that room where he could hide something that size. It wouldn't exactly fit under the bed. No, I doubt it would be in his room if they didn't see it when taking pictures. He must have given it to someone already."

I thanked her for her time and handed her my card. She excused herself to grab a few of the maids and sent them my way. The ladies I spoke with were very polite but didn't have much else to contribute. They seemed to mirror the thoughts of their boss with regards to Daniel; he and his friends often made lewd remarks toward them.

Everyone seemed to think Daniel was trouble, but no one could give a credible theory on how he would have pulled off this theft, especially considering the short turnaround between his parents going to bed and when the bust was discovered as missing. Short of someone following him home for the handoff, which the security footage would show if that was the case, there just wasn't anywhere to hide it.

His sleeping in also contributed to my theory that he was innocent. If he had taken the sculpture, he would be rushing to get it out of the house as quickly as possible, as soon as the police had gone, and his parents had left for work.

While lunch was served to the household, I chatted with Ben, the chef. He mirrored the praise of what a good employer the Schwartz family was, but he was one of the few members of the staff who remained on site when all the family members were home. He might not join them at the dining room table, but sound carried through to the kitchen during their meals.

"If you want my honest opinion," Ben started, "Mr. Schwartz has always been excessively hard on Daniel." I perked up. This was the first person to show any sympathy for the boy. "I've been working for the family for years, so I've watched that kid grow up, and he always seemed

FRAMED

like he had such a bright future. But Mr. Schwartz beat him down over and over again. Nothing was ever good enough. If Daniel got an A, why wasn't it an A Plus? How could Daniel ever expect to take over the family business unless he was exemplary in all things, he'd say.

"Over time the A's turned to B's, then C's, and lately Daniel has seemed to give up trying to win his father's approval. He's started to get angry and act out. It's a rare night when Daniel is home for dinner, and when he is there's always some verbal sparring going on. It's gotten to the point where he either stays away most nights or he gets home early enough to snag food from me before his parents get home, taking it up to his room to eat. After the last meal they all had together, I'm surprised Daniel's still under this roof."

"What happened at the last meal?" I practically held my breath in anticipation, not wanting to run the risk that Ben might clam up.

"Mr. Schwartz basically drew a line in the sand. Said his boy would never amount to anything, wish they'd never had him, so on. Outright said he would never pass on the business to Daniel, that he'd rather sell it off than watch his son 'bring ruin to it like everything else in his life'. Poor kid ran out of the room so fast, I couldn't tell whether he was more hurt or angry. Bit of both, I reckon."

I felt the impact of those words as keenly then as Daniel must have that night. I'd had similar words said to me throughout my childhood, minus the family business part of course, mainly when my parents were drunk or coming down off a high. It hurt more than words could describe to hear things like that from your parents, the ones who brought you into this world. The ones who were supposed to love you unconditionally. And even all these years later, with my parents long gone, the pain remained.

I thanked Ben for his candor and assured him that nothing he said would be reported back to the Schwartz family unless it was absolutely critical to the case. I didn't think we'd need it, but it could speak to the motive for Daniel to commit this crime.

Finally, it was time for the interview I'd been the most excited about, but also dreading. If Daniel did this, I'd have to completely re-evaluate my gut. We now had motive of sorts, along with means and opportunity, but there were still some things that just didn't add up.

One of the maids led me up to Daniel's room, and I knocked on the door. He stared for a moment after he opened up, trying to place who I was. It seemed to click, since he opened the door further and said "I wondered when you'd show up. Are you here to arrest me?"

I paused, confused. Was he confessing? "Did you do something I should be arresting you for?"

He looked up, hopeful. "Well then, why are you here?"

"I figured we could talk. It sounded like you had something to say this morning, but we didn't get a chance to hear it."

His face sagged with relief. I could tell this kid was scared and trying so hard to put on a tough front, sure that he wouldn't be heard and that we would just take other people's opinions of him without giving him a chance to tell his side of the story.

"I really did set the alarm last night," he started, jumping right in. "I don't know how it got turned off, I swear. I always set the alarm as soon as I get home. Then I grabbed a drink from the fridge, came upstairs, and started playing video games. I didn't hear or see anything. I had my headphones on, and I keep my curtains closed all the time so I can sleep in, plus they block the glare on the TV.

"When Dad woke up and saw his stupid bust missing, he stormed up here and banged on the door. I didn't even hear that over the sound of my game, so he barged in and started screaming at me. I could barely understand him and didn't know what was going on until I went downstairs and saw police showing up to take pictures in the foyer."

"Daniel, why do you think your parents assumed you didn't set the alarm? Is it often disarmed when they wake up?"

He shook his head vigorously. "No, never. I've got no idea why they thought I forgot, I guess they're just so used to blaming me for everything. Though, I guess I have been messing up a lot lately." He hung his head in shame. "Maybe this is my fault, and I made us a target somehow?"

I knew I shouldn't divulge critical details of our investigation, especially to a suspect, but I figured I'd be safe with something he could find out on his own if he really tried.

"I doubt it, Daniel. From the looks of it we're leaning toward either an inside job or a real pro. The majority of crooks leave heaps of evidence behind, but your house was spotless. You can rest easy knowing it wasn't your fault."

ELLIE HOHENSTEIN

It was definitely too early to assure him of that, but I didn't seem to be able to help it. I saw so much of myself in this kid who had lost his way, and I wanted to show him it got better.

"I usually volunteer at the youth center on Tuesdays and Thursdays, if you ever want to show me your gaming skills. And if you need to talk—about the case or really anything at all—I'm just a phone call away. Don't let all my swagger and awesomeness fool you," I joked. "I was a lot like you at your age. There's still time to turn it around."

I handed him my card and headed back toward the door. I paused at the frame and took a quick look around the room. Definitely no spots in here to hide that sculpture. I let out a sigh of relief. "I mean it kid, you ever need anything, you call me."

He nodded to me, a thoughtful look on his face, then turned away to play his game.

I headed back out to my car, stopping in the office on my way out to thank Mrs. Finch for her time and accommodation. I left a small stack of my business cards in case any other staff members had information they wanted to share.

Since it was almost lunchtime, I decided to stop in at a little café on my way back to the station. It was mostly a coffee house, but they served some small meals as well.

The ding of the bell on the door was drowned out by the low hum of chatter when I arrived at the café. Rather than a traditional dining room, the shop was laid out with couches and chairs grouped together with small tables, creating a much more casual, relaxing feel. Whenever I had a case that I was stumped on, I would pack up my files and come here to work, the change in scenery and the caffeine helping to stimulate my thought processes.

I was a little early for the lunch rush, so by the time I had gotten my drink and placed my order, there were a number of seats open—including my favorite spot in the corner.

The armchair was backed into the corner, with windows extending out on either side. There was a low table in front shared with an adjoining couch. There were a couple of people seated on the other end of the sofa and adjacent chairs, but they were far enough away to not be able to see what I was working on. This spot allowed me to observe the patrons, the passersby on the street, and the workers, all without compromising the security of my classified case information.

I had cracked many cases in this very chair. I could learn so much about how people thought, how they acted, how they were motivated, just by watching the patrons of the shop. Most of the baristas and cashiers knew me by name, but not what I did for a living. I found that people changed how they acted when they knew you could arrest them. It helped that I rarely dressed like a cop, but I actively tried to keep my occupation a secret in my personal life.

It was like people thought I would be looking for an excuse to dig up their past crimes, their secrets, and make them pay.

All I wanted was good food and coffee, and maybe someone to share it with.

I draped my jacket over the back of the chair and settled in with the file Ryan had given me. Hopefully, I'd be able to come up with a viable alternative suspect or at least a way to clear Daniel of suspicion. My food arrived, and while I ate, I flipped through the papers. I couldn't shake the feeling that we were headed in the wrong direction investigating Daniel. That we were going to have to waste time checking off boxes to rule out what didn't happen before we could get a chance to figure out what did.

Daniel absolutely had access, and while he might have expected to have more time to stash or get rid of the bust, it would have only been a few more hours before his father woke up and discovered it missing. I really needed to check in with Ryan to see if he had gotten a chance to examine the video surveillance to make sure Danie; had not handed off the bust to someone waiting outside.

But I just couldn't lock onto the theory that Daniel had done this. I had a gut feeling that there was more to this, and my gut was usually right.

I started making some notes, highlighting a few irregular employees for Ryan to speak with. He should have more information on the Schwartz and Son staff once I returned to the station, and I felt confident that we would find something there. Hopefully we would uncover a connection to all the robberies in our chain of cold-cases, but I'd be happy just solving this one.

We could question the gang kids together, my way of helping Ryan build out his informant network. For my own, I made a list of people to check in with about the

FRAMED

bust, as well as get some outside opinions of Daniel and his involvement in the gang.

Satisfied with my plan so far, I ordered one last cup of coffee, giving myself a few more minutes to look over everything before packing up and returning to the station to review the plan with Ryan.

I generally tuned out the sound of the bell on the door, lost in my work, but for some reason when the chime rang out this time, I looked up.

And then she walked in.

Chapter 3

Alexis

There was a slight chill in the air as I walked down Main Street toward my favorite cafe. I probably should have worn a jacket, but I always felt so *alive* after a heist. Even half a day later, my blood was thrumming through my veins, and I couldn't get rid of the smile on my face.

The last few hours at the office had breezed by. I generally tried to keep my mornings light after pulling a job, on the off chance I managed to get some sleep. I'd only had one session, and I decided to take a long lunch break and walk across town to my favorite place to celebrate the successful heist.

As I walked, I replayed last night in my mind. The job had gone flawlessly. The Schwartz family had been on my list of targets for years after hearing Daniel talk about how his parents disregarded him and treated him like he was

FRAMED

just an ornament to bring out at parties, pretending to be a happy family.

I tried to be patient. There were other clients in worse situations, but a few weeks ago Daniel's father had told him he would never be good enough to take over the family business. His father would rather sell off their family's legacy than pass it down to his inept hands. As if any of that was Daniel's fault, and not his father's own failings as a parent. These high-class people believed they could substitute parenting with an endless stream of nannies and tutors, and the children would still love them and turn out fine. Daniel was hurting for a real role model and, knowing he would never get that at home, he found one somewhere else. Only this "role model" would lead him straight to jail, or worse.

I had been seeing Daniel as a patient since he was a young teen acting out by breaking things around the house, and I'd thought we had been making real progress until he met "J-Dog", the low-level recruiter of one of the local gangs. The thug had done his job well, feeding Daniel false promises and making him feel seen and valued, telling him all the things I tried to get the Schwartz family to say and actually mean. J-Dog's involvement led to Daniel committing a string of small crimes, but when his parents got involved and started paying people off, I began to wonder how long it would be before the rebellion escalated and Daniel ended up hurt.

So, I planned my heist.

Daniel had mentioned the bust in a session around six months ago when his parents acquired the piece. His father had bought the sculpture through their antiquities business, taking a loss to get the bust in his personal collection for well below market value. I wondered if the police would have something to say about that. I'm sure Mr. Schwartz didn't expect a theft to reveal his indiscretion. Daniel had mentioned how creepy the bust was, displayed in the foyer so when you walk in the door it's staring right at you.

I tried to keep the kids out of my planning, at most getting some insight on what would make the biggest impact for the parents to lose. I took care to not ask Daniel any more about the sculpture, driving his focus elsewhere during our sessions.

Unfortunately, Daniel had also been my way in. I had spent a few nights watching him from a distance and learning his habits, so I knew he regularly came home late in the evening. For a troublemaking teen, he kept a fairly consistent schedule, heading home around eleven each night.

My assistant, Jess, had hacked into the security company a few weeks before and repositioned the cameras to leave enough of a blind spot for me to sneak up to the house from the surrounding woods. I waited for Daniel to get home, snuck in the garage when he opened the door, and waited for him to get out of sight before silently following into the house.

After I heard him walk up the stairs, I waited another five minutes before disarming the alarm with the code Jess had uncovered. She could probably have hacked back into the security company to disarm it remotely, but that would require for me to tell her the moment I was ready to enter the house, and we never risked communication devices on

FRAMED

my jobs. We also wanted to make sure that when they reviewed the alarm, it was shown that it was manually disarmed. Each family member had their own unique code, and I'd smiled as I entered the numbers that I knew would make Daniel's father see red.

I had snagged the bust quickly and headed back out through the garage, clicking the lock into place behind me as I pulled the door closed. My car was parked about a mile down the road in a small gap in the trees. Before I'd pulled away, I made sure to rustle the leaves up and shift the dirt back around to disguise any potential tracks. One final review had me satisfied that no one would look twice at the spot.

The bust I had taken was now locked away at my drop point, waiting for my fence to pick it up. The buyer had already paid, but I had an agreement worked out with the fence to hold my payment for a few weeks until the heat died down, just as a precaution. The profits from the sale would be funneled back into my practice slowly, made to look legitimate through sessions that were actually pro bono. I was fortunate that I was one of the top psychiatrists in the city and catered specifically to the upper class with "troubled" kids. I could charge an obscene amount for each session and the parents would happily pay it, if only for the status of having me as the doctor if word ever got out that their child had to see one in the first place.

The bell on the door sounded my arrival at the café. I paused just inside the doorway to get my bearings and to breathe in the smell of roasting coffee and sandwiches. I felt a slight prickle on my neck, the awareness of having eyes on me carefully cultivated through years of training to be invisible. I scanned the crowd until my gaze caught on a man sitting in one of my favorite fluffy chairs, tucked away in the corner by the window. He had his arms on his knees while he bent over a stack of papers, appearing to be working on something.

He was casually dressed in a plain black T-shirt and jeans, his brown hair was tousled in a just-rolled-out-of-bed look. He was a little scruffy and had slight bags under his eyes, like he had been woken *far* earlier than he wanted to be. The two empty cups of coffee on the table in front of him along with the third in his hand made my hunch likely. Either that or he really liked coffee.

But his green eyes were locked on mine, and for a moment I couldn't look away. His mouth was slightly opened in a stunned expression, almost like my appearance had taken his breath away. No, that thought was clearly the high of last night talking; assuming that he was so captivated by me would be a whole new level of arrogance. I needed to calm down. Still, I couldn't help but follow this pull in my gut and have a little fun. I smirked at him then turned to approach the counter to place my order.

The cashier was chipper as I walked up, "Good morning! Welcome to Coff-ay All-Day, what can I get for you?"

"One latte please," I replied. I wasn't particularly hungry yet, so I could wait and grab food before I left. This way, I'd also be able to grab something for my assistant as a surprise for her.

FRAMED

I paid for my coffee and stepped to the side, being careful not to look over at him while waiting for my drink to be made. I didn't want him to think I was creepy, staring him down before I approached. I took my phone out to double-check the time and my calendar. I had an hour and a half before my next session. It was a bit of a walk to return to the office from here, but I could stay a while and still have time to eat and prepare for the session.

When my order was up, I put my phone back in my purse. The wait had allowed a little nervousness to sneak in, some innate fear of rejection, but I pushed it down, put on a casual smile, and silently chanted my inner mantra to psyche myself back up. It was something I pushed all my patients to do—the first step to being able to do something is believing you can do it. Self-confidence is one of the most underrated keys to success.

With a restored bravado, I turned and walked straight to the empty spot on the couch beside his chair. He had returned to studying his stack of papers, but he looked up as I approached. He closed the folder, blocking the files from my sight and leaned back in the chair to sip his coffee. To those not paying close attention, his actions might have seemed casual, but I could tell it meant two things: I was not supposed to see what was on those pages, and he was definitely interested in having a conversation with me.

I could understand the desire for confidentiality, but I made a living out of getting people to spill their secrets, and my curiosity was instantly piqued. Would he be a tough nut to crack, or an open book?

38

"This seat taken?" I asked, indicating the empty couch spot.

"Please, help yourself," the stranger replied, inviting me to sit down. His voice was smooth and deep; I could probably listen to him talk for hours. I had a few patients that had shrill, high-pitched voices and sometimes those sessions were a pain to get through.

Up close I could see a few things I hadn't noticed before, like his chiseled jawline, and a sculpted body hugged by his shirt. I guessed he was in his early thirties, close to my age, and clearly attentive to his physical health and exercise. He had a slight tan, belying a decent amount of time spent outside rather than being stuck in an office all day. His scruff appeared predominately well-maintained; maybe he just skipped this morning's trim. His eyes were sharp with intelligence—and interest—as I sat down, as if I were a fascinating new puzzle he couldn't wait to figure out.

"I suppose the spot *next* to my favorite chair would still be acceptable since the best seat in the shop is otherwise occupied. Not only is that chair the most comfortable, but I can look at the people outside going by and still take in all that's happening here. I always find people-watching fascinating." I held my breath, waiting for him to seize the opportunity to pick up the conversation or to dismiss me and go back to perusing his files.

He met my smile with a grin of his own. "This is my favorite escape for the same reason. I'm surprised we haven't had the occasion to fight over it before today."

"I don't make it to this shop as often as I'd like. It's a bit of a 'special occasion' place for me. I have a decent

FRAMED

coffee machine at my office, so I can generally get by with that, and there are a handful of restaurants closer that I generally grab food from."

"Special occasion? And what are we celebrating today?" The way he said "we" had me tingling inside. Having someone to celebrate my victories with was something I longed for, but the secrets I had to keep made it hard to have a successful relationship. I had plenty of my own secrets, but I also kept those of my patients. It was hard to talk about your day when you couldn't give specifics about the progress patients made or the challenges they were facing, which at times felt so close to my own experiences as a child that it could be hard to keep my emotions under control.

But his words also had me thinking of all the ways I could "celebrate" a successful job. The adrenaline rush I got from stealing needed an outlet, and right now I didn't have a good one, hence the sleepless nights. The best release I got was speeding down the dark highways to my drop site in the next town over, with my loot in the trunk and music blaring.

I obviously couldn't tell him that I was celebrating stealing a multi-million-dollar sculpture from a prominent family that treated their child like trash. So, I gave the simplest answer, the ultimate feeling that I got when my whole body was thrumming with the rush of the heist. "Being alive."

It was the truth. My day-to-day life was fine, helping kids through therapy brought joy and a sense of accomplishment to my life with the hope of sparing a child from the same troubles and pains that I experienced.

But nothing made me feel more alive than the heist. The fear of potentially being caught, of doing something that you weren't supposed to do, that shouldn't even be possible, and getting away with it… that was a thrill few would get to experience.

I used to tell myself all the excuses in the book. I had to steal to eat, I needed to put myself through school, I had to buy an apartment, on and on. But I had finally decided to just own it. I *like* stealing. If I was going to do it anyway, I could at least use it as a way to put some good out into the world. I started targeting the parents of the rich clients I treated, but only the ones who truly deserved a swift kick in the ass.

I'd realized the only thing rich people valued was their money, and the art they used to flaunt it, so that's what I used to substitute the physical justice the kids deserved but would never get.

"I'll drink to that," he said with a chuckle. He held out his hand, "I'm Jake, by the way."

"Alexis. It's great to meet you, Jake." I shook his hand then settled in against the armrest. "So, what are you escaping from?"

"Huh?" He crooked his eyebrow in confusion.

"You said this place was your escape, so what are you escaping from?" It was second nature for me to push the burden of the conversation onto the other person, just like my body language was calculated to appear relaxed and casually interested. It decreased the pressure of the situation and put a client, or conversation partner, at ease. Jake clearly also had some experience interacting with people, or at least with women, leaning in and giving me

FRAMED

his full attention. His disarming smile made it easy to actually feel relaxed instead of just appearing so.

"Oh. Nothing special, just the normal wind and grind of the workday."

"And what is it that you do?"

He considered, as if deciding how best to explain what he does. "I work for the city," he said simply.

"It's a bit early for lunch, shouldn't you be at the office? Or are you one of those super important people who can breeze in and out as they please?" I laughed. He chucked as well.

"Nothing so exciting. Just lucky enough to have a flexible schedule and an understanding boss. How about you? What type of office has a 'decent coffee machine'? Office coffee is supposed to be terrible as a rule."

"I may have had a hand in picking the coffee machine, and I made sure it was only the best. Some days I need the caffeine just to keep a smile on my face." That would not be the case today. I don't think I had stopped smiling since I sat down. And it wasn't just from last night's lingering excitement.

"Then you have a very understanding boss too." I hadn't told him what I did for a living. He didn't seem to make a fuss about it, either not noticing my dodge or not pushing me on it. After all, he had mostly dodged the question too.

"We cater to a certain client base, and they expect to have something good to drink while they wait."

"So, you're saying it's good coffee, and you guys give it away for free? Sign me up. The coffee at my office might actually be sewer water." His eyes sparkled with amusement.

"Well maybe you will have the occasion to try it sometime." It wasn't likely since I generally treated children. Jake also seemed well-adjusted, not likely to need therapy himself. I'd been surprised before, but I had a fairly well-developed gut when identifying those in need of professional counseling.

"I think I'd like that," he said sincerely.

We chatted a little longer but all too soon it was pushing time for me to leave. I wanted to see him again, but I needed to play this goodbye carefully, to toe the line between desperate and confident. There was a decent shot he would ask for my number, but I wasn't one to leave things to chance. I excused myself to grab another drink.

I ordered a few quick sandwiches to take back to the office and another cup of coffee for the walk. I also asked the barista what Jake had been drinking and ordered one to be delivered to him after I left. I wrote my name and number on the cup, unsure whether I was being daring or chickening out of giving him the chance to ask—or not.

When my food was ready, I grabbed the bag and returned to gather up my things. "I'm so sorry, Jake. I just saw the time and I'm afraid I have to run. It was great meeting you. I hope we get the chance to fight over that seat again soon," I said with a wink.

I left before he had the chance to stop me. He watched me walk away, confusion on his face. I looked back through the window, smiled at him, and raised my drink.

The walk back to the office offered me an unfortunate chance to dwell on our interaction and overanalyze the

FRAMED

entire event. Jake had been sexy and smooth, attentive while still keeping the conversation casual. He had seemed flirty, but had I imagined it? Was my mind influenced by my adrenaline from last night's activities?

Distracted, the walk passed by quickly and I soon arrived back at my office. My practice took up the entire top floor of one of the few high-rises in the business district. I had four session rooms set up with different types of furniture to best accommodate my client's preferences. One room was designed for small children, filled with toys they could fidget with and bean bag chairs for them to sit on.

I also had two waiting areas, one for adults and parents to relax in while their child had a session, and one for children to play before or after their sessions or for siblings while they waited. The children's room had a TV playing cartoons continuously but was separated from the other waiting room with a door to muffle the sounds while still allowing visibility.

When I stepped off the elevator my assistant's desk was the first thing I saw. Jess greeted me cheerfully with a knowing smile. She and I had met in college after she had caught me pickpocketing a few of the frat boys at a party one night. She critiqued me on my technique, and we were friends and partners ever since. Her long hair changed color every few weeks, a vibrant red for now, and she also liked to keep things interesting by wearing colored contacts. I half suspected she was always switching it up so she could disappear at any time, or so she would never be recognized unless she wanted to. She could stand out

44

when it suited her, but she was also able to disguise herself and fade into the background when necessary.

She helped with both of my businesses. With her technical skill level, she could do any job she wanted, or none at all and just hack her way to financial freedom. I kept her happy by providing top-of-the-line equipment and the time to basically do anything she wanted as long as my schedule was maintained. We managed the practice together and kept no secrets from each other.

Jess had set up security protocols at the office and in both of our homes to protect all of our data and she maintained a separate server to manage the information on my heists. Somehow, she had it set up so that whatever she accessed couldn't have its location traced back to our offices. She was free to hack into anything she wanted, on my dime, and she earned a share of my proceeds for her help when I needed it—in addition to the generous salary she earned from my practice.

I dropped the bag of sandwiches on her desk as I walked in.

"Ooh, for me?" she asked with intrigue.

"Of course! My thank-you for being such a great partner." I grinned, grabbing mine out of the bag. "These are the best sandwiches in town, I think. Plus, I had some great company while I waited. I might have met someone!"

"WHAT!" She knew I had a hard time dating, which was basically the opposite of her life. She operated under a "why choose just one guy" lifestyle and was constantly going out with someone new. "Give me his name, I'm gonna find everything."

"No! I only know his first name and I don't want anything spoiled. Let me get to know this one the old-fashioned way!"

"Ugh, fine... What's his first name then?" She pretended to look disappointed. Maybe some of the disappointment was real, but she knew I was a secret romantic and would never spoil it for me.

"Jake. Oh, he was so handsome and charismatic. I tried to do a power-move and left before he could ask for my number, but then left it on a coffee cup for the barista to deliver once I was gone. I'm not sure if he's going to call though. At the very least it saved me the humiliation of him *not* asking for my number... Maybe our connection was all in my head, but it definitely seemed like he felt it too."

"Ooh, nice one. I wonder if he's going to do that dumb guy thing and wait three days to call."

"I sure hope not, the anticipation is already killing me. I need a client to distract me," I laughed. "Who's my next session?"

Jess handed me some folders. "You have two appointments already scheduled for the afternoon, but Daniel Schwartz also called to see if we could fit him in today. I'd like to give him your last spot, if that's okay. It would have you staying a little bit past five."

"Definitely. Let him know, and if that doesn't work for him then move whatever you need to fit him in whenever he wants."

I grabbed the file and walked into my office to prepare for my sessions.

Through my first two sessions, I couldn't help but let my mind drift to the upcoming one with Daniel. It was too early for him to have been cleared of suspicion, but I was confident that he would be eventually. I wasn't sure what to expect out of this session. Would he be angry? Upset? Happy that his parents had been victims or that the bust was gone?

His time finally approached, and I was waiting in the lobby with Jess for him to arrive. When he arrived, I directed him to choose a room. I bid Jess a good evening, since she would be gone before our session ended as it would run over the normal business hours, then I followed Daniel.

He was standing by the window looking out when I entered the room, and I paused to see if he was waiting for me before he sat. Manners had been drilled into his head through a few years of cotillion classes, even if he liked to play thug nowadays.

"Would you like to sit, Daniel?" I asked gently when he didn't move.

"No, you can though," he replied, not looking away from whatever he saw outside. "My house was robbed last night. They took that stupid sculpture Dad bought a few months back."

"I'm sorry to hear that," I started slowly. He might have made the connection that he mentioned the bust to me and then it got stolen, but he had said his parents had been flaunting it about and bragging to everyone they could.

FRAMED

"Do you feel unsafe at home because of the break-in?" I continued, directing the conversation toward his feelings.

"No, at least not like that. Mom and Dad blame me. They say I didn't set the alarm, but I did. I know I did. But somehow it was already deactivated when Dad came downstairs during the night and the stupid bust was gone."

"Well, I'm sure the fact that you set the alarm will become evident through the course of the investigation. The security company should have records of when it gets activated and deactivated." Would he wonder why I knew that? "At least, the company I use does." That should cover me.

"Yeah, you're probably right. It's just so damn frustrating!" He gently hit the window frame with the bottom of his fist and turned to storm further into the room. "They never believe what I say, and they don't trust me. Even though I've never forgotten to set the alarm before.

"If I had, I could at least understand why they wouldn't listen, but Dad deactivates it every morning when he goes downstairs! None of the staff has codes so Dad has to do it before Ben, the chef, comes in to cook breakfast. But this time, the one time we get robbed, it's not on. 'Something went wrong, must be Daniel's fault'" His mock voice of his father was actually fairly spot-on, based on the few conversations I'd had with the man.

"If you truly feel they never believe you, then why do you think it's bothering you so much that they didn't believe you this time?"

48

My question pulled him up short. He walked over to the chair and sat down, running both hands through his hair.

"I guess because this time is different. This time I really didn't do anything, and I never gave them any reason to think I had. I know I've screwed up a lot lately, so if I had broken something, gotten arrested, or whatever, and they had assumed it was my fault then fine, I deserve that. But not this.

"Plus, it's like they had me doubting *myself*. I knew I set the alarm, but all of a sudden, I was thinking 'well maybe I didn't.' Dad criticizing me is bad enough, but when Mom joins in, she just gets into my head. I swear sometimes I feel like no one listens to me but you." He paused for a moment, then corrected himself. "Well, that might not be true. The detective looking into the robbery stopped by this morning to talk to me. He seemed to listen."

I was instantly on alert. "Did he make you feel pressured to talk to him, or uncomfortable in any way? You know, you're still a minor so he probably shouldn't have been talking to you without a parent or lawyer present." If this shady detective pretended to be Daniel's friend in order to get him to slip up and confess to having something to do with the robbery, I would be pissed. It would set his trust issues back months, at least, and could end up with serious consequences for Daniel.

"No, not at all. I really felt like he believed me."

As we talked some more, Daniel seemed to become more grounded.

"You know what, it serves Mom and Dad right, having that ugly sculpture stolen. They shouldn't have had it in

FRAMED

the first place, and now they don't. Maybe the police will even look into whatever shady thing Dad did to get it.

"Thanks, Dr. Lee. I'd better head home now so I can catch dinner before Ben leaves." He stood to go, and I followed, patting him gently on the back.

"Just remember, you can call my emergency line at any time if you need me, Daniel. I'm here for you."

After he left, I grabbed my things to walk home.

Back at my apartment, I popped open a new bottle of wine in one last celebration of my successful heist. I settled in on the couch with my glass and a book, ready to finally relax and get some rest. It would, without a doubt, be an early night for me.

Just as I cracked open the book, my phone rang from the table beside me. I checked the screen to see who was calling but didn't recognize the number.

Anticipation filled me instantly... Could this be Jake? Would he call so soon? If it's him that must be a good sign, right?

"Hello?" I answered the phone tentatively.

"Hey there, Alexis? It's Jake from the coffee shop this morning." His voice was just as smooth as it was in person—all deep, sexy, and cocky, as if he knew I had been waiting for this call all afternoon.

Well, two could play that game.

"Oh, yes. The chair thief, how could I forget?" I challenged back.

"Exactly," he laughed. "Glad to have made an impression. I wanted to thank you for the abandonment issues I now have, after you rushed off so abruptly this morning. And for leaving me your number so I can try and win back some dignity after not being able to react in time to ask for it."

"Well, Jake, it sounds like *I'm* the one who made the impression, if you're ignoring that silly three-day rule about when to call."

"Can't argue with that." I could hear his smile through the phone. This guy definitely thrived on a challenge, and it seemed like he loved my spunky side. "So, I was hoping you'd let me have the privilege of taking you out some night this week. There's a great new Italian place that just opened up near the coffee shop, or I know a great little dive bar if that's more your scene?"

"How about we start with dinner, then maybe go to the dive for some drinks if that goes well? Does Thursday work for you?"

"Sounds perfect. Text me your address, I'll pick you up at 7."

We said goodbye and I squealed in excitement. I flopped back down on the couch and brought up my messenger app to let Jess know about this development.

Now, I had to figure out what outfit would work for both a nice dinner and drinks at a dive bar...

Chapter 4

Jake

The next morning, I asked the chief to sign off on officially pursuing other suspects than Daniel. Ryan and I had spent the afternoon reviewing the security footage and chasing down gang members to look for what Daniel might have done with the bust if he had taken it. We had come up short on both accounts. Daniel hadn't left the house again after coming home, and no one else was evident on the footage waiting outside for him to pass the sculpture off to. While it wasn't definitive proof that he was innocent, the lack of evidence of guilt—in addition to him not having the means or connections to sell the bust—seemed like justification enough to shift our focus elsewhere.

Our warrant for Schwartz and Son's finances, and the clearance for the forensic accountant, had come through. Ryan and I rode together to their office to serve the warrant, bringing a handful of uniformed officers to collect files. The accountant was planning to meet us there.

On the way, we discussed the employees Ryan intended to interview while I oversaw the collection of evidence. We expected the forensic accountant to take a day or two for a cursory look at their records, then it could be a few more if there was anything to merit further investigation.

The Schwartz and Son antiquities house was a two-story building in the historic district of town. The marble building itself might have been as old as some of the items they sold, with the stone appearing a faded gray color. The ornate carvings around the doors and windows had been beautifully preserved, qualifying the building for landmark status.

The main floor was laid out like a museum, with art lining the walls, artifacts in glass cases, and a placard for each item giving details about the artist and the specific piece. I checked in with the secretary at the main desk and asked her to have Mr. Schwartz come down, but without her mentioning who was here to see him. She called Schwartz on her desk phone and insisted that he report to the lobby immediately.

While we waited, I browsed through the showroom, examining a few of the pieces on display, and allowed my mind to drift to Alexis. I had been ready to throw the rest of the day away and spend it talking to her after just a few minutes of conversation, much to my own surprise. I generally couldn't wrench my focus away from a new case, getting lost in the puzzle it presented, but there was

FRAMED

something about Alexis that had my mind emptying of any other thoughts. She was beautiful, with long, dark hair, and a vibrant smile that could light up the room. Her slight yet curvy figure captured the attention of every part of my body, and I couldn't look away. Her deep blue eyes had radiated sass and mischief as she approached me, and her bold confidence took me by storm. Once she'd asked to sit down, I'd been hooked.

The conversation had been light, and I didn't learn much about her, but that only left me desperate to find out more. When she raced out of the café, I was worried I'd have to resort to extreme measures to run into her again, but right after she disappeared from sight, a barista had ambled over with a drink for me, Alexis's name and number written on the cup. I had to fight the urge to call her right then, but programmed her number in my cell and made a plan to call her that evening, once I'd settled at home for the night. Now, I just had a few more days until I could see her again, and I couldn't wait.

I turned my attention to the next piece of art as I continued my walk around the room. Each piece had a placard that gave the name of the work, the artist, the year it had been created, as well as any special details about it. There were some artists I had actually heard of, such as Manet, Degas, and Rembrandt, but there were many more that were unfamiliar. I could never understand how paint on a canvas, or carved clay or stone could fetch such high prices. Sure, the works were nice, and they were clearly very old, but it just wasn't my thing. I couldn't get past knowing all the good the same money could do in the hands of people who needed it.

ELLIE HOHENSTEIN

Finally, Gerald Schwartz entered from an elevator at the back of the room, dressed much nicer than the last time I had seen him, in a three-piece suit and bowtie. The suit was unflattering on him, emphasizing his weight issues. The high collar of his shirt made it look like he didn't have much of a neck and gave him a bit of a double chin.

"What is the meaning of this?" he said angrily as he noticed the handful of officers behind me.

"Mr. Schwartz, I'm sorry to inform you that we have a warrant to collect the records of all transactions dating back the last five years, your employee files, and of course financial statements. We have our department accountant here to review the data; he will need to be set up in an office and given anything he asks for.

"These officers are here to facilitate the collection of records, and I will be supervising as the detective for the case. I can assure you, sir, that all this is well intentioned, just trying to make sure we can turn up that missing sculpture of yours."

I couldn't help the smile that crept in as his face turned a deeper shade of red with every word I spoke.

"This is an outrage! I won't stand for this! I'm the *victim*. You can't come barging into my place of business and demand to see my files, I won't have it."

"Well, sir, actually we can. That's what this piece of paper here says. You're welcome to look it over, call your lawyer even, if it makes you happy, but in the meantime, we're going to start our collection."

FRAMED

I motioned for the accountant to come over. "Now, this here is Mr. Briggs, should I have your secretary show him where to set up?"

Briggs had been working with the department for a few years. He was a small and quiet man, best suited to working alone and undisturbed. He was exceptionally fast while still being detailed in his analysis, and I trusted no one more with this job. The secretary came rushing over and led him over toward the elevator, chatting politely as they walked away.

During the whole exchange, Mr. Schwartz's eyes never left me. He glared at me with his arms crossed over his chest, then finally relented. "Fine, all our offices and records are kept upstairs, take what you need. But you best believe my attorney will be speaking directly with the chief, and you had *better* use all this information to find my bust."

He turned abruptly and stormed away, pulling out his cell phone as he walked. I instructed my team to head upstairs and begin collections, while I waited with Ryan at the front desk for the secretary to return.

Once she was back at her desk Ryan gave her the list of employees he needed to speak with. There were a handful that had worked here at least five years and we were looking for any connection to the other cold cases of art theft we had. Any of them could be operating as a fence and using their connections through the business to sell the stolen items. The secretary led us to a conference room upstairs, then located the first person on Ryan's list and directed them over.

56

ELLIE HOHENSTEIN

I listened in on the first interview, then left Ryan to finish the rest while I walked around to check in on the officers collecting the records. They were boxing up files and one of them was copying digital information from the company server over to flash drives to take back to the station for analysis. With any luck, one of these employees would turn up with some shady connections and give us our first fresh lead on the string of thefts.

Satisfied that things were moving along well, and that Schwartz was not trying to hide any files from us, I went back downstairs and asked the secretary to give me a tour of the place. She showed me a variety of pieces, proving more knowledgeable about the art than I expected.

The showroom was organized to have a thorough mix of styles, artists, and mediums through the whole layout, ensuring that a customer would have sight of every piece on display when looking for something to match their specific tastes. It was an interesting marketing strategy, but the secretary assured me that it was very effective in selling multiple pieces to a single customer, often helping them branch out from their usual style.

While we walked, my thoughts drifted back to Alexis, wondering if she liked art, and what pieces she might find interesting. She had said she liked watching people at the coffee shop, and there could be a sort of art to that, learning the human behaviors that drove one's actions.

I'd have to ask her thoughts on our date on Thursday, perhaps I could plan a second date coming here, or to a museum. It was an effort not to try and text her or call her and start really getting to know her, but I always enjoyed

FRAMED

face-to-face interactions better and wanted that view when discovering more about her.

One thing I had learned over the years as a detective was that most of the communication people did was with their body language. You could tell so much about what a person was feeling from the way they carried themselves. Alexis exuded confidence and poise, and her snarky attitude had thrilled and surprised me. Her clothes and accessories made it evident she was well off, but she also felt down-to-earth in a way that few of the people I had met with money did.

By the time we had made it through the showroom and the auction house, officers were filing back downstairs with filled boxes. I went upstairs to check in on the status and was pleased to find that they were almost done. With the last of the boxes carried out, and the flash drives sealed in an evidence bag, I dismissed the officers back to the station to begin looking through everything.

Ryan was on the last of his interviews, and Briggs had settled into a spare office to go through the financials. I assigned one officer to stay with the accountant as protection, just in case. It also helped to have an extra set of eyes on site to observe anyone acting strangely or possibly shredding documents we may have missed, and I knew Briggs's eyes would be glued to his screen, oblivious to the rest of the world.

Once Ryan was done, we headed back down to the lobby, asking the secretary to pass along assurances to Mr. Schwartz that we would have all his files returned in about a week. After we got settled in the car, I asked Ryan how his interviews went.

58

"Not much to report. Some of them were involved in either the purchase or the sale of a few of the items that have been taken over the years, but they didn't seem to remember who they had sold them to. I didn't exactly expect anyone to jump up and say, 'I stole that and sold it on the black market,' but no one seemed nervous, or at least no more than expected when talking to cops."

He shuffled through the notes he had taken, skimming down the pages as he spoke.

"I recognized a few names on some of the sale reports of other items run through Schwartz and Son, generally listed as agents, that I think I've seen under suspicion of dealing in stolen art, but I'd need to look deeper to confirm. None of them were on transactions involving our missing items though. At the very least they could point us in the right direction if we can find the right leverage before we talk with them.

"I also asked about Mr. Schwartz and how it was to work for him. Mixed reviews there, some called him an ass while others said he was great to work for. No one seemed to hate him enough to steal from him, though."

"So overall, a... bust," I said with a laugh. Ryan rolled his eyes, not appreciating my attempt at humor. "Well, back to the drawing board, I guess. Maybe our warrant will turn up something, and it sounds like we've got a few leads we can chase down."

"There was something that one of them did say. It could be nothing, and might not be connected, but one of the guys said that Schwartz was always taking first dibs on anything they brought in, buying it for his personal collection. Like with the bust, it came in through the business and he bought it from here. But this guy questioned how Schwartz could have afforded it.

"The company doesn't make that much margin on what they sell after commissions and such. And most of it stays in the company's retained earnings with only small dividends paid out to Schwartz on top of his salary. This guy didn't think that Schwartz would have had the millions needed for this just lying around."

"Hmm, could be something. If he blew all his spare cash on this piece, then maybe we're looking at insurance fraud. Schwartz would definitely have the connections to sell it, but I'm not sure if he'd be willing to risk the humiliation of the theft for it—could be bad for business. Let's give Briggs time to dig up something before we question him."

"Sounds good. Where are we headed now?" he asked as I drove past the turn we would have usually taken.

"Now? We're hitting the streets."

It took considerable time and effort to cultivate a Confidential Informant relationship. The biggest hurdle was informant's fear that you were going to betray and arrest them. There was no shortcut to establishing the trust required for them to tell you the really good stuff, especially when it implicated them in some way or had the chance of them being outed as a snitch. I had spent years assembling my few trusted informants, but Ryan was just getting started.

In my experience, there were two ways to start a good CI partnership. The first was to arrest someone for some minor crime, then make a big show about deciding to let them off if they could give you something that was helpful.

The other way was to go undercover and get to know the person as if you were also a minor criminal and see what they let slip. This second method required a lot more time to let them get to know the fake you and was largely dependent on your acting skills. That type of relationship could also implode if the informant discovered you were a cop in the wrong way.

I decided in the interest of time we would drive around the sketchier parts of town and see if we spotted anyone who was recently arrested for a small crime. We could follow them from a distance and hope we got lucky enough to catch them in the act of something else.

"You still review the recent arrest reports every day, right? The ones with the mugshots?" I asked Ryan.

"Yeah…" He looked a bit nervous about where we were headed and why I was asking.

"Good. Alright, Rain Man, let's see if you can find us someone to tail. We've got a few hours. Eyes on the window, let me know if you recognize anyone." Ryan had almost a photographic memory, so he should be able to identify someone from their pictures if they were skulking about.

"Awesome," he said sarcastically. He didn't look nearly excited enough about this. Ryan had yet to understand the value of a good CI. I generally kept my informants to myself, not bringing him to any meetings I held with them; it was a delicate balance and they tended not to trust new officers.

FRAMED

We drove around for about an hour, careful not to take the same street more than two or three times in case anyone was watching. My black Honda Accord was nondescript enough, and there were plenty of them on the road, but I didn't want to take any chances that someone would catch on to what we were doing.

Finally, Ryan perked up and pointed out the window. "There's one," he said, motioning to a guy standing outside a convenience store.

I didn't slow down or stop. Instead, I headed to the closest parking lot. I reached into my back seat and pulled two sets of workout clothes from my gym bag. I handed one to Ryan.

"Uh, what's this for?" he asked. His nose was scrunched up like I'd handed him rotten garbage.

"Relax, they're clean. I keep a few spare sets in here in case I need to go incognito. I could probably lose my tie and blend in okay, but your dress shirt, slacks, and polished shoes scream 'outsider' at best and 'cop' at worst.

"This is part of why I usually dress so casually. For one, it's much more comfortable. Two, you never know when you're going to need to blend in with a crowd. Always be prepared for any situation. I've got a suit in the trunk too in case the occasion called for it. Now, put those on real quick. The windows are tinted dark enough that no one should be able to see in if they're looking, but you never know who might notice if we take too long to get out of the car."

We both changed quickly. I was in jeans and a collared shirt, which could pass for casual enough if I was alone, but since Ryan was changing into athletic wear, it would

62

be best if we both looked like we were on a jog. Ryan was close to my height and build, but his thick muscles made him a little bulkier than me. The shirt would probably be a little tight, but his physique really helped sell the narrative I was going for.

Ryan laced up the extra set of sneakers, which fortunately fit him, and we both secured our holsters to our thighs beneath the shorts and tucked our badges under our shirts before getting out of the car. We jogged back to the convenience store, but the guy was no longer loitering in front. After a quick look around to make sure he wasn't visible further down the street, I motioned Ryan toward the building. We slipped inside as if we were planning to buy some drinks or needed a bit of AC to help us cool down from our run.

We split up, wandering down the aisles, and I caught sight of our target grabbing a few bags of chips and packs of candy, then stuffing them in his pockets. This would be too easy. Some small-time criminals just couldn't resist the five-finger discount, even when—possibly especially when—they had just gotten out on bail.

We watched the guy wander through the store, slowly making his way toward the front. To the casual observer, he might have been browsing, but he kept his eyes locked toward the check-out as he neared the door, ready to make his escape when the cashier looked away. He got his chance as one of the other customers asked for something off the back shelf, and he bolted out the door.

"Stop! Hey, he's stealing!" the cashier shouted as the door slammed closed, too late to do much about it. He was stuck behind the counter, and the store probably had

FRAMED

a no-chase policy anyway. Ryan and I took off after the thief; I pulled up my badge to show the cashier as I passed.

"Willow Springs Police, stop right there!" Ryan shouted as he ran out the door and pursued. The suspect slipped into the next alley, no doubt hoping to use it to escape, but he must either have been unfamiliar with the area or had terrible luck because it was a dead-end. Ryan and I caught up quickly, and he surrendered without a fight.

"What's your name, sir?" I asked. It was always best to start off friendly since we were hoping to be able to let this guy go.

"Ray. Ray Smith." He looked defeated, hopeless.

"Well Mr. Smith, you're under arrest. You have the right to remain silent, anything you say can and will be used against you in a... court... of law." I trailed off, pretending to be distracted by recognizing him. "Say, Ryan, doesn't this guy look a bit familiar?"

"Oh yeah, I think someone brought him in a week or two ago. Petty theft, if I remember right. You'd think he'd have learned his lesson after that." Ryan said, darkly. I shot him a glare. We were trying to get this guy to work with us, not insult him. Ryan had a long way to go in building his CI skills.

But I had to follow the trail Ryan laid. "That's right. Hmm, a repeat offender? I hear Judge Scott's been cracking down on that lately, issuing stronger sentences. Just last week he sentenced someone to how many years for petty theft?"

Ray visibly paled. He started stammering, cutting off Ryan's reply, begging us not to take him in, pleading on

64

behalf of his family and children—an often-used ploy to try to make us sympathetic.

"Hmm… what'd we take today? Chips and some candy? Small time. I bet all the other thieves you know are small-time too. Not much you can offer us to let you walk," I teased, dangling the bait to see if he'd be willing to turn snitch.

"No! I know others who take big stuff—stuff they can't even use for themselves and have to flip. I can take you to the pawn shops they sell to. Buying stolen stuff is illegal too, right? And a much better bust than someone who just stole some snacks."

"Nah, we've got folks on most of those places already. You're going to have to do better than that. I'm talking big, big, stuff. Know anyone into art?"

He tapped himself on the head as he thought. "Art? Art, hmm… No, not off the top of my head."

I started walking him back toward the convenience store, at which point he started to panic. He grabbed my arm to stop me. "Wait, no. I can find out! I can ask around and find someone who knows something, I swear! Please. I can't find out if I'm in jail, and there's no way I can get bail money again."

Got him. He may not be able to turn up anything, but it was worth a shot.

I sighed, pretending to give in to his pleas.

"Alright, Ray, tell you what… This here is Ryan." I waved my hand in his direction and Ryan smiled a cruel smile. If he couldn't catch flies with honey, then fear would have to work this time. "You're going to meet him on this corner in *exactly* three days. That's Friday at…" I

FRAMED

checked the time on my watch, "...three o'clock. You will tell him everything you can find out about who might have stolen a sculpture lately, or what happened to it.

"If you are even one minute late, Ryan and I will personally appear at your trial for your last arrest. Now, we're going to go back to that store, give the nice cashier back the chips and candy, and act like we're taking you in. When we get out of sight, we will let you go."

Ray happily agreed, then put on a contrite expression as we entered the shop. He apologized profusely to the cashier and swore he would never return. We escorted him out of the store, then a few blocks away we removed the handcuffs.

"Remember, Friday at three o'clock. Be there," Ryan said fiercely. We turned away and walked back toward my car.

"Dude, we've *got* to work on your technique. We want to charm them, not make them piss their pants," I said, grinning.

"Oh, I thought we were doing good-cop, bad-cop?"

I burst out laughing. I supposed it was a fair guess, but next time I'd be clearer about what we were trying to do.

"Alright, kid. I think that's enough Miyagi-ing for today. Let's head back to the station."

I dropped Ryan off in front of the station but decided there wasn't much for me to do until my team finished sorting through the evidence. I could try to help them, but the analysts had a system down. I ended up getting in the way the last time I tried. They basically banned me from going through files and such with them, but I wasn't really complaining.

ELLIE HOHENSTEIN

I decided to spend the rest of my afternoon at the youth center. The chief knew how important this place was to me, and he didn't mind me occasionally taking a few hours out of the workday to volunteer. It was basically recruiting for the police department, plus I was helping keep the kids out of a future life of crime. That's where he had discovered me, after all.

The youth center was an old factory that had been converted into a safe and sometimes even fun space for local kids to hang out. Many of them were from poor families and came to the shelter to eat, not getting sufficient nourishment at home. Others were escaping mean or abusive parents, if only for a few hours. And some of the kids were truly homeless, having run away from either foster homes or troubled families.

There were offices for the staff and volunteers, keeping them separate from the children to help the kids feel safe; many of them had issues with authority and were slow to trust the administrators. Cameras were placed all over the facility so the administrators could monitor for safety.

There was a gym with basketball courts, a volleyball net, and exercise equipment set up to keep the kids healthy and in shape. A relaxation room was set up as well with couches, TV's, video game systems, and some toys for smaller children. For those with unsafe homes or nowhere else to go, there were also two rooms set up with bunk beds, and locker rooms with showers and spare clothes in all sizes.

There were a few kids mingling around when I arrived, their ages ranging from around ten to seventeen. I greeted those that I knew and headed toward where some of the

FRAMED

older kids were playing basketball in the gym. Since I was already wearing workout clothes, I decided to join in with them. I had played here a lot when I was younger, but I was a bit out of practice now.

I'd had my fair share of struggles growing up. Despite their drug addictions, my parents managed to stay just under the radar of the law, so I hadn't ever been removed from their "care". But it had been a hard childhood. I'd had to spend more time taking care of them than they had taking care of me, even at a young age. As I got older, I'd also become angrier with them and my poor lot in life. Other kids got happy families, supportive parents rather than the piss-poor ones I had.

So, I had found a new family in one of the local gangs, doing what I needed to for survival. Two of my friends were a few years older than I was and tried to look after me, keeping me away from the really bad stuff, but I still got picked up a few times for minor things like breaking and entering, petty theft, and disorderly conduct. I was lucky, the officers that caught me had always seemed to feel sorry for me and let me off with warnings.

Chief Douglas, a detective at the time, had responded to calls about me on a few occasions, but had never properly arrested me, instead recognizing my anger at the world as loneliness and a lack of direction. I didn't have any hope for my future, thinking I'd follow in my parent's footsteps and ruin it for myself anyway. He tracked me down at the youth center and spent a few months convincing me that I could be more, that I could be better.

Once I turned sixteen and could file for emancipation, he helped me through the process and let me stay at his house. He made me finish high school and enrolled me in the police academy once I graduated. I had quickly become an all-star. Thanks to keeping up my exercise routine and finally getting enough to eat at mealtimes, I was in peak physical health. Plus, my experience on the streets had helped me think more like the criminals I was chasing. I held one of the best arrest records in the force for a few years before being promoted to detective, and the sky was the limit from there.

But as much as I loved what I did, I never felt like it was enough. I wanted to *stop* kids from getting arrested in the first place, not just catch them when it was too late. There had to be more I could do to help the underlying cause of why these teens turned to crime in the first place.

That was a big part of why I came to the youth center two or three nights each week. I worked with the staff to get kids interested in the programs they offered. I did what I could to follow up on bad home situations. I took any reports of bad or overwhelmed foster parents or abusive families to social services for formal investigation. They always made sure it looked like a routine check-in to protect the kids that confided in me.

I had managed to recruit a few kids to the force over the years but had yet to feel like I was making a significant impact. There were just too many of them. But until I could figure out a better way, I would keep coming back.

Chapter 5

Alexis

I gossiped the first hour of my morning away with Jess, planning my outfit for my upcoming date and speculating about Jake. Since I wouldn't let Jess look him up, I had to describe his physique in excruciating detail, and recap a play-by-play of the call last night. It wasn't a long call, but Jess made me repeat it a few times until she was satisfied. I was finally saved by my first patient of the day, Ralph McGill.

Ralph's parents owned a small chain of high-end restaurants in the city. This often required them to work nights and weekends, so Ralph struggled with feelings of neglect. I had encouraged his parents to prioritize time with him, but they hadn't yet taken my advice, so I was trying to work with Ralph to recognize other ways they showed him their love.

ELLIE HOHENSTEIN

His nanny brought him to the office promptly at nine-thirty, and I went out to greet them. Jess got the nanny settled in with an espresso while I let Ralph choose the room he wanted to meet in today. He was twelve years old and was starting to want to be treated more "grown-up", so he chose a room with a simple set of chairs and coffee table rather than the room with toys.

I closed the door behind us and settled into the chair across from him once he sat down. "How are you doing today, Ralph?"

"I'm alright... school's getting a little tough, but I think I'm starting to get the hang of percentages." Ralph said excitedly.

"That's fantastic. You know, I sometimes struggle with those, maybe you can show me a few?"

He pulled a workbook out of his backpack and spent a while teaching me fractions and percentages. Despite the distraction of the tutoring session, it seemed like something kept popping back in his mind, causing him to act uncomfortable for a few moments. Then he would shake it off and dive back into teaching.

After the fifth instance of him trailing off mid-sentence I decided to seize the opportunity to get him to open up. "Ralph, are you alright? Is there something you'd like to talk about?"

He set down his pencil and sat back up in the chair. I continued, trying to help soothe some of his nervousness. "It's alright, Ralph. Whatever you tell me will be just between us. I'm here to listen."

"I saw my dad do something bad..." he said, reverting to a more childish tone, proving his discomfort with the

FRAMED

topic. "They let us out of school early the other day and I heard voices in his office and when I walked in, he was naked with a woman, but it wasn't my mom…"

An affair didn't surprise me, Bill McGill was a notorious flirt. He had brought Ralph to some sessions early on just so he could try and flirt with Jess. He never seemed to notice the disgust written all over her face at his attempt at picking someone up while his son was in therapy a few feet away on the other side of a door.

But for Ralph to catch Bill in the act, that was a whole new level of low.

"And how did your father react when he saw you?"

"The lady screamed, and he yelled at me to get out. He was really mad, but it was an accident! I didn't mean to interrupt him; I was just scared that someone was in the house. The housekeepers never close the door when they go in there. In the shows I watch, the bad guys always break in when they think no one will be home. I was trying to be brave… I was just gonna open the door a little, then call the police."

I was sure that, in his fear, his father raising his voice hit harder emotionally than it would normally. I had heard Bill was quick to anger, and he was used to dealing with adults in his restaurants, so he didn't have a lot of tact when it came to talking with children. There had been many confrontations that I had helped Ralph work through.

"Where did you go after you left the office?"

"My room… I hid under my blankets, but I didn't cry this time. I practiced my breathing like you taught me."

A little pride surged through my chest. Ralph had made a lot of progress with his self-awareness and self-esteem in the past year, and the willingness to actually listen to my advice was one of the reasons I loved working with kids over adults.

"And did your dad come to your room later to explain what happened?"

"Yeah, he came and told me the woman was just a friend and said they had spilled drinks on themselves, but I'm not dumb. I said he was lying, but that only made him more angry..." Ralph trailed off and fear took over his eyes. "He said I can't tell my mom. That if I said anything to her then I'd be responsible for hurting her, for ruining her life."

I kept my expression schooled into calm. Ralph was upset enough; he didn't need my gut reaction to make him feel worse.

"That must have felt like quite a lot to ask of you, to keep that secret for him."

To put the burden of that secret, and the weight of ruining a marriage, onto a child's shoulders was unforgivable.

"It's not fair. He's the one that messed up, why would I have to take the blame for something he did? Do you think my mom would really be upset with me if I told her?" He was looking for hope, but I knew all too well that, when it came to these kinds of things, the hurt person rarely acted rationally.

I pondered for a moment, deciding how best to phrase my answer in a way that might help him.

FRAMED

"I think that sometimes when we get told bad news, we don't always express ourselves the best. It's just as true for grown-ups as it is for children, especially when it feels personal. And it's possible that your mom might not react well if you tell her, and she might take it out on you, at first, in her pain. If you choose to tell her, you need to be prepared for that.

"But what you choose to do is up to you. Your father can't control how you will handle it, and neither can I. I can promise you, though, that I will be here if you need someone to talk to. No matter what you decide."

He seemed to feel a bit bolstered by that. He changed the subject, telling me that he was ready to move on, and we chatted about whatever came to him for the rest of the session. By the time we wrapped up he appeared much lighter.

I walked Ralph back to the lobby and thanked the nanny for bringing him. I asked her to pass along the message that when the parents had time, I would like to chat with them about how their son was progressing. They had not had a review with me in almost a year, rarely being willing to take the time out of their busy schedules.

My next session passed quickly and Jess had already left for lunch by the time it finished. I grabbed my purse from my office and locked up the practice on my way out.

I had a weekly lunch date with my dear friend Vivian. With my hectic schedule between patients, heists, and volunteer work, I spent a lot of time focusing on the lives of others. This was one of the few routines I kept for myself, just enjoying the time with a friend and trying to put work out of my mind for the hour. The restaurant was

74

a short walk away, and, ironically, was owned by the McGill family.

By the time I arrived, Vivian was already seated at a table on the front patio. We both loved to eat outside, and we usually ensured it was an option when selecting the restaurant. She waved me over and stood up to hug me. "Hey, Lex! Good to see you!"

Vivian Bellefonte had moved to town around a year ago. We ran into each other at a charity event and hit it off instantly. She came from a well-off family in New York, but had wanted to get away from the pressures of the family name, so she moved out to Willow Springs. She was a socialite in every sense of the word, and it seemed her only job was spending her family's money. Still, she had dived right into the community, always looking for a cause to donate to, so I knew she had her heart in the right place.

"I love your outfit, Viv! Is it new?" I swear she never wore the same clothes twice. Today she was dressed stylishly in a light cream cashmere sweater that looked far more comfortable than anything I owned, sleek black slacks, and red high heels to match her bright red lipstick. Her tall, thin frame was a perfect model figure, toned but still supple where it counted. She wore a large black sun hat over her short blonde hair, and thick Burberry sunglasses shielded her blue eyes from the bright day.

"Of course! You know me, I was out at the stores the other day and felt this sweater and about *died* it was so soft. I just had to have it. There's not much time left for me to enjoy wearing long sleeves now that spring is almost here. I had to seize the opportunity."

FRAMED

I laughed. Vivian was always so *extra* about everything, but that was part of why I loved her. She was just so open and carefree. I'd never seen her with anything less than a smile on her face.

The waiter came over to take our order and returned quickly with our drinks. Vivian and I chatted about all we had been up to since we last had lunch last week, or at least I talked about all the *legal* things I had done since then. Jess was the only person in my normal life that knew my secret.

Though my time with Vivian was helping cheer me up, I still hadn't been able to shake my anger about the situation Ralph's father had put him in.

Once our meals were delivered Vivian called me out on it. "Lex, hun, what's up? You look like someone kicked your puppy. If you had one. What's going on? Is it something to do with a client?"

"Sorry, yeah there was this kid whose dad put him in an impossible situation and it's just stirring up a lot of old emotions for me. And it really sucks because this kid is so awesome, and he's been making such good progress in our sessions, and I'm afraid this is going to set him back."

If I was honest, part of the reason this session had rattled me so much was from my own childhood. Cheating was a bit of an emotional trigger for me that brought up all kinds of trauma. My mother had cheated on my father and when he found out about it, they argued while driving home from dinner one night. Not paying attention to the road, my father had swerved into oncoming traffic, and the accident took both their lives and left me in critical condition. I had pulled through, but I'd had no family left, not any that wanted me anyway.

I was only ten when they died. I spent the next eight years bouncing around foster homes, angry at the world. It was a miracle I was able to get into college at all, but once I saw my opportunity to make a better life, I jumped all-in.

"That's terrible!" Vivian patted my hand in reassurance. I'd told her a little of my time in foster care, enough for her to know I'd had a rough go of it and understand why the children's charities were so important to me. "I hate people who can't take responsibility for their own actions. And to pass it off onto their child—truly despicable. I wish there was some way he could feel the pain he's putting his son through."

I wondered for a moment if I had let more about Ralph's session slip out than I meant to, but what she said distracted me as an idea popped into my head. There *was* a way I could make Bill feel his son's pain. It wouldn't be a direct connection, but Bill McGill had just made it to the top of my hit list.

I'd even find some way to make sure he made the link between what he did and the theft—something in his collection had to be related to affairs or secrets.

As soon as I got back to the office I would get Jess to start planning. I didn't usually pull back-to-back jobs like this. I preferred to wait for the trail to go cold on the last one and for folks to relax their security a bit, but if I waited too long then he might end the affair or his wife might find out and start divorce proceedings, split up their

FRAMED

belongings, or at least put everything under a microscope, which would make it a lot harder to steal anything.

Decided, I smiled mischievously at Vivian. "You know, I'm betting karma will take care of him after all."

Chapter 6

Alexis

I gave Jess the rundown on my plan before my next client arrived, and she began searching to see which items in his collection would make the most impact, if stolen. We would reconvene after my last session, at least to make a plan on identifying what pieces the McGills might hold, if not make a selection and iron out the finer details of the heist.

The afternoon was blocked off exclusively for local children from impoverished families that I had met through various charities or programs. These children had just as many problems as my upper-class clients, but generally lacked the resources to get the help they needed. I could only imagine how different my life would be if there had been someone with my training to talk through my issues with.

FRAMED

I did everything I could to make the kids feel more comfortable in my posh office. I ensured that none of my usual clients would come to the office, so the kids or the parents wouldn't feel judged, or less important. I dressed more casually so they didn't think I believed I was better than them. I also made sure to have snacks and drinks that they might be more familiar with, like the store-brand sodas. I always offered them the name brands as well, but I found that simply having the option of something they were used to made them feel more at ease.

I never charged the parents or social services for these sessions, knowing their money was needed elsewhere and therapy was something they would otherwise go without. I had helped many children cope with the loss of a parent, or handle situations where they were struggling with pressures from their family to help pay bills, or even just having a hard time in school. Over the years, many of the children I had seen were able to balance their responsibilities better, or more adeptly handle their emotions to produce positive relationships, managing to start better lives for themselves as adults.

It was a difficult burden to bear, hearing the stories some of them told me about the conditions of their foster homes, and not being able to report the foster parents thanks to confidentiality restrictions and there not being an imminent threat to the child's safety. But I made sure to anonymously arrange for donations of things like clothes, shoes, and school supplies to those families. When I was in foster care, any money that was donated to my home went to new clothes or dinners out for the foster parents, rather than coming to us kids, but supplies generally made their way down to us.

One of my patients, Lacey, was in for a session today. She was around thirteen and was escorted by a representative from her school. If we met after school hours, she usually would come by herself, or with her younger sister, Sarah, in tow. It worried me that she would wander freely about the city, but I remembered having to do the same at her age; my foster parents didn't have a car that could transport all the kids in the house at once and there were younger ones that couldn't be left alone. I had learned early how to use public transportation out of necessity.

Lacey's parents had passed away about a year ago, and we were working through all the upheaval of moving to a new home, new school, and being surrounded by new people. Her eight-year-old sister was also in the house, with the two of them having managed to be kept together, but Lacey felt responsible for taking care of her and protecting her from some of the larger kids in the home who were bullying them.

I was working with social services, trying to call in a few favors to get them moved into a home where they would be the only children. I believed that might be the key to helping both girls since it would feel like a smaller change for them compared to their old life. It would also allow the new foster parents to get to know them and establish a real connection. If they were really lucky, they might even find a family looking to adopt them. But for now, they were stuck with the Jacksons.

FRAMED

"George and Patrick were picking on Sarah again," Lacey was telling me. "I tried to get Mrs. Jackson to make them stop, but she was too busy taking care of Kelly and wouldn't listen. So, I pushed George down, away from Sarah, but he hit his big, stupid head. It started bleeding and, of course, that's right when Mrs. Jackson came into the room. Funnily enough, she had time to yell at me, but not time to help Sarah. Then Patrick told her I started the whole thing, and she believed him over me."

The Jacksons meant well, and when they only had a few kids in their care they were actually fairly good foster parents. When the girls joined the house, they had made accommodations to give them a room to share separate from the other kids. They lived in a four-bedroom home but had eight children staying with them. Lacey and Sarah were in one room, two other girls had one more, and the three boys they kept shared the remaining room. Kelly was only a few months old, so the Jacksons had her crib set up in the bedroom with them rather than having a nursery. It was recommended for infants to sleep in a room with parents for the first year anyway.

While I couldn't speak from experience, I had counseled a handful of new parents and it seemed like the first few months were usually the hardest. With so many other kids in the house I imagined that the Jacksons were working overtime trying to keep the baby healthy and calm.

But I also understood that Lacey was feeling deprioritized. She was accustomed to having her family's almost undivided attention, and adjusting to a new baby entering the home would be hard enough even without everything else she was having to deal with.

"What was Mrs. Jackson doing with Kelly when you went to ask her for help?" I needed to get Lacey to think through the whole situation. I knew the Jacksons were good people, just overwhelmed.

"I don't know, she was crying or something. And Mrs. Jackson was trying to walk around with her."

"Could she have possibly been trying to get Kelly to go to sleep? Sometimes that can be very difficult, especially with a lot of noises going on around."

Lacey looked down, sheepishly. "Yeah, that might have been what she was doing…"

"And when she came into the room, what do you think she was coming to do?"

"Well, she didn't have Kelly with her, so maybe she had gotten her to sleep by then. She might have been coming to see what I needed. But she still didn't believe me when I said George started it!"

"Did she say that she didn't believe you?"

"Um… no. She just said that it wasn't okay for me to shove George."

"And do you think that shoving George was the best way to handle the confrontation?"

"Probably not. But he was teasing Sarah, and I needed to protect her."

That was the real issue with the whole confrontation. Without parents, Lacey was feeling the pressure to fill a parental role for her sister rather than being able to just be a kid. I couldn't tell her not to look out for her sister, so I just needed to encourage her to enjoy the parts of being a child while she could.

"Of course. Have you thought of ways you and Sarah could be home less often, maybe some extracurricular activities you could get involved in at school? That might also help you build some new relationships and feel more comfortable with the new environment."

She considered. "There is a cheer team, and they meet with a beginner group from the elementary school. It looks kind of fun, and I used to do gymnastics when I was younger. But I'm not sure I have much cheer in me anymore..."

"Maybe joining the group could bring some cheer back into your life." I chuckled quietly at my unintentional pun.

Lacey left my office looking a little bit brighter and hopefully feeling a little more comfortable with her place in her home. I knew Mrs. Jackson would never purposefully ignore her pleas for help or allow a small child to be bullied there. The only reason she was so overwhelmed was because she couldn't bear to say no when asked to take in a new child; she cared too much.

Lacey was in a terrible situation, but she didn't realize how much worse it could be. When I was her age, I was placed in a home where it was a challenge just to get fed. The couple who ran it never technically denied us food, but we weren't allowed to eat outside of specific mealtimes. Dinner was served at five o'clock, sharp, and if you weren't there when it began then you couldn't join the table.

My school started and ended late since the city schools shared buses, and we weren't dismissed until four. Like

Lacey, I was bullied by the older kids in my home, so I avoided them at all costs. This included taking the bus home. I chose to walk instead, finding the streets safer than the transportation provided by the school. At first, I didn't have money for the public buses. It took over an hour to walk home, so I missed meals more often than not.

So, I learned how to steal. It started with small things— a pack of chips here or a candy bar there—and I got caught more than I'd care to admit, but I was still young and scrawny enough that most of the shop owners took pity on me and gave me what I had taken anyway rather than calling the police.

Soon, I had developed a real knack for a simple lift. I started to get a little more risky, snagging extra items and selling the contraband snacks to kids at school. This got me bus money, which both got me home for dinners and broadened the territory that I could hit. I tried to make sure to not steal from the same place too often, feeling slightly guilty about taking from those who didn't deserve it.

I started to target stores that appeared to be involved in wrongdoing. Some of them had employees actively selling drugs in the store, or allowed someone to set up in the shop. Others were just guilty of treating their employees like trash. Those were the ones I relished stealing from. I developed an addiction to the rush I got from the heist.

By this point I was starting to fill out better, so when I got caught, the victim's version of taking pity on me involved calling my foster parents. After a few times of

FRAMED

having to rescue me, they would complain to Social Services that I was "difficult" or a "troublemaker" and I would get bounced to a new home. As I got older, the homes I landed in got worse, and I had to double down on my stealing habits. My talents grew and so did the scale of my targets.

I hit my first museum at sixteen and used the profits to start saving for college, determined to have a better life. I partnered with a few rising stars of the underworld while trying to find my groove, but it wasn't until I met Jess that it really felt right.

Jess knocked on my office door and popped her head in. "You ready to get started?" she asked.

"Let's do it."

Jess locked the front door of the practice, and turned out all the lights in the lobby so it would look like no one was here. I lowered the blinds and disconnected my computer from the office server and connected to our secure remote one. We turned on the two TVs in my office, which I usually used for background noise while I worked or to keep tuned in to the local news in case anything was reported about my jobs. We could have just used one, but the second screen allowed Jess and me to both display information when planning jobs.

Closing the door behind her, Jess returned to my office and we both sat at the small conference table in the corner. She hooked up to one TV and I hooked up to the other, then she started bringing up pictures of various paintings and small sculptures.

"These are the pieces in the McGill family's collection. Bill has a handful of original paintings, a few reproductions, and some small statuettes or custom pieces. The reproductions and the custom works probably wouldn't fetch much on the market but could hold sentimental value."

"What about the layout of the home? Are any of the pieces prominently featured where it would be the most obvious when it's gone?"

Jess leaned in and searched the files on her computer. "Looks like... Ah ha!" She pulled up the blueprints for the home. Her diagram had red, blue, and yellow dots that popped up details of the piece located in that spot when hovered over. There was one in the foyer, three in McGill's private office, two in the dining room, at least ten in the family room, and one or two in each of the bedrooms.

"Okay, I put this together based on pictures from the last party they held. It was around a month ago, so this might not be the most up-to-date diagram. Each red dot represents an original painting, the blue dots are reproductions, and the yellow ones are sculptures.

"There aren't any security cameras inside, so I couldn't get a more updated view. But I also looked back to the last two social events and the pieces were in the same place, so I don't think it's likely the McGills have moved them around. Their financials don't indicate that they would have gotten any new pieces that would have prompted them to shuffle things around either."

"Alright, so it looks like the majority of the original paintings are in his office, with a few scattered around the shared spaces," I said. "In fact, that's the only type of art he has in his office. I think he spends a lot of time working

FRAMED

there, so that would be a way to guarantee he notices it quickly. Plus, it's clearly a point of pride for him to have his favorite works in there. Did he truly open the office during their parties for others to enter?"

It didn't make sense for a private office to be a space displayed during events, so I was surprised we had the detail on what works were featured in there. Jess clicked a few more buttons on her computer and brought up pictures from the last event, which looked like a private party for Ralph's mom's birthday. The office featured a solid wood desk, with a surprisingly simple design, large enough to have a computer monitor in one corner and space to lay out papers for a work area.

Also in the office were shelves lined with books, awards, and knickknacks. Some of the titles were visible from the pictures, and I noticed that they seemed to be mostly celebrity autobiographies and a few financial books for managing companies or investing.

There was a fireplace set into one wall, and a handful of lounge chairs placed around it with small tables for drinks, indicating that the room doubled as a men's parlor during the social gatherings, which explained why it was open and photographed.

The walls were lined with awards for their restaurants, pictures of the McGill family at grand openings, and a few family portraits. Finally, the three paintings were proudly displayed, one directly across from Bill's desk and the other two on each side of the fireplace. Those were the only adornments on those walls. If any one of those went missing, it would be obvious from the moment he walked into the room.

ELLIE HOHENSTEIN

So, I had three paintings to choose from.

"Alright, what are the pieces in the office? This will be like a triple whammy. Not only is it clearly the most important room to Bill, we'll be taking one of his favorite pieces, and it's the room where Ralph caught him having the affair. It's poetic justice at its finest."

"Okay, go to the folder labeled 'Options'; I sorted the details on the various items by room and then by specific piece. We can each bring up the files on one on the screens and then see the other from the computers," Jess instructed me. I did as she asked, selecting the "Office" folder, and saw three items listed: *Still Waters, Firesound,* and *The Secret.* I opened the files on *Still Waters,* seeing the record of the sale, details of the artist, and pictures of the piece. While I pulled those up on my TV, Jess brought up the details of *Firesound* on hers.

"First up," Jess began, "*Still Waters.* This piece was painted in 1947, by artist Gregorio Dumont. Bill acquired it three years ago through Schwartz and Son for around five hundred thousand dollars."

The painting depicted a calm lake at sunset, the vibrant oranges and deep reds blended seamlessly, reflecting off the water to create an almost blinding effect. There was a small log cabin to the side, coated in shadow from trees behind it. The grass separating the cabin and the lake was lush and full, sprinkled with stepping stones and wildflowers.

It was a beautiful piece. I checked the blueprints again and saw this one was displayed to the left of the fireplace. *Firesound* was perfectly positioned to mirror *Still Waters* on

89

the right. There was something poetic about the juxtaposition of the two opposing elements.

Jess continued with the highlights of the paintings. "*Firesound*, created in 1840 by Francesco Calvano was acquired seven years ago. Looks like a black-market deal for this one… He spent about three hundred thousand plus traded another painting away to get it. Since it's likely stolen property, there is no insurance policy on this, and he's not likely to report it to the police if you take it. It'd be a good option and would really hurt. We could probably get around seven or eight hundred thousand for it."

I looked at the digital image of the work. A dancer was depicted mid-twirl in a raging inferno. It was impossible to tell if the flames were coming from her as she spun, swirling around her like a tornado, or if she was catching fire and doing a last dance to her death. I supposed it could be interpreted either way, but it was clearly a passionate piece. I could wholly understand why Bill would be captivated by it—I could hardly look away. It spoke to my inner turmoil as well as to the me-against-the-world attitude of my teens.

I definitely was tempted to take it, but I was afraid that if I did then I wouldn't be able to let it go, and hanging on to my spoils would both negate my good Samaritan excuse and was a foolish way to get caught. My methods worked because nothing could be directly traced back to me. I appreciated many of the artworks that I had taken over the years, but I knew that once I started collecting, it would be impossible to stop. It was kind-of like the *don't get high on your own supply* rule that drug dealers followed.

Jess and I both opened the documents for the final piece. "*The Secret* was painted by William Fisk in 1858," she reported. "If you're looking to send a message, this one might do it. The painting depicts a man seducing a woman, while another woman watches from the shadows. It looks like the couple is hidden in a grove, but it's impossible to tell which one might be being unfaithful. I wonder why McGill chose to put this one in his study, or if his mistress asked him to. Did Ralph have any idea how long the affair had been going on?"

"No," I replied. "He just found out about it but there's really no telling. You know Bill was always a flirt, so it might not have been the first, and it probably won't be the last. Having the painting displayed probably feels like a power-play to him, highlighting his infidelity right under his wife's nose."

Jess rolled her eyes. "Fool's move for him. If he gets caught that would be one messy divorce with all the restaurants they own together. Plus, they have a lot of other assets to split. His wife, Alison, has her family money too. They signed a prenup when they got married, so any infidelity means that the only things up for grabs in the divorce are assets acquired or which had significant appreciation during the marriage, like the restaurants did. So, she would walk away with a lot more than he would."

From my experience that tended to be the way it went. The ones fooling around were usually the ones with more to lose, making it just another rush to get off on during the affair.

However, this was definitely the piece to steal. If I was lucky, the wife might catch my hint and start her own

FRAMED

investigation and get herself out of the marriage if that's what she wanted. It's possible she was having her own extra-marital affairs, but Alison had never struck me as one who fooled around the few times I had met her at charity events. She was approached often enough by potential partners, but family was important to her and she always politely but firmly dismissed them.

"That's the one," I said confidently. "Now let's figure out how to get it."

Jess nodded and closed down the other files, while I moved the image of the painting to my TV screen for inspiration.

"Okay, first and foremost: security. They use a company called Starforce, which uses satellite transmissions to communicate with their home office. Honestly, I'm shocked that the McGills use such a faulty company, but it's good news for us.

"The satellite signals are notoriously spotty, so alarms deactivate due to glitches all the time. They also don't even fully turn on if the satellite is misaligned, but you can't tell from the home that it didn't take. Weather can also cause some issues for the signal, so if you're feeling up to taking the painting out and risking the elements, then a stormy night could be a good option.

"The picture itself is about half your height, but maybe only two feet wide, so it will be a little awkward to carry. Extraction from the frame would be the best option, but only if you have the time."

This is why I loved Jess. She not only had all the background information on all the pieces that the McGills owned, but she had also found time to start looking into

92

the security. She knew by now the way I thought and operated, and had just given me a huge head start.

"Thanks, Jess. I really appreciate all the work you've done. So, let's think through if this makes sense. First, I need to study Bill's habits a bit, see what time he usually goes to bed, or find out if there are any nights he will be out of the house. I also need to get some information on Alison, to make sure I don't get interrupted by her. I've got to find a way in, ideally before he sets the alarm or hope for a system glitch—maybe even cause one?

"Then, assuming I get in, I need to find a way to make it to the office undetected and back out again, so I need information on what staff members stay on-site and their routine. It looks like the office is in the back corner of the house, so it might make the most sense to go in that way. Do we have any pictures of the back yard or patio from the events?"

We spent the rest of the evening brainstorming how to infiltrate the house, running through every scenario we could, given the information gaps we had. I'd spend my nights for the rest of the week watching the house. Jess would again move a security camera for me a few days early so I would have a clear way in and out, I just needed to identify which camera to choose. By the end of our session, we had the makings of a good plan.

Chapter 7

Alexis

The rest of my evenings might belong to the McGills, but I'd be spending this one with Jake. Despite the looming heist, I had found myself looking forward to tonight for the past few days, unable to think of anything else during my down time.

I hadn't been on a date in what felt like ages. Between work, volunteering at the local shelters, and planning out my heists, I didn't have many nights free. I also didn't go out many places to meet new people. When not riding a high from a successful job, I was fairly introverted, more comfortable with one-on-one conversations and happy to sit at home by myself reading the night away. I could mingle at parties and charity events, but it was incredibly exhausting for me.

My excitement for going out with Jake was new for me. I don't think I had been this excited about a date...

probably ever. There was just something about him, an air of mystery perhaps, that had me on my toes wanting to figure him out. I had texted him my address shortly after he had called the other night, and I wasn't sure how timely he would be. Planning the heist had managed to keep me distracted most of the day, but now that the date was imminent, my nerves were starting to creep in.

I had chosen a light blue dress, which had the effect of making my eyes look a deeper and darker blue by comparison. It was a solid color but had multiple layers. The silk underlayer wrapped over itself at the front while coming up at an angle, creating an inverted V between my legs. There was also a sheer layer on top, adding a touch of modesty to an otherwise sexy look. The dress was a little longer in the back than the front, and there was a spotted texture pattern inlaid on the sheer layer.

I paired the dress with silver heels and jewelry and planned to bring a silver clutch for my phone, ID, and credit cards. I wasn't sure how tall Jake was since I had not seen him standing, but I was generally short enough that the extra two inches of heel didn't make me taller than the average man.

My makeup was modest, highlighting my eyes and lips, with a light blush to add color to my cheeks. I preferred a natural look, but also wanted to make sure I looked like I had put in some effort. I stood in front of my bathroom's floor-length mirror at ten minutes to seven, giving myself a final look to make sure I was satisfied with my appearance. I did a quick twirl, nodded, and made my way into the kitchen for a quick drink of water to calm my nerves.

FRAMED

Before I could get to the kitchen, there was a knock on the door. So much for calming my nerves—instead they skyrocketed at the sound. I hurried through, skipping the drink, and headed toward the door. I checked the peephole to make sure it was Jake, then opened up to greet him.

"Hiya, handsome," I said in a teasing voice, leaning against the doorway. But there was no real joke there, he looked even better than I remembered.

I had met causal Jake, maybe even just-rolled-out-of-bed Jake. This man was something else entirely. His hair was styled lightly on top to appear soft and lush but was trimmed shorter on the sides and back. His facial hair had been shaped up, full but not bushy. His dark gray casual button-down shirt had subtle textured vertical stripes and made his bright emerald-green eyes pop. He was wearing nice jeans and loafers, appearing the casual yet dressy way men were able to pull off.

He was taller than I imagined, stretching four or five inches above me, even in my heels. His shirt pulled tight across his defined chest, and the sleeves were partially rolled up, revealing muscular forearms. In his hands he held a small bouquet of white roses. I gave him points for choosing something a little different, yet still incredibly romantic.

"Hello, yourself," he chuckled in that deep, smooth voice. "Wow… You look absolutely incredible." The sincerity in his voice made me stand a little taller and brought a big smile to my face. "These are for you," he added, holding out the roses for me to take.

ELLIE HOHENSTEIN

"They're beautiful, thank you. Would you like to come inside while I grab something to put them in?" I stepped back to let him into the apartment.

He followed me into my living room, and leaned lightly against the back of my couch, taking in the view. My kitchen, dining area, and living room were all one large space, a small sunroom with access to a deck off to one side. Through the kitchen was the hallway leading to the two bedrooms and my in-home office.

The living room had a gas fireplace with my television mounted above, bookcases built into the wall on either side, shelves were filled with my collection of fiction works. I liked to read a variety of genres, but there were more romance novels than I cared to admit. I was a hopeless romantic despite the lack of hope in dating I had for myself.

I strode into the kitchen and grabbed a vase from the cabinet. "Would you like a glass of water or anything before we go?" I called out to him. He politely declined, so I grabbed my clutch and we headed out the door.

He led the way out of the building and over to a sleek black car. He opened the door for me to get in, a total gentleman. The interior was spotless and there were air freshener inserts in the vents emitting a tropical scent.

He got in the car and cranked it up. Pulling away, he asked, "So, how was your day?"

"It was really good, actually. Had a bit of an issue to solve at the office but I think I'm well on my way to getting it worked out. How about you?"

"It was fine, just waiting around for people to get me the things I need before I can actually get anything done.

FRAMED

Pretty typical with city funding." He laughed, like it didn't bother him at all.

"What is it you do with the city then? We didn't talk much about it the other day," I pressed. I wanted to make it through tonight without revealing my job, but if he needed to talk about something then I was happy to share my part to get him to open up.

"Bah, let's not talk about work. Work is work, but I'd like to focus on getting to know the real you." He shot me a charming smile, dismissing my question. He either really didn't want to say, or it was possible he couldn't say. I was familiar with the need to keep some secrets, and if he wasn't able to talk about his job much then I'd at least be in familiar company.

"Sounds good," I laughed. "Alright, let's see what type of music you like." I turned on the radio, and it was set to a pop music station. He started singing along with the song, horribly off tune, but enjoying every moment of it. I burst out laughing again at the show, impressed by his easy confidence in revealing a flaw so early into a first date. If he was this open already, I had high hopes for truly getting to know him over the course of the evening.

"Alright, so pop music, any other presets programmed for your favorite stations?"

"I've got one for rock, two pop stations, one R&B, and one country station. I can listen to just about anything, except commercials. But honestly, I usually hook my phone up and play music off a streaming service. No commercials that way, and I can easily pick my playlist to suit my mood."

"I do the same. I've got a playlist for almost every occasion, and I'm constantly listening while I work. The background noise helps me focus."

We chatted about our favorite artists, songs, and concerts we had attended the whole way to the restaurant, the conversation flowing easily.

Jake had made a reservation, so we were able to be seated immediately. The waiter approached and asked us for our drink order, Jake got scotch and I ordered a chardonnay.

"I've actually been wanting to come here for months," I started, looking around at the crowd. "A few of my friends know the owner and were invited to the grand opening party, and they have been raving about the food ever since. I think they said that the head chef actually spent a month in Italy while crafting the menu and recipes, so it's incredibly authentic."

"The owner just paid for him to take a month to go around Italy tasting food? Sign me up," Jake laughed. "Seriously, that's amazing. And it looks like that was a good investment for him, I've never even heard of some of these dishes. Every Americanized Italian restaurant has the same basic menu, so I'm excited to try something new."

"I can't even imagine spending a month in a different country. I've always wanted to travel, but I didn't have the money when I was younger and then, once I did, the timing was never right. I've dreamed of going somewhere with a friend or a partner. It seems to me that those kinds of experiences are always better off with someone by your side."

FRAMED

"So where would you go if you could go anywhere in the world? Say you won the lottery and could quit your job, sky's the limit…"

I didn't mention that I could have quit a long time ago with the money I made off my heists. I had kept enough that I would be set for life if I made some good investment decisions.

"Hmm, everywhere? Seriously, I'd probably get a one-way ticket to Europe, to start, and just go where my heart led me. No itinerary, just taking in as much as I possibly could of the cultures. I'd hit the tourist spots, of course, but you can't really get a feel for the country in those areas—they try too hard to cater to the visitors. I'd make friends with some locals and get them to take me to their favorite spots."

"That's smart," Jake said. "I've never really thought about how the tourist spots might be different from the rest of the country. I wouldn't even know where to start trying to find places to go outside of well-known spots."

The waiter returned to take our order. I went for Chicken Alfredo, one of my favorite items on any menu. I didn't want to run the risk of getting something I didn't like while on a date.

"I'll try the Cod Arracanato. I like fish, it sounds interesting."

So, Jake was a bit of a risk-taker, at least when it came to food.

"When I was really young," Jake began after the waiter had taken our menus and walked away, "it was always a bit of a hit or miss whether the meal would be any good, and it was always a 'you'll eat what I make, or you won't eat' situation. So, I learned quickly to eat just about anything and to just be appreciative of having a full stomach."

"I think that's a good philosophy, but I kind of went the opposite way. I didn't always have a guaranteed meal, so I made sure that when I ate, it was good enough to keep me going until the next one."

Jake nodded. "I was able to take a bit more control when I got older. I actually ended up cooking a lot of the meals for my family, so I got pretty good at it. But it definitely took me a few years of eating burned food to get that way. We didn't have money for cookbooks, so I had to figure it out by taste, trial and error, and if I got it wrong, I'd have to eat it anyway. It really added a layer of appreciation for those who can create an incredible dining experience, though. I like to try something new every chance I get, and I usually take the wait staff's recommendations. If they like it, I'm sure I will too."

It sounded like Jake's childhood might not have been sunshine and rainbows, and if he was comfortable opening up about it then I would too if the topics came back up. Talking about being an orphan and growing up in foster homes was a bit heavy for first-date conversation, but he did say he wanted to get to know the real me. Or at least the part of me that didn't include criminal activity. Baby steps.

We talked about our favorite dishes until the food came, which was delicious. It was like my taste buds had taken their own month-long trip to Italy. Jake said his meal was equally delicious and he offered me a bite. He even fed it to me, which I found adorable and romantic. He scarfed down every bite of his, and still asked if I wanted to try a dessert.

"I can't believe you've got enough room!" I laughed at his suggestion. "I feel like I could explode."

"I'm just glad you didn't order a salad," he replied good-naturedly. "I have a pretty heavy exercise routine and I tend to eat a lot to keep my energy levels high. I'd have needed a second dinner after this if I'd had to cut back to impress you."

I winked at him. "I'm pretty impressed as it is."

He grinned. Though I was sure I couldn't eat another bite, I agreed to try whatever he picked out. He ordered a chocolate and berry panna cotta tart, which nailed two of my favorite flavors, so I had more than my share of the dessert even though I was full.

After we finished, the waiter brought the check, and he snatched it up. I tried to play the *no, really, I can pay for my share* game, but Jake was a true gentleman and wouldn't hear of it. He paid cash and told the waiter to keep the rest as a tip. We were free to go whenever, but I wasn't ready for our night to end.

"Alright, I have to ask. You're an incredibly handsome, confident, smart man, who is a total gentleman. Why on earth are you still single? It seems to me like you're the whole package."

He rolled his eyes a little and snorted. "While I agree wholeheartedly with your assessment, I've never found anyone who really gets me. They see the 'handsome, confident, smart gentleman' but don't really look past it. I had a rough upbringing, and my job can be pretty tough and heavy. Most women I meet are only interested in the surface level, and I haven't felt like I'd be able to talk to them about the real, hard stuff. And there are always going to be things that I can't talk about. They assumed I was trying to keep secrets, or play games, but they just didn't understand that I had my reasons."

He had gotten a bit somber, like this was something he truly struggled with. I lightened the mood back up with a wink. "Well, I think there is *great* value in having a few secrets. Keeps the mystery alive. Some women use so much makeup that their entire face is a secret." He laughed. I continued on, more seriously, "You should be entitled to yours until you decide it's time to share."

Jake smiled at me and reached out to grab my hand across the table. He ran his thumb over the top of it gently, and I was acutely aware of every spot our hands touched. Butterflies had invaded my stomach and, in that moment, I thought it was the happiest I'd been in a long time.

"So, are you up to keep this night going? The dive bar I suggested has darts and a few pool tables. I could let you win a few times, really earn those first-date points." He gave me a confident smirk.

"Let me win? We'll see about that!"

We made our way back out to his car and he drove us to the dive bar. It was a small place, and the bartender greeted Jake by name and handed him a beer. I ordered one as well, then Jake led me over to the pool tables. One was free, so we racked up the balls, each grabbed a cue, and he *graciously* allowed me to break. Three balls went in, all stripes.

"Shit," Jake said, bringing his hand to his forehead in disbelief.

FRAMED

"Did I mention that my job in college was bartending at the local dive bar?"

It was only a few nights a week, enough to have a legitimate reason for why I was always flush with cash, despite not having parents to help pay my way through school. I also found that bars were the best place to gather information and meet other crooks.

"Why, no… No, you did not." He looked thrilled, like this had suddenly become a real challenge. "I guess I'm solids then."

We played a few more games, then switched to darts, which I also dominated.

I was amazed how easy it was to talk to Jake. The conversation flowed smoothly, and even the small lulls didn't feel awkward. Jake was flirty and smooth, and seized every chance to touch me—a small hand on my back here or a graze of my arm there. Each time he brushed against me I got tingles in the spot that shot straight down to my core, anticipation building with each occasion.

Unfortunately, I knew I needed to get moving to head over to the McGill house to start my recon. I faked a yawn, convincingly enough to not offend Jake, and he offered to drive me home.

When we arrived at my building he jumped out of the car while I was still unbuckling my seatbelt, running around to my side to open my door. He held his hand out to help me stand and didn't let go as we walked into my building.

I unlocked my door but didn't go inside just yet. Instead, I leaned against the frame and turned back to face him. "I had an incredible time tonight, Jake. Thank you so much."

"It was great. You're really something, Alexis." He leaned in slowly, giving me time to pull away if I wanted, and his lips gently touched mine. Fireworks exploded in me, and nothing mattered in the world except the feeling of his kiss. His beard and mustache lightly scratched at my face in a pleasant sensation as he moved, and his tongue lightly teased at my lips, taking the kiss further. I wrapped my arms around his neck, and his came around my waist, pulling me closer. Time seemed to stand still for a moment, but all too soon he was pulling away.

"Can I see you again soon? Tomorrow, maybe?" he asked nervously.

It was a very quick turnaround for a second date, and I needed to spend my time tailing the McGill family, but the only word running through my mind was, "Yes."

His whole face lit up and he leaned in to kiss me again. This kiss didn't last as long, but still lit my whole body on fire. He kept his forehead against mine for a few moments longer.

"Sounds great. I'll text you tomorrow and we can figure out the details."

He unwrapped himself from me and stepped back, looking almost like it pained him to do so. I could understand the feeling, the absence of his body against mine left me immediately missing him, even though he was standing right in front of me.

"Goodnight, Alexis," he said, walking backwards toward the elevator.

FRAMED

"Goodnight, Jake." I twisted the knob behind me without turning away, and kept my eyes locked on his until the door closed between us. I sighed and leaned my head against the frame, reliving the kiss that had shaken me to my very core.

After a few moments, I pulled myself together and headed into my room to change. I dressed in all black then slipped on a jacket to hide my ensemble from curious eyes on the walk to my car. Turning out of the resident parking deck, I started my drive toward the McGill house.

It was time to plan a heist.

Chapter 8

Jake

I tossed and turned all night long. I couldn't stop thinking about my date with Alexis. I felt the ghost of her kiss lingering with me the whole way home, the heat of her body as I tried to sleep.

She was stunning. My breath had caught when she opened her door. It had been a few days since I had seen her, so I was beginning to worry that I might have imagined her beauty. I had a habit of glorifying things in my mind, remembering them as better than they actually were. But I may have even underestimated her in my memories.

Her dress made her eyes look a deep sapphire blue, and her makeup was only lightly done, accentuating her natural beauty. Her olive skin seemed to glow with some inner light, and her smile was blinding. Her outfit was sexy and

FRAMED

not overly dressy, which was perfect since we ended up going to the dive bar after dinner.

I was shocked at how easily our conversation flowed. I still held some things back, wanting to wait to mention that I was a cop in case she reacted badly. She seemed to understand and didn't pressure me to talk about work. I'd had dates before where I tried to avoid talking about my job and the woman just kept asking and asking, until I finally relented and told her that I was an officer. Then they would always get awkward, thinking through everything they might have said that could implicate them in wrongdoing.

But with Alexis, she just agreed and changed the topic, no questions asked. I had been so nervous, especially since the conversation had been steered toward work so quickly once we got in the car, but I was relieved that she didn't make a big deal about it.

It was easy to talk to her about anything, from music to travel or food. I even shocked myself by bringing up a bit of my childhood; it took me by surprise when I found the words on the tip of my tongue. I usually waited until third or fourth dates to mention that I'd had troubles in my youth. If I was asked about my family I would generally just say they had passed on and leave it at that, not wanting to get into the drama about the drug abuse and neglect. I'd gotten over it, in time, primarily thanks to the support the chief gave me once he took me in. He was much more of a father to me than my own had ever been.

But Alexis seemed to get it. The brief comment she made about a similar struggle made me both relieved she could relate to me but also sad that she had suffered. It sounded like her situation might have even been worse than mine, if she was forced to miss meals.

I was blown away further when we made it to the bar and she kicked my ass up and down the pool table, and then roasted me in darts, to boot. Her history of bartending might also explain why she seemed to be so easy to talk to; some folks had a habit of pouring their hearts out to the bartender once they've had a few too many. She had probably gotten used to listening to folks, turning her attention into a money-making opportunity.

It was an exercise in self-control not to ask to come inside when I dropped her off at her apartment. She had accidentally let a yawn escape at the bar, though she tried to cover it up, so I knew she was tired and putting on a good show hiding it from me. But the way her body responded to mine when I kissed her, I'd like to think a new wave of energy might have rushed through her.

And that kiss. Holy crap, that kiss. That kiss was what dreams are made of... at least my dreams last night. The feel of her in my arms, leaning against my body, it was like electricity lighting me up inside.

I knew I had to see her again as soon as possible, rules of dating be damned. And I was going to go all in. The real me, one hundred percent. I knew exactly where we were going to go for the evening, the best place to show her what was truly important to me. Lay it all bare, and hope to God she liked what she saw. Because I knew that if I spent much more time with her, and it was anything like last night, her walking away after finding out the truth would absolutely break me.

FRAMED

Today would be agonizing, having to wait until after the workday was complete to see Alexis again. But fortunately, Ryan and I got some good news from the analysts yesterday evening. They had found dirt on Gerald Schwartz that we could use as leverage to see if he would flip on any of his employees if they were involved in any of the thefts over the last five years.

On the surface, the accounts all looked clean, and the employees didn't appear to be involved in any illegal activity. However, the tip from one of the people that Ryan interviewed had led us to look closer at the purchase and sale of the bust. Ryan talked to the appraiser and found a smoking gun. Briggs, the accountant, had also found a discrepancy in the equity accounts of the balance sheet that we could use as a bargaining chip before coming down hard on Schwartz.

Ryan had scheduled Gerald to come into the station, under the guise of giving him news about one of his employees. Telling people you wanted to interview them, much less interrogate them, didn't always work out for the best. They might claim they were too busy, or even make a run for it. I achieved the best results when people believed we were trying to help them, to do them a favor.

It also had the benefit of many of them coming without a lawyer, not asking for one until it was too late. Was it unethical? A bit, maybe. But we got a lot more criminals off the streets this way, so I was of the opinion that the ends justified the means. The ones who were smart knew not to talk to the police without an attorney present, and would either come to every interaction with one, or would ask for one as soon as they walked in the door. Others just *thought* they were smart, or at least smarter than us, and figured they couldn't possibly be caught and didn't want to risk looking more guilty by asking for their attorney to be present.

Schwartz would be in around ten, so I didn't need to rush into the office this morning. I took my time getting ready, I had a hot date tonight after all, then took the scenic route through town to the station. I stopped by a drive-thru coffee shop, deciding I'd treat Ryan to something special this morning. He always seemed to have coffee for me on the early-morning calls, so it was time I repaid the favor.

Unsurprisingly, Ryan was already at his desk when I walked into our office. He was completing a final review of the forensic accountant's discoveries and the major findings that our team recorded from all the employee files.

"Morning, Ryan! I got a surprise for you," I announced, setting down the coffee as I passed by his desk. "One mocha latte, from that little shop you're always raving about."

"Wow," he said, raising his eyebrows. "The date last night must have gone really well. I don't think I've seen you in this good of a mood in... ever?"

I laughed. He was probably right. "Oh, it definitely went well." I grinned mischievously. "I'm actually seeing her again tonight. This girl is really something else."

"Are you going to let me run a background check yet?" Ryan didn't have the same appreciation for a little mystery that I did, and it drove him crazy that I wouldn't tell him Alexis's name so he could look her up. I'd sneaked a look at her license last night when the waiter had carded her for the drink, and discovered her last name was Lee. Since I knew her address from picking her up at her place last night, I had all the information we needed for a simple background check, but I shook my head.

"Absolutely not. You know I like finding it all out for myself. That's half the fun of being a detective, working out the puzzle, uncovering the information bit by bit. Why ruin that?"

He sighed, but nodded. "Fine then, but don't blame me when she turns out to be a serial killer or something."

I laughed again, shaking my head at the ridiculousness of Alexis being some kind of criminal. I was pretty good at reading people, and I could tell that she was innately *good*. No matter what hardship shaped her youth, her inner light had not been extinguished.

Schwartz arrived promptly, dressed to the nines, which seemed to be his business attire. I supposed that with the clientele he catered to, an air of sophistication was required at all times to make the best impression.

We met him in the lobby, and I walked over to shake his hand while Ryan stayed at the door to keep it open. "Thanks so much for coming in, Mr. Schwartz. Please, right this way." He tried to head toward one of the meeting rooms accessible from the lobby, generally used for the more casual interviews to decrease the pressure to the interviewee, but we directed him through the security door instead.

"Aren't we meeting in one of the rooms out front?" he asked, beginning to look a little nervous as we marched him toward one of the interrogation rooms.

ELLIE HOHENSTEIN

"Oh, I wouldn't want to risk this information getting out, so we're making sure we won't be interrupted." I reassuringly replied. Or at least I hope it *sounded* reassuring. It was so much harder to get them into the interrogation rooms when we had to use force. Some folks panicked and tried to run through the bullpen, full of officers, to escape. Idiots.

Ryan held the door open as I escorted Schwartz inside. The room was utilitarian by design, containing only a table with two metal chairs plus one additional chair against the wall. The table was bolted to the ground, one less potential weapon in the room.

Ryan held his hand out, "Have a seat."

Schwartz scrunched his nose up as he sat down on the uncomfortable metal chair on the far side of the table. He was facing a two-way mirror, and we had a surprise waiting for him in the observation room on the other side of the glass. Ryan took the chair across from him, while I leaned against the wall beside the glass, my arms crossed in a confident, laid-back pose. Ryan got to play tough guy today, and for now I would appear like I was just along for the ride.

"As you know, Mr. Schwartz," Ryan began, laying a closed folder down on the table, "we've been looking through your company's records of all transactions over the last five years, which includes acquisitions, sales, employee records, and so on. I'd like to give you the opportunity to tell me if there is anything you'd like to share before we go over what we found."

"Share? Of course not, I have nothing to hide," he said, looking side-to-side as he spoke, a clear indication that he

FRAMED

did, in fact, have something to hide. "I'm sure whatever you found has a perfectly reasonable explanation."

Ryan shook his head, as if disappointed that Schwartz didn't come right out and confess to wrongdoing. "Of course, of course. Alright then, Mr. Schwartz. I'd like it if you could walk me through these transactions related to the sculpture that was recently stolen from your home."

He pulled a few documents out of the folder and lay them down in front of Schwartz. One was an image of the bust, another was the financial records of acquisition and sale from the company, and there was also the appraiser's report valuing the bust.

The documents showed that the company had acquired the sculpture for two-point-five million dollars from a private owner. The item had been authenticated and appraised before the sale, valuing the sculpture somewhere around three-point-five million, meaning the company had gotten a great deal and would likely have made a sizable profit on the item if it had gone to market or been sold through the auction house.

The bill of sale showed that Schwartz had only paid one-point-five million dollars for the same piece, which put the company at a financial loss of a million dollars.

Schwartz looked over the documents and confirmed, "Yes, I sold the sculpture to myself at a loss, which as the owner of the company is my right to do. Ultimately the loss just means smaller dividends for me, so it's no big deal. It was a common enough practice when my father was running the business, I can't see why it should be any different for me."

ELLIE HOHENSTEIN

I took the opportunity to pop into the conversation, taking an easygoing tone. "Well, there's two things that make it different, actually. The first is that you don't own the company."

At that, Schwartz jolted out of his seat, face red, and slammed his hands down on the table. "I beg your pardon, sir. That company is *mine*. I've poured my entire life into it! How dare you say it's not mine?"

I kept my confident smile. "You're right, I meant to say you don't own *all* of it. Did you know that your father left a small portion of the business in a trust to your sister? A very small portion in fact, only about two percent of the business, just enough to make a decent college fund for her children. Well, she passed away, what, ten years ago? And that trust, that two percent, passed right on down to her children. The same children who haven't seen a dime of those profits that you've been collecting these past ten years."

Schwartz was literally shaking with rage by this point. "That good-for-nothing wench never did anything for this company, her ownership claim is ridiculous!"

Ryan jumped back in, "Ridiculous, it may be, but that share is hers none-the-less. Now, you may not know this, but while your father was doing the same thing, he owned the whole company. But since you share a piece with your sister's family, that makes your sale an embezzlement. Add in the commission you paid to yourself for the sale, which is really just icing on the cake, I think you can see where we're going here."

FRAMED

We had Schwartz, there was no getting out of this for him. But it was possible that he might not know that. It was time to see what he did know.

Schwartz seemed to run out of steam. He fell back in his chair, pale, murmuring "embezzlement" over and over, trying to make sense of what was going on.

"Look," I said gently, kneeling down next to him, "you didn't know that the ownership had passed to her kids, we get it. I'm sure that we can talk to them and convince them not to press charges, assuming you can pay them the balance they're owed after all these years. They're grown now, and I'm sure that would be quite the payday for them. They wouldn't even have been able to access the funds until they came of age anyway. So really, no harm no foul, right?

"But there's something we need in return. Now, you claim to not know who took your sculpture. And we believe you, really we do. The biggest problem is that we have five years' worth of thefts to answer for, same as yours, with no evidence to follow. These all look like inside jobs. Now, a lot of those pieces ran through Schwartz and Son at some point or another. We want to know if any of your employees might be involved, either taking the items themselves or fencing them for the true thief. If you can give us this, then I'm sure we can help you work something out with your sister's kids."

Schwartz was almost in tears, shaking his head. "I wish I could, really. I would tell you if I knew anything. But all of our people are carefully vetted. We run frequent background checks on them, complete with financial analysis. There's no way any of them could be involved."

ELLIE HOHENSTEIN

We'd suspected as much, but we had to try. I turned and walked back toward the wall, nodding to the mirror as I went.

A few moments later the door opened and two people in crisp, black suits walked in. "Mr. Schwartz, we're from the IRS. I'm afraid you're under arrest for embezzlement and fraud," one of the newcomers said, pulling out a set of handcuffs.

"Fraud! What on earth are you talking about?" Schwartz looked startled as the agents pulled him up to stand, locking his hands behind his back.

Ryan turned in his chair, one arm resting on the back. "Oh did I forget to mention that part? I knew I was forgetting something. That's the other difference between what you did and when your father ran the business." He chuckled as he pulled out another sheet of paper.

"Our analysts caught something weird with the documentation on your company's purchase of the bust—the digital file of the appraiser's report seemed to have been edited after the rest of the documents. Of course, we followed up with the appraiser to confirm why that might have been the case, and he was more than happy to turn over his copy of the report. This is the appraiser's *real* assessment of the bust's value, which shows it only being worth two-point-one million dollars, and it's dated *after* the sale went through. It seems that you were in quite the hurry to purchase the bust from its previous owner. So much so, in fact, that you got swindled.

"The new report was falsified and backdated not only to look like your company made a winning purchase, but

FRAMED

also to allow you to take out a significant insurance policy on the sculpture. Of course, you never planned for a crime to have us digging into the financial history of the piece, but we had to check. Especially after it was your code that disabled the alarm on the night of the robbery."

"My code? That's outrageous! No, Daniel didn't set the alarm! It was his fault that the piece was taken!"

I pushed back off the wall, drawing in close to Schwartz, letting him feel some of my anger at his insistence of his son's guilt and refusal to hear the truth.

"Actually, the security company proved that Daniel did set the alarm when he came home that night. It was deactivated a few minutes later using *your* code. Your code, which, according to you, no one else knows. You're lucky that our findings on the fraud negate your insurance claim, or else we'd be pretty certain that you stole the bust yourself to make up the loss."

"I want my lawyer," Schwartz demanded.

"I'm sure you do." I snorted. It was a little late for that. "Take him away."

At that, the agents dragged Schwartz out of the room, reading him his rights as they went. Since his crimes were at a federal level, they were moving him to their office in the next town over rather than booking him at our station. We had turned over all our findings to their team for evidence in their case, so less paperwork for me. Win-win.

I clapped Ryan on the back, congratulating him on a successful interrogation. Now, if only we could carry that momentum to finding the sculpture and catching the thief.

Chapter 9

Jake

Ryan and I walked back to our office, our spirits soaring—for the moment—from the rush from catching one of the bad guys. It wasn't every day that we uncovered embezzlement and fraud, especially when the whole thing started with a home robbery. But my mirth faded as I remembered the bust was still missing.

I fell back into my chair and ran my hands through my hair. "That was fun, but what are we going to do about the bust? We still have no idea who took it."

Ryan didn't take defeat easily, but I knew he was just as stumped at this point. We'd been here before with the previous thefts, so we knew the routine even if we were reluctant to admit it.

"With the fraud negating the insurance policy that takes out Schwartz as a suspect. Daniel's out too since he definitely wouldn't have had the resources to fence the

FRAMED

item or the time to hide it between when he got home and when the police showed up. You already made the rounds with your CI's earlier this week to ask about the painting and Daniel's gang involvement, did you get any leads from that?"

"No. The folks who had heard of him said that Daniel was just a patsy for some thug called J-Dog, not involved in anything serious. He wouldn't have had any enemies, either. No one has heard of the bust being sold in the city either, my guess is whoever is handling the fencing is doing it from a different town. It could be across the world by now."

"So I guess it's going up on the wall," Ryan said with a sigh.

We had all the unrecovered items in our string of cold cases posted up on the wall of our office, practically running a border around the room, there were so many. This thief was incredibly good, we just had to hope they would slip up one day.

At this point, I wanted to meet the person behind the thefts more than just catching him. Every case presented a new challenge, and I wanted to shake their hand for being such a worthy foe. I was borderline envious at their ability to think so many steps ahead, to keep every scene so pristine without any evidence we could use. I often wondered if I might have turned out the same if I hadn't been taken in by the chief as a teen.

"I'll let the chief know," I said dejectedly. "We'll pack up the evidence and leave it unsolved for now. You're still planning to meet with that possible snitch we bagged the other day, right?"

"Yeah, I'm going out at two to make sure I beat him there. If he doesn't show I'm going to be really frustrated for wasting my afternoon. I don't know how you stand to work with these crooks."

I laughed. Honestly, I found myself fitting in better with many of the criminals I worked with than the officers on the force. Some of them took the job way too seriously, like Ryan, and I knew sometimes you had to color outside the lines to get the job done.

"You find the ones that are connected enough to know a lot of what's going on, and who really, really don't want to go to jail. They are much more motivated."

I got up and walked out of the office to try to find the chief, the damper on what would have otherwise been a banner day.

I found Chief Douglas in his office. He waved me in and motioned for me to sit in the chair in front of his desk.

"Good work on the Schwartz case, Jake. It was an unexpected twist, but these white-collar busts make great headlines, so thank you. Would you like to be included in the interview this time?"

The chief knew me better than that. I never chased fame and was happy just getting to solve the puzzle.

"You go on ahead, Chief. See if Ryan wants to, though. The kid did most of the hard work and he's got a bright future."

"How is his training going? He's been a detective for a few years now, do you think he's ready to break out on his own, maybe lead a new partner?"

I hesitated. "Ryan is good... He's got decent instincts and a sharp mind, but I'm not sure he's quite ready to

FRAMED

spread his wings yet. He's so rigid, unwavering in his beliefs. More force than finesse. Maybe he just needs a few cases where he can take the lead but have me there as backup."

"Sounds good," the chief said. "Maybe we'll get lucky and something truly interesting will happen here soon. Any updates on our mystery thief?"

My frustration became visible. "No, it looks like this bust from the Schwartz case is another one going unsolved. We've come to a dead end; there's just no evidence. Do you think we could get some help from federal agencies?"

"Perhaps. I'll drop a line out to the Art Crimes department up in D.C. The value of everything is getting up there, maybe we just need some fresh eyes on it."

He thanked me again for my hard work, then asked me to close the door behind me on my way out.

The rest of the day passed calmly, spent filling out the paperwork to close the case and packing everything away. Around four, I left to go home to change for my date with Alexis.

I dressed casually, in a simple logo tee and jeans. Tonight I was showing her the real me, all of me, and there was no better way to start than to dress exactly how she would find me on a normal evening or weekend.

She had texted me the address of an office building to pick her up at, saying she would meet me out front. She was sitting on a bench in front of the skyscraper when I pulled up, checking out something on her phone while she waited.

"Hey pretty lady! Need a ride?" I joked as I rolled down the window. She jerked her head up and a huge smile lit up her face. Knowing that I was the cause of her smile inflated my ego to the size of the building behind her. I just hoped that she would still smile at me after she learned about my past.

"Hi!" Alexis exclaimed, walking over. I got out quickly and ran around the car to greet her with a quick kiss and to open her door. She laughed at my chivalry but thanked me.

"Always the gentleman, aren't you?"

"I try to be. Especially for a woman who deserves it." I gave her a flirty smile and a wink, then walked back to my side of the car.

"Am I overdressed?" she asked, eyeing my outfit. "We can stop by my place really quickly and I can change?"

She was dressed professionally, a deep purple blouse with some frills along the neckline and a pair of gray slacks. Nothing too fancy, but would be slightly out of place at our destination. Then again, I thought she would stand out no matter where she was.

"Hmm… Nope, you're perfect." I grinned and we headed off.

She looked a little nervous as we drove through some of the sketchier parts of town, or maybe she was just confused and it was my nerves causing me to misinterpret her reactions. I pulled into the parking lot of the youth center, easily finding a spot up front. Very few of these kids had cars, but there were spaces for the staff and the few kids who did drive.

FRAMED

"What are we doing here?" she asked cautiously as we got out of the car.

I steeled myself, bracing for disappointment if she wanted to leave. "I know this isn't exactly the best place for a romantic date, and we don't have to stay long if you're not comfortable, but I wanted to show you something real about me. I know I alluded a bit to not having the best childhood, but I didn't go into much detail since it's not really great first-date conversation. My parents were drug addicts, and this place became my haven.

"My parents had struggled with drugs for as long as I can remember. Growing up, I was always having to take care of them, cooking and cleaning, trying to pick up small jobs to help keep a roof over our heads. Other kids ran a lemonade stand for fun things, or to get a little extra cash for a new toy or game, but I did things like that just so we had food to eat. Eventually, I got angry and started acting out, which of course didn't help anything. I'd come here when things were really bad, sometimes for a few nights at a time. I got really lucky though. When I was fifteen, I met someone who recognized my potential, and he worked to get me away from my family. He took me in and helped me turn my life around."

I was shifting my weight back and forth while I talked, making eye contact as much as I could but I was so afraid about what her reaction might be. As I brought my short speech to a close, I glanced up and saw a soft smile on her face.

"Let's go," she said gently as she took my hand, leading me toward the building.

124

I laced my fingers with hers and gave her hand a quick squeeze, her actions meaning more to me than I could say. I opened the door for her, but as we walked through the halls, things started to get a little strange.

There was a chorus of almost everyone we saw saying "Hey, Lex!" as we passed. Alexis would smile, wave, nod, or even say hello in return to each of them, greeting a handful of them by name. We passed the center director's office, where he was standing in his doorway talking with a staff member.

"Oh! Hey Alexis, Jake. I didn't realize you two knew each other!" the director said cheerfully. Alexis saw my stunned expression and saved me from answering.

"We met by chance earlier this week, in fact," she told the director. "He took me out to a lovely dinner last night and is showing me his old stomping grounds today."

"Oh Jake, you've found an absolute angel!" The director clapped his hand on my shoulder and gestured to Alexis. "This one here pops by every other week and the kids absolutely love her. She's even got a few of them coming up to her swanky office, and every time they come back they go on and on about her. She's made such a difference in these kids' lives, we can't thank her enough.

"And Alexis, it's a miracle that you've never ran into Jake here before! He's here a few nights every week. Although he's usually off in the gym or the rec room, so I'm not sure your visits would have collided much." He laughed and wished us well for our visit, mentioning how the kids would be thrilled that two of their favorite volunteers were getting together.

FRAMED

Once he was out of earshot, I turned to her with my eyebrow crooked. "An angel, huh?"

She laughed. "It was kind of him to say, but no. These kids are mostly angels at heart. I have a few centers I rotate through in Willow Springs and some of the surrounding towns. You'd be surprised how often children that are considered 'troubled' are just confused and in need of someone to help them understand all that is going on in their lives. They need someone to talk to—someone who will truly *hear* what they're saying. That's all I really do. The rest is on the kids."

"So why this?" I asked. "Why pick troubled children to help? Why is this important to you?" I wanted to know her story, even more so now that I knew this passion was something we shared.

We moved to the rec room and sat down in a couple of chairs. There were a few younger kids in here, but none that I was familiar with. They were mostly playing games at the other end of the room, so we had a bit of privacy.

"I grew up a lot like you, actually." She gave a small, sad smile, as though taking comfort in the fact that we shared these experiences even if they were bad. "My parents died in a car accident when I was young. I was ten, and I almost didn't make it myself."

I couldn't help but interrupt. "You were in the car with them?"

"Yeah, I was left in critical condition for a few days but pulled through. When I woke up, I had lost everyone. You know how they say there are five stages of grief? Denial, anger, bargaining, depression, and acceptance? Well, I spent most of my teen years in the 'anger' stage. I was

126

angry at my mom, for cheating on my dad, angry at my dad for not paying attention to the road while driving after he found out, angry at my aunt, who had been estranged from my father and didn't want to take in his orphan, but especially angry at myself for not knowing how to stop being so angry.

"And of course, with anger came trouble. I acted out a lot too, and things went downhill fast. But unlike you, no one found me to help pull me out. I had to do it myself. I worked to find ways to pay my way through college, and that's when I was finally able to move past my loss and start making a better life.

"I want to help other kids who might be feeling the same things. Hopefully, I can use my experience and training to make it so they don't have to fight through the same issues I did."

"So, you're a shrink?" I asked. That would explain how she was so easy to talk to and why she never pushed me for more than I was ready to share. It was literally her job. I still loved it about her, though.

Alexis crinkled her nose at the term. "Psychiatrist. I went to medical school and everything."

"That's incredible. You took a weakness and turned it into a strength, all on your own. And rather than just sitting pretty, charging an arm and a leg for your sessions you're using it to help those less fortunate. A lot of people would take their new life and run, refusing to look back to when times were tough."

She waved me off, seemingly dismissing the idea that she was doing something out of the norm, or better than someone else would have done. "My past is a part of what

FRAMED

made me who I am. I would have been a completely different person if I had access to someone like me when I was a kid. I might not have chosen the same path, but I like to think I would have been successful in other ways."

She had a point. If I had found someone I could talk to—really open up to—back when I was a teen, I might not have gotten into as much trouble as I did. I'd definitely had issues; I still did really. A good shrink would have helped me see that it wasn't my fault that my parents had addiction issues, that my feelings that they chose their addictions over me were valid but that it wasn't a reflection of my value. And I might know those things now, but I could have tackled those issues in my teens rather than carrying those burdens into adulthood and allowing them to impact my relationships.

"I'm sure you would have, but I think I like this version of you more," I said with a smile. Lightening the mood, I challenged her: "And I think you like me too, but the big question is whether you will still like me after you see me get my ass kicked by a bunch of teenagers at basketball."

She barked a laugh and jokingly replied, "I think you mean will I still like you after you get your ass kicked by a bunch of teens, *and me*?"

"Absolutely. Let's do it." I led the way into the gym where a few kids were playing, and I asked if Alexis and I could join in the game. She kicked off her heels and joined one team while I joined another. Her team won handily; Alexis even scored a few baskets. I bought us all ice cream from a truck nearby after the game, Alexis and I sharing a bowl.

It certainly wasn't the mushy romantic type of date, but in my opinion, this was so much better. I felt like I had finally found someone who I could truly be myself with, who would understand some of the pain I still carried from my youth and wouldn't judge me for it. Someone who I could heal from those wounds with, and work together to grow into stronger people.

I didn't understand how I could feel this strongly, this soon, but Alexis Lee had some kind of spell over me and I hoped that would never change.

Chapter 10

Alexis

I didn't see Jake over the weekend, but he was never far from my thoughts. Our date on Friday was by far the most interesting and unique one I had ever been on, but it was also the most meaningful. Jake had opened up so completely that I was having trouble reminding myself that we were only up to the second date. I was falling for this man hard, and I wasn't sure how to slow down, or if I even wanted to.

Even though we didn't see each other, we texted lightly through the weekend, no serious conversations, just enough for a little "I'm thinking of you" reminder here and there. I was hoping to be able to see him again soon, I just wasn't sure when that would be. My nights would be filled with recon work this week and I didn't want to have to end our next date early for that. I felt bad enough about having to leave the first one when I would have very much liked for it to continue.

I spent the weekend trailing the McGill family and their staff in preparation for my heist. By Monday, I was reasonably certain I had their routines down, but I wasn't planning to actually steal the painting until Thursday. That would give me a full week of studying their habits, which so far seemed to be the same each day, but I wanted the additional time to be sure. A week still wasn't much history to base my plan on, but I was operating on a tight timeline to ensure the most impact.

Bill, Ralph's dad, seemed to work at one of the restaurants most nights, coming home consistently around eleven. This left Ralph with a nanny all afternoon, from the time he got home from school until he went to bed. It was no wonder that the poor kid felt neglected by his parents. The nanny clearly loved him, but it wasn't the same.

I was leaning toward the idea of sneaking into the house before Bill got home, avoiding the risk of being interrupted altogether. The nanny was a live-in, the only staff member who stayed in the house, but she was an older woman who went to bed shortly after Ralph did. That would give me a window of around an hour to get in, get the painting, and get back out.

I hadn't seen much of Alison McGill, Ralph's mom. She had been home Thursday evening but had left Friday and had not returned over the weekend. She was an unknown that I would need this week to uncover. Her routine could throw off my entire tentative plan or could lead to me having to push back my timeline.

FRAMED

Also mysteriously absent was the mistress that Ralph had mentioned during his last session. I wasn't sure if this meant that his father had decided to end the affair rather than risk Ralph telling his mother, or possibly they just didn't see each other very often, especially over the weekend while Ralph would be in the house.

Ralph was coming in for his weekly session this morning, and I would use the opportunity to gather some more information. I felt guilty involving him, but I didn't have much choice with the short timeline I had given myself. I wouldn't allow him to give me any information like alarm codes, nor did I ever manipulate my patients in any way to help me with the thefts. The kids were innocent, and I made sure to keep them that way.

Also on my docket for today was Daniel Schwartz. He had switched his regularly scheduled appointment last week and moved it up after my break-in, but his father had been arrested on Friday on charges of fraud, so he had called that afternoon to see if we could switch his session around again this week. I hated that he had to wait through the weekend, but my schedule Friday had been packed and then I'd had my date with Jake. Daniel had my emergency line number though, so I knew that if it had been urgent, he would have called me.

When I got to my office Jess greeted me with a freshly made espresso. I was operating in a mildly sleep-deprived state, staying up until around three each morning watching the McGill family. Some days it felt like I'd only been asleep a few minutes. Over the weekend I'd grabbed catnaps where I could, but it was certainly not sufficient rest. I'd make sure to take a solid nap before I went in for

132

the painting, ensuring I was operating at the top of my game. This was the shortest timetable I'd ever given myself for a job of this size, so I'd need to have all my wits about me during the heist.

I ran quickly over my notes from Ralph's last session and made a mental list of questions that I needed to ask, both as a follow-up for him, and investigation for myself. The nanny brought him up right on time, as usual, and got settled in for the next hour. Ralph picked the same room we had met in last week, and we started our session talking about how school had gone the previous week.

It seemed to take forever for him to get relaxed enough for us to talk about something real, though it probably felt longer than it actually was due to my nerves and the necessity to get the information. I was finally able to bring the conversation around to the affair almost fifteen minutes into our session.

"So, Ralph, last week you told me something you discovered about your father. Do you want to talk about that?"

"Oh… yeah, I guess we can. Dad and I talked the night after we had our last session. He told me that he had told the lady that he couldn't see her anymore; that he loved my mom and was happy with her. And since he wasn't going to see the other lady anymore, I didn't need to feel like I needed to tell my mom anything."

So, he had ended the affair, or at least had told Ralph that he did. It could really be either, but if he ended it then that would explain why I hadn't managed to catch sight of her.

FRAMED

"And do you agree with him that you don't feel like you need to tell your mom?"

Ralph considered this for a few moments. Last week he had been more concerned about his mom taking the hurt out on him, but it seemed like now he was thinking about what would be best for her. That was incredible growth for someone his age, to think of how their actions affect others and not just doing something to make themselves feel better.

"I'm not really sure what I want to do. I don't want to hurt her, so I feel like I shouldn't tell her, especially if there's nothing to tell anymore. But then I think of how I felt when I found out that my friends at school were talking about me behind my back, and how angry it made me. I wished that they would have just come talk to me when they'd had a problem, instead of making fun of me when they thought I wouldn't find out. And that makes me think that my mom would rather know about it so she knows that something was wrong and can decide how she wants to fix it."

"You worry that you're taking away her decision by not telling her?"

"Yeah, I think so. It was really hard last week before my dad talked to me. I was angry at him for how he treated me and wanted to make him suffer too by telling her, but I couldn't stop thinking about how he told me she would be mad at me for telling her. I didn't want to lose her. But it got a bit easier when I didn't have to see her every day."

"Why didn't you have to see her every day? Was she too busy at one of the restaurants?" I tried not to appear

134

too interested, but this could be critical information for my upcoming heist.

"No, she went to a spa or something for something she called a 'wellness getaway' or something like that. I can't remember the words she used, but she won't be back until Friday."

That was perfect, I didn't need to bother knowing Mrs. McGill's routine. All I needed now was to have Jess figure out what spa Mrs. McGill was staying at and set up some kind of alert in case she checked out early. That only left me with Ralph and the Nanny, but as long as his father was working at the restaurants that night, I should have plenty of time to get the painting.

"So, have you forgiven your father for the way he reacted when you found him and the woman in his office? You seemed angered and a little scared by his yelling."

"I guess so. I mean when I get surprised or caught doing something I'm not supposed to I don't always act the right way. Sometimes I get mad, so I get why he reacted the way he did. But I'm still having some nightmares about it. They're getting better, but his face was so angry. I see it when I close my eyes at night, and it can be hard to fall asleep."

Ralph and I talked a little longer about his relationship with his father and what steps he might take this week with his mother out of the house to try and repair it. He didn't seem too convinced that my suggestions would work, but he promised to think about it. I wasn't positive he was ready to forgive his father quite yet, but I had certainly learned that you never knew what might happen. You only get one father, after all.

FRAMED

Daniel came by in the afternoon. When taking the bust I'd had no idea that this would end up happening, but I felt like it was just icing on the cake. I wasn't sure of the details, but Daniel had mentioned before that he thought his father had done something shady when purchasing the sculpture, but I hadn't realized it was something outright illegal.

I tried to make sure I didn't appear too eager to hear the news, starting the session cautiously.

"So, Daniel, can you tell me about why you wanted to move up your appointment this week? Has something happened with the case of the theft you told me about before?"

I had to act like I didn't know that his father had been arrested, as I hadn't seen it explicitly published anywhere. The only reason I knew was because Jess and I had been watching so closely. Jess had hacked the police department's crappy server a while back to see what the latest updates were on the items we stole. She added an alert to her search program after every time I pulled a job.

Daniel grinned, like his father getting arrested was something he was thrilled about. "Karma, that's what fucking happened. Dad got arrested on Friday. I don't think it's public yet—with so much money on the line, the IRS doesn't want to spook all the folks making trades at the antique shop—but they said the charges were because he faked the appraisal to get a higher insurance policy, and that he embezzled from the company."

Daniel genuinely looked giddy. I'm not sure if he realized that his father was probably going to jail for years, and that he wouldn't be able to help if Daniel got into

136

trouble again, but I couldn't begrudge him a little excitement. Gerald, Daniel's father, had told him that he would never be fit to run the business, but it looked like Gerald wasn't fit either if he had to falsify an appraisal.

I really couldn't have picked my target any better. I didn't know all the ins-and-outs of the law when it came to business-related crimes, but I was hoping that buying the item from his own company at a loss was at least frowned upon. Thanks to the falsified appraisal, the insurance wouldn't even pay out so the whole cover-up was for nothing.

"And how do you really feel about your father possibly going to jail? That could take him away from you when you might need him."

"Nah, he wasn't much good to me anyway," Daniel said, dismissing the notion, "Except for writing checks. And I can do that myself. I've got a ton of money in my trust that isn't tied up with the business, plus I think Mom's gonna take over to keep it running. Honestly, Doc, without Dad there to tear me down I'm probably going to be able to cut back on my sessions."

That would be good if he was ready, but I didn't believe Daniel should quit therapy until he at least got away from that gang he was fooling around with. If I could get him to that point, I'd happily wave goodbye and watch him head down the path toward a successful life.

"Well, we should probably wait to see if he actually gets convicted, and how you're feeling at that point, but I hope you are right.

"What about the robbery?" I asked, needing a hint of what my own fate looked like as well as how Daniel's next

FRAMED

few months might go. "Do you still believe you will be blamed for the piece going missing?"

"Nah, that detective came by over the weekend and told us that they had reached a stand-still in the case and would have to wait until new evidence was found, or something like that. Oh, and get this! He made sure to tell my mom that I *did* set the alarm that night, and that it was my dad's code that disabled it. If anyone was going to be the prime suspect in the theft, it would have been him. I bet they might still try and pin it on him, but I'm not sure since the insurance won't pay out anymore."

"Well, that is good news for you that you aren't being considered, and it must have felt nice to be vindicated about the alarm."

"It was awesome. Mom couldn't believe that it was his code that turned it off. She doesn't even know the code, so there's no way it could have been anyone but Dad. She started mumbling about him sleepwalking or something, like he would have turned off the code in his sleep. It was so dumb, I burst out laughing when she said it."

"So, what will you do from here? Are your friends going to think it's 'cool' that your dad was arrested?"

"I don't know, maybe. But I don't care. I was mostly just hanging out with them to piss Dad off. Some of them are cool, but hanging out with them always felt off, you know? Like when they'd push me to break into places, but never follow me in. Or they'd say they were gonna be the lookout while I stole something, but when I got caught, they were gone. It's like everyone's out for themselves, which wasn't much better than home."

ELLIE HOHENSTEIN

I hoped he really meant that, and that he wouldn't fall back in with those folks when the novelty of having his father gone wore off. He still wouldn't have a role model, and his mother would be under added pressure running the business, leaving even less time for him than she used to have.

I might suggest to her that it would be a good opportunity to get Daniel into the office, to help her out and to build their relationship back up. At least, I would if I could get her in for a conference. I imagined that would be even more difficult after today.

We talked a little longer before he left and, overall, he seemed to be handling everything well. The best news of all, I was in the clear on the Schwartz heist. Jess confirmed later that day that the police had officially resigned the case, leaving it unsolved unless more evidence surfaced. In another week the payout from the sale should come in.

Now unburdened, I was coming for the McGills.

Chapter 11

Alexis

I was in great spirits by the end of the day. I had a solid plan for the heist, assuming the next few days of surveillance didn't show anything new. The Schwartz case seemed to be closing, plus things with Jake had been going so well.

I knew it would be a few more days until I could see him again, but I didn't want Jake to think I had gotten cold feet after he opened up at the youth center. He had appeared so worried at first, but all I could think when he was telling his story was: *Finally, I found someone who can really understand me, what I went through.*

I was reasonably certain he hadn't taken the same path that I did and gone into clandestine activities, but his past had challenged him at every turn and instead of breaking he had taken his experiences and used them to put good back into the world. He genuinely wanted to help those kids at the center make better lives for themselves, to rescue them like he had been rescued.

For a moment I dreamed of a possible future for the two of us. We could have a giant house out in the suburbs, adopt or foster troubled teens and give them a loving home, and set them up for success. With the money from my heists, I could organize scholarships or grants that they could receive so they could attend college, never knowing it was me that funded it or where the money came from.

We could have dogs and cats, then train them to be service animals for the kids. We could throw events for the youth center to help keep the kids doing wholesome activities rather than getting involved with the gangs.

And we could be *happy*. A family—something neither of us had been given a chance to truly have.

But how would he react when he found out about my stealing? That I was still a criminal, even if I used it for good—taking from those who deserve it and giving to those in need? Could he love me even with all that? I'd just have to make sure we had as strong of a relationship as possible before coming clean about it. That way he would love me too much to walk away after learning my secret.

I decided that I didn't want to wait until after the heist to continue developing our relationship. There was no reason I couldn't call him and talk while I tailed Bill. Sitting in my car watching a mark was fairly boring anyway. If something interesting happened, I would just end the call.

I settled in, hit the dial button, and steeled my nerves. What if he was a text-only kind of guy? I didn't think so since he called me that first night to set our date, but he didn't exactly stay on to talk after we agreed to a time, so I was a little nervous that he might not enjoy this.

He answered on the third ring, "Hey there, I was just thinking about you." His voice gave me goosebumps, I swear.

"Good things, I hope," I flirted back.

"Haven't found any bad things about you yet, so you're in luck. How was your day?"

"It was really good actually. Had a few patients that seem to be making some real progress. That always makes me happy." I paused for a few moments. "Sorry, I'm not used to having anyone to talk about my successes with."

"No need to apologize," he said with a chuckle. "I'm glad I'm the one you wanted to tell. I feel the same way sometimes, I could tell people about my time hanging out with the kids down at the center but unless they experienced how hard that life can be, they just don't understand how big of a deal it really is. I might not be a shrink," he added with a slight tease in his voice, "but I know how hard it can be to reach troubled kids."

"So, what about your day? Anything exciting happen?"

"No, it's been pretty quiet lately. I actually wish I had more to do." His tone turned back to flirty as he continued, "You see, there's this girl that I've been seeing this past week and she's all I can seem to think about. It's starting to affect my job performance and I think my coworkers are getting tired of me talking about how beautiful and smart and incredible she is."

I couldn't help but laugh, "Oh really? Please, go on."

I settled into the seat of my car and chatted with Jake for almost an hour. We were still learning about each other and neither of us had much experience dating anyone seriously. We had jumped into such heavy topics on our second date, and while it was amazing that we were able to get to the real stuff without any issues, I was enjoying learning the little things about him as well.

My next few nights continued in the same pattern. I would spend the mornings treating patients, then the evenings talking with Jake while I staked out the members of the McGill family and staff. Everything seemed to be coming together with the plan Jess and I had come up with.

Finally, the day of the heist came. I canceled my afternoon trip to the youth center so I could go home and sleep. I needed to be fresh for the event. I woke up shortly before dark, dressed in all black, and grabbed my cap and gloves. I didn't wear a mask during heists, not wanting to impair my vision. Instead, I relied on the cameras not being able to see me at all thanks to Jess repositioning them, but I needed to protect the scene from traces of hair or fingerprints.

I made sure every single strand of hair was restrained and trapped while on the job, and all my skin was covered except for my face. I also wore protective shoe covers indoors to make sure I did not leave any footprints or track in any unexplained materials. While outside, I always walked on my toes so that any footprints left looked more like animal tracks. I'd even thought about going so far as to buy shoes with points on the toes that mirrored deer tracks, but I hadn't felt it necessary yet. With the

FRAMED

forecasted storms, I probably wouldn't need to worry about footprints anyway.

I drove out to the McGill estate and parked my car in the trees, down a path I had found when staking them out. It got me close enough that I wouldn't have to carry the painting far, which was good since it would be large and heavy. It was fully dark by the time I arrived, and I had to navigate to the spot without the benefit of my headlights since I didn't want to tip off any of the staff on my way in. The alcove I had discovered wasn't visible from the road, so I was safe leaving my car there while I was watching and infiltrating the house.

I got within a hundred yards of the tree line and climbed up a sturdy tree with low, thick branches. I made my roost where I could pull out my binoculars and watch the house. The branches were strong enough that if I moved around, they wouldn't shake too much, and the tree was far enough back that if they *did* shake, no one should be able to see it anyway. I settled in to wait for the house to grow dark.

Even in the dark, the McGill home was impressive. When Jess and I had reviewed the blueprints, we saw that it was around eight-thousand square feet. It was built into a hill, three stories in total but the lowest one was below ground in the front, opening to the side. That level contained their garage, a theater room, home gym, and a bonus room. The main level was used for entertaining, with multiple parlors, a large kitchen and dining room, the office, and a great room for the family. All the bedrooms were located upstairs.

ELLIE HOHENSTEIN

The exterior of the house resembled a small castle. Each corner had a rounded room, similar to a tower. The house was made of gray bricks and stonework, with arching doors and windows. Outdoor spotlights were placed behind the bushes to shine up on the walls, illuminating the home in a soft glow. I silently thanked the McGills for making my job of monitoring the house easier with the lighting. Ralph and the nanny both had rooms along the front of the house, so I would be able to see when they turned in for the night.

I had called the restaurant that Bill was supposed to be working at tonight to check that his plans hadn't changed. I'd used the guise of making a reservation for that night, and once I had been told that they were fully booked, I pretended to be outranged and stated that Bill was a personal friend, and I was sure he would get me a table if he saw me. The hostess had confirmed that he was planning to be in that night, and I was more than welcome to try my luck.

That meant that the only non-family member remaining in the house was the nanny. The light in Ralph's room had been dark all evening, which was unusual. I thought back to our session on Monday and vaguely remembered him saying something about a day off school on Friday, so perhaps he was staying at a friend's house. That could mean that the nanny had the night off and might change up her routine, but the woman hadn't gone to bed later than nine a single time in the past week, so it seemed unlikely to interfere with my plans.

Sure enough, the light in the nanny's room flipped on around eight-thirty, then off again around nine. I waited

FRAMED

for another half hour to be sure that she was well and truly asleep and wasn't planning to leave the house. I started to move towards the house.

Now, it was time for the fun part.

The first step was interrupting the satellite signal for the security system. I was lucky that it was a cloudy night with thunderstorms due to start shortly after I would leave. That should provide reason enough for why the signal might have gone out if they look into it. Jess had said the alarms deactivated randomly from satellite issues, so no one should question why the alarm malfunctioned tonight.

Jess had managed to acquire a signal jammer for me. This machine was supposed to interrupt satellite signals but leave cell phones undisturbed. It was pocket-sized, which meant that I could hold onto it while I was in the house without too much inconvenience. I only needed to leave it running for a few minutes, just long enough to disconnect the alarm if it had been set.

I walked around to the back of the house, keeping to the trees. I had inconspicuously marked two that lined up the entrance of my path towards the house, outside of the view of the camera Jess had repositioned a week ago. Approaching the home, I turned on the jammer. The range was fairly small, so only the desired target was affected in more densely populated areas. I needed to stand right next to the house to be sure it would work.

I waited around five minutes, still as a statue, then headed for the back door. My lock-pick set was one of the most useful investments I had ever made. It was the best set on the black-market and had never failed me. I finessed

146

the pins in the lock and turned the knob once I had everything lined up correctly. The door swung open silently, admitting me to the house. I took two more minutes to put on my shoe covers and make sure I didn't hear the beeping of an alarm, then turned off the jammer and stepped inside.

The back door had been the closest entrance to the office, but there were still a few rooms I had to cross to get there. I tip-toed my way through the house, the soft carpets muffling my steps. The house was well-made, and none of the floors creaked as I moved. The opulence of the house was mirrored in the interior, with artwork and expensive trinkets all over the place. There were crystal dishes holding candies in each room, fancy chandeliers, and anything that would show off the family's wealth to those who visited. If I hadn't had a specific target in mind, there would still be plenty of options of items to take and get a good payday.

When I reached the office, I was pleased to find it unlocked. I hadn't been sure if Bill would find it necessary to lock up his business dealings from the house staff, but apparently he either had the information secured inside or he trusted his team. His wife helped run the restaurants, and there would be no need to hide it from her. I hoped this was simply the habit, and it wouldn't be unusual for the door to be found unlocked tomorrow.

The layout of the room was exactly the same as it had been in the pictures from the latest party they had thrown. The painting I'd selected was on the wall opposite the desk as we had expected, but was a bit larger in person than I had expected.

FRAMED

As part of my preparation, I had gotten a picture of a similar size and weight that Jess and I assumed it would be and had practiced carrying it around my apartment to get used to the handling. While the reality was not significantly off in size, the frame looked to be solid gold, which would be much heavier than I had practiced. This left me with two options, I could either take the picture out of the frame and leave the frame in place, or I would have to be more careful when setting it down while opening doors, and lighter on my toes when walking through the woods to ensure I didn't leave footprints.

I decided that leaving the frame behind was too much of a risk, both from an evidence standpoint as well as the time it would take to remove without damaging the canvas. I could go for a slash-and-grab, but that would significantly reduce the value of the piece. After an examination of the mounting hardware used, I pulled out a few tools and began disconnecting the hooks from the frame. The weight of the frame meant that the hooks had been reinforced in the wall to ensure the security of the hang, but the bolts came out of the back of the frame easily enough. I pocketed the screws so there wouldn't be anything from the frame left behind.

Gently lowering the frame to the ground, I got a feel for the weight, adjusting my stance and hold appropriately. Satisfied, I headed out the door, making sure to close up behind me so everything would be left just as it had been before I got there.

I inched through the house, cognizant of every sound around me. With no deadbolt on the back door, I was able to turn the lock on the handle before pulling the door closed behind me.

I kept my footsteps as light as I could walking back toward the trees. My movements within the trees could be written off as activity from the wildlife that was sure to live there, but human footsteps through the yard would be noticed. I kept to my toes, hoping any remaining indentations after the coming rain might be written off as animal steps.

Snagging my binoculars off the tree as I went, I headed back to my car and loaded the painting into the trunk, laying down my back seat to accommodate the size and covering it with a blanket. Once I'd pulled out of the alcove and navigated back onto the road, I got back out to check to make sure I hadn't left any tire marks or signs that a car had been there.

I still had approximately half an hour before I expected Bill to return home, but there were a few other houses off of this road, so if he came home early he would hopefully assume that my car belonged to a guest of one of the neighbors. Satisfied that all was well, I got back in my car and started my drive out of town.

My drop point for this painting was two towns over, and it would take at least an hour to drive there. But that was fine with me. I was riding high on the success of another mission. Everything had gone off without a hitch.

I found myself wanting to call Jake, to talk to him about my win and to celebrate with him. I knew that I couldn't really tell him about this, not yet at least, but the idea that it might be possible in the future added to the smile I wouldn't be able to shake off all night.

FRAMED

For now, I turned up my music and sped down the road. Another job well done.

Chapter 12

Jake

As soon as I walked into the station on Friday morning, I could tell something had just happened. Officers were mobilizing, getting ready to head out to a scene as I went up to my office. Ryan had beaten me in, as usual, but appeared to be gathering up his stuff to leave.

"I was just about to call you," he said as I approached. "Alison McGill reported finding her husband's body in his home office this morning. Everyone's on their way to their estate; the coroner will meet us out there. Do you want to ride together, or should I drive separately so I can come back early for research?"

"Did she give any details of what we should expect at the scene?" I asked.

"She said there was a lot of blood. So, I'm guessing murder rather than natural causes," Ryan replied.

FRAMED

I started to get excited. "We don't get many murders in Willow Springs, outside of gang violence. This will be good experience for you. Stick close to me through this whole investigation. I'll show you some of the things to look for, and help you with the questions we need to ask that differ from other crimes. Also, people experiencing a sudden loss are sometimes distraught and need a gentler tone, so we've got to be extra careful about how we approach the witnesses.

"Let's ride together. I'm not sure what condition Mrs. McGill will be in, so I'll lead the initial interview with her while you observe. This is only your second or third murder investigation, right?"

"Third," he confirmed. "That sounds good. I'll take notes so you can focus on the scene and interviews."

On our drive to the estate, we discussed theoretical investigation tactics for murder cases. Most of the officers were already on site when we arrived, scattered around the grounds and the house taking pictures and cataloging evidence. They had left everything in its place, marked with numbers so the evidence could be easily matched up to the logs back at the station. They were waiting for us to observe the scene in its original state before they started collecting everything. Mrs. McGill and the staff members had been cordoned off so they couldn't interfere.

Ryan and I planned to see the body before we went to talk to Mrs. McGill. We already knew it was in the office, which was in the back corner of the house, but we inspected the rest of the main floor before heading to see it. I pointed things out to Ryan as we walked through, such as the front door showing no signs of damage to indicate

152

ELLIE HOHENSTEIN

a break in, or at least not through this entrance. There was nothing to indicate anything out of the ordinary in the rooms, so we proceeded to the scene of the crime.

The office had double doors that were open wide. We could see Mr. McGill's body lying face down in the middle of the room, the plush white carpet stained red around his head. His head was toward the desk, as if someone had knocked him down while he had been walking in that direction. His arms were by his sides, indicating he had not tried to break his fall, possibly instantly knocked out or even killed by the first blow. There was blood splatter on the walls and floors, but no murder weapon was in sight. He was dressed in a T-shirt and baggy chef's pants, which led me to believe that he likely had been killed last night after he returned home from working at one of the family's restaurants.

"Were you able to find anything that might have been used to kill him?" I asked the officers. They shook their heads. It was likely the killer had either taken it with them or had stashed it somewhere.

I walked around the room, pointing things out to Ryan as I observed them.

"See the blood spatter here? These splash patterns show multiple distinct hits." I indicated how there were arcs, slung back off the weapon with each strike. I also illustrated on the victim's head where the different hits had landed. "The first probably knocked him out, but something with this small of an impact radius probably wouldn't have done much more than break the skin, and definitely shouldn't have caved the skull in like this. You can see here that there were other points of impact, all in

FRAMED

the same general location but not perfectly in the same spot.

"The weapon could have been something sharp, but it wouldn't have had to be. We're probably looking for a handheld object, made of metal. There's no glass or wood splinters to indicate it was either of those materials. The cause of death is pretty obvious at this point, but the coroner will still do an autopsy to make sure there wasn't something else at play."

I looked around the room to see if anything appeared to be missing. Being unfamiliar with the house, it would be harder to spot anything out of the ordinary. My gaze snagged on a bookshelf against the wall near the body. On one shelf, three matching awards were displayed, but they were spaced strangely, as if there should have been four.

I donned a pair of gloves and picked one of the awards up. It appeared to be made of gold, heavy and solid. The base was circular and thick, and the topper was a large star with rounded points. It was labeled "Best Restaurant in Willow Springs". I carried it over to the body and lined up the base with some of the impact marks on McGill's head. They were a match.

"Looks like we've found *what* the weapon was, we just need to find the right one."

A crime scene tech took some last pictures of the body, with me holding the award next to it to indicate my theory, then we gave the coroner permission to touch the body. He was able to use the internal temperature to confirm that Mr. McGill was killed last night, likely between the hours of ten and midnight.

ELLIE HOHENSTEIN

I walked behind the desk to get a different perspective. As I looked across the room, I noticed that the wall opposite didn't appear to have any adornments. This struck me as strange given that all the other walls were decorated with either art, awards, or pictures of the McGill family. I also noticed something small on the wall, but couldn't tell from this distance what it might be. A closer look revealed some kind of mounting hardware, possibly for a heavy painting or a television.

"There's something missing from this wall," I indicated, pointing to the mounting hooks to make sure that the techs took photos. "We need to either ask the wife what used to hang here, or see if we can find out from the staff or friends that may have visited recently. If all that fails, maybe we can find some pictures from a recent party." The McGills were notorious for throwing a party to celebrate almost anything. I supposed that entertaining must be a calling for them, given that they were in the restaurant business.

"It's possible that McGill took the picture down on his own, or at least had a staff member do it, planning to switch it out for another piece, but I figure that he would have waited until he had the replacement ready. This space was in his direct line of sight when sitting at the desk, so I doubt that he would have the spot empty for an extended period. Ryan, make a note to ask the staff when the picture was removed. That might give us an indication on whether this case was actually a robbery gone wrong." Ryan nodded, writing down everything I said. He was attentive, soaking up all I had to teach him today.

FRAMED

I made a final assessment of the room to ensure there wasn't anything else that we needed to examine in person rather than through the pictures the techs were taking. Satisfied, Ryan and I headed back out to the front yard to speak with the staff and family.

"Alright," I said to Ryan as we walked. "We'll start with his wife for two main reasons. The first is that when we have a murder in a home like this, it is almost always a friend or family member who commits it. Someone who would have a reason to be in the house, in the same room as the victim. The wife is the primary suspect when that's the case, until evidence proves otherwise.

"Second, she just lost one of the most important people in her life. Bill was her husband, business partner, and the father of her child. I expect her to be a mess right now, regardless of whether she did this, and she needs to feel prioritized. She needs to know that we will act quickly to ensure that justice will be served.

"If this was a robbery, then it's likely that Bill interrupted the crime in progress, and that the thief panicked and attacked. Hopefully we will find some evidence, like skin under the fingernails, that we can use for DNA analysis. This is honestly unlikely since he was hit from behind. It would mean he either turned his back on the thief, or the thief could have hidden and attacked when Bill walked in. I don't want to rule anything out at this stage."

We had reached where the witnesses were waiting and I approached Alison McGill with my hand extended. "Mrs. McGill, I'm Head Detective Jake Griffin. I want to start by saying that I am so sorry for your loss. I can't

156

imagine how hard this must be for you, especially since you were the one to find your husband."

Alison was a petite woman with short brown hair. Her green eyes were puffy and ringed with red. She had been crying rather heavily when we arrived, but was now down to only a light sniffle and occasional tear. She was dressed in comfortable, but expensive-looking clothing; not workday wear, but certainly not pajamas.

"I hate to ask this of you now, but would you please walk my partner and I through what happened this morning?"

Tears began to fall harder as she spoke. "I got home from a week at the spa just this morning. Possibly around seven? Bill usually gets in late at night and sleeps in, so I expected to find him in bed. I went up to our room to unpack my suitcase, but he wasn't there.

"I called out for him as I walked back through the house, and I woke up Darcy, the nanny. She didn't have to take Ralph to school today, so she was enjoying sleeping in. She hadn't seen Bill, and she sleeps like the dead when she takes her pills, so she wasn't positive if he had even come home last night.

"I came back downstairs and noticed the office doors open. Bill never leaves them open, so I knew something was wrong. Then I saw him... all that blood..." She started crying in earnest. I grabbed a pack of tissues out of my pocket and offered one to her. I always brought a pack or two to murder scenes, it was a small way I could help loved ones of the deceased on one of the worst days of their lives.

FRAMED

"Do you need a minute?" I offered. "I know this is hard, and I can't thank you enough for being strong and going over this. It's important that we get the best information right off the bat, so we can act quickly to catch who did this."

"No, no. I'm alright." She took a deep breath to calm herself back down, then continued, "Once I found him, I called the police right away."

"Thank you so much, Mrs. McGill. Where is your son this morning? You mentioned the nanny didn't need to take him to school today, but I don't see him here."

"He stayed the night at a friend's house. They have today off school, and we try and let him stay with friends when that happens, to make a special occasion even better. I called the friend's mother and asked her to keep him until we get all this cleaned up, possibly another night if needed. I don't know how I'm supposed to tell him about this." She broke out in tears again.

It was never easy to tell a child that their parent was gone. No matter the relationship, this would leave a gaping hole in the kid's life. I couldn't help but think of all the good Alexis had done for the kids at the youth center, maybe she would have time to talk to the McGill kid and help him through this. I made a mental note to bring it up when the time was right.

"We're going to need that mother's name before we leave, but I have one more question for you about when you came home this morning. Was the alarm on?"

"Now that you mention it, no it wasn't. Bill always sets the alarm when he gets home, but we also have a terrible security system. It disconnects all the time, something about the satellite signals having to be lined up just right. Bill has a friend who was an investor in this company, and they swore it was going to be the next big thing once they got all the kinks worked out, but that was years ago and it's still terrible. We've never had any issues with break-ins around here though."

That wasn't strictly true, I'd been to a burglary only a mile or two from here, courtesy of our favorite ghost thief mastermind. But many of the people in the one percent that had been hit specifically requested that it not be publicly broadcast, going so far as to pay the media outlets not to air the story.

"Do you have a place where we can review security footage, or do we need to contact the company? I'm guessing the alarm deactivating doesn't stop them from getting a copy of the feed?"

Alison shook her head, "No, we have to request the footage any time we want to review, and Bill had it worked out where the request had to come from him, not me. Sometimes there is a delay when the satellite link gets interrupted from the weather, but you should be able to get what you need from the security company in a few hours."

I thanked Alison for her time, then gave her my card in case she found or thought of anything else that might be relevant to the case. The only other staff member who was on site at the time of the murder would have been the nanny. We questioned her, but she confirmed that she was asleep and hadn't heard anything; she usually took sleeping pills on the nights that Ralph was gone so that she could get the best possible night's sleep. We got

FRAMED

statements from the rest of the staff, which was basically us hearing "we left before he got home" over and over again.

The biggest thing we uncovered was that the painting now missing from the office had been there the night before when the cleaning team left. So where had it gone?

Back at the station, Ryan and I had managed to identify it by looking at photographs from recent events the McGills had hosted. He printed the images and showed them to one of the specialists over at Schwartz and Son, using the connections he had made in our last case. The painting was called *The Secret* and portrayed an affair. It made me wonder if there was another reason behind its selection other than just being a highly valuable piece. If Mr. McGill was having an affair, it might add another suspect to our list, or have given the wife a reason to lie and murder her husband.

We had called the spa that Mrs. McGill had reported staying at, which confirmed that she checked out early this morning. It was around an hour away, and she had left by six, which was when the resort woke all its guests for an early morning yoga session. It was unlikely that she would have driven back into town in the middle of the night to kill her husband, then back to the spa, only to come back a few hours later, but I'd seen crazier things happen. Especially since it was convenient that her son had not been home that night.

There wasn't much we could do to confirm the nanny's alibi that she was asleep and hadn't heard anything, but we collected a urine sample to have our lab look for traces of the sleeping pills she claimed to take. We had an officer

160

dispatched to confirm with an independent doctor that those specific pills would cause someone to not be woken by a possibly violent struggle across the house. The nanny had also confirmed that all the staff had left for the night before she went to bed, and that only the house manager had a key to get back in.

The house manager had gone home and was with her husband all night long, the security cameras in the parking deck of her building confirming that neither her car nor her husband's had moved during the night. Security footage showed no one coming or going from the property other than when McGill came home at eleven. Based on the coroner's estimate of the time of death, it was likely McGill was killed shortly after he arrived at the house.

With the theft of the painting in the same room as the body, we were primarily operating under the assumption of a break-in gone wrong. Many first-time killers took the murder weapon with them in a panic after what they had done, but the strange part was that there was no other indication of alarm. Nothing in the house was knocked over in a mad dash to escape, or had any bloody handprints on it, which we would have certainly expected given how brutally in McGill's head was bashed in.

And they had still taken the painting, which from the picture would have been incredibly heavy and bulky, and probably the last thing that I would have chosen to take right after killing someone. There were a number of smaller pieces that also held value. They could have wiped down the frame to remove any traces of fingerprints, and then taken something smaller on their way out.

FRAMED

Unless this robbery was a job, and the thief had been hired to find that item specifically. We would have our resident hacker take a look online to see if they could find any postings on the dark web looking to hire someone to steal the painting, or anyone trying to offload it. This was the normal practice when investigating high-dollar art thefts like our cold cases, but our mystery thief was incredible at covering their tracks. With any luck, this was someone else, someone not as skilled at evading the law.

Actually... "Ryan," I said to get his attention away from where he was reviewing the photos and evidence log at his desk in our office. "The only thing that would indicate that this was a theft rather than a targeted murder was the missing painting. There was no other evidence of a break-in. Security cameras did not show any cars other than Mr. McGill's coming or going, nor anyone else walking away from the house, especially carrying a bulky painting. And yet it was gone."

Since the house was empty other than staff and Mrs. McGill, we had done a full sweep of the house to make sure the painting was not still in the home. So how had it been taken out? My gut was screaming at me that this was the work of our mystery thief. They had never escalated to murder, though. This was so far out of the M.O. that I almost wanted to dismiss the idea. But everything about the theft fit too perfectly.

"What if this is the same person as our cold cases? The lack of break-in evidence and the high-dollar target lines up with the M.O., and for someone who hasn't been caught after five years, I'd imagine that being interrupted would have been enough to cause them to panic and attack McGill. But would they still have enough composure to carry out their heist after murdering someone?"

Ryan immediately agreed and jumped on board with the theory, helping me map out what might have happened.

"Alright," he said, getting excited. "This might just be the best thing that ever happened for us. I mean, it's horrible that someone is dead, and I feel terrible for the family, but if you're right, we might have our first real evidence on this guy. If there was a struggle, we might have DNA. And this might make the guy sloppy when it comes to the next heist or to disposing of the murder weapon. It's a bit soon for his normal timeline between jobs, but other than that it all fits!"

He gazed up at the pictures ringing our walls, the items that our thief had taken and we hadn't been able to recover or close the case. The way Ryan was glaring, it was almost like he was personally offended by their presence on the wall, even though he was the one that had hung them there. He had become my partner only three years ago, so he wasn't involved in all the cases but had gone back and printed off those from before we teamed up, as motivation to catch this guy.

"Okay, let's treat this as a robbery then," I directed. "Go back and canvas the scene to see if you can identify the thief's way in or out. Look for anything you can find that might indicate how they escaped unnoticed, and where they might have parked a vehicle to transport the painting. It would have to be an enclosed vehicle like a car or van; this guy is way too smart to ride a motorcycle with

FRAMED

a painting this size strapped to him, too much risk of damaging it.

"I'll go to the security company and request footage for the last week to see if we can identify someone casing the place. They only sent last night's footage over earlier. We also need to interview them about the alarm issues and see why there was no alarm set this morning—so two birds and one stone, as they say."

With a renewed sense of energy, we both headed off for our tasks. I visited the security company, but they mainly confirmed that they were still working out the issues with the satellite signals causing alarms to disconnect without warning or notice. It looked like the alarm had been set by the nanny before she went to bed, but was disconnected sometime around nine-thirty. There were thunderstorms in the area, which regularly caused their signals to fail, so the disconnect was being attributed to that. The alarm wasn't armed after that point, so McGill hadn't set it once he got home.

I wondered if McGill had been concerned about the alarm being off when he got home, or if it was so normal that he didn't think about it. He also didn't set it back once he was inside. I always set my alarm once I know I'm in for the night, but I supposed some people only set it when they went to bed. With his wife out of town and his son gone, would McGill have been expecting a late-night visitor?

Ryan called me shortly after I finished up at the security company, also having come up short. He hadn't found any signs of entry on any of the other doors, and didn't see any evidence that someone had moved a giant painting through the trees, though it was difficult to be sure since the thunderstorms knocked down some branches and would have likely flooded any potential footprints.

I asked him to mention to Alison that, if she was interested in having her son talk to someone about the loss of his father, I knew a great psychiatrist. I didn't give a name, but said he could tell her to call me if she wanted more information.

It sometimes felt like it was impossible to get moving on our cases while having to wait on everyone to give us the necessary information. We either had to wait for the security companies, the coroner, the officers to log the evidence and get everything into the system, the lab to analyze everything… It always seemed to move so fast on TV and in movies, but real police work took a lot of time. Time that we might not have if our killer was on the run.

Around the end of the day, though, I received what felt like the best information I'd ever heard. The crime scene techs had collected an unusual hair sample from the floor in the office at the McGill house. Long, dark hair, too long to be Alison's, and too dark to belong to any of the staff.

It seems that our killer, possibly our master thief, was a woman.

Chapter 13

Alexis

It was another morning riding high after a job well done for me. The only thing that might make it better would be a chance encounter with Jake again. I stopped at the coffee shop on my way into work, just in case, but no such luck. I hadn't texted him yet today, planning to give him a call later to schedule another date.

I was dying to see him since today marked a week since the second of our back-to-back date nights. We had talked every evening except yesterday. While I felt like I was getting to know him well, there was no substitute for being able to see his face and touch him. There was also a lot of communication through body language that I was missing out on. He seemed to be experiencing the same feelings that I had, but it was hard to know for sure without seeing him.

ELLIE HOHENSTEIN

Slightly disappointed, but still in good spirits, I grabbed a drink for Jess and myself and headed into the office.

"Mmm, coffee," she said happily as I walked in. "It must have gone well then?"

"Without a hitch," I replied with a grin. "A week or two from now we should be seeing a nice little payday."

"Fantastic!" She handed me a few folders containing my patient files for today. "Here you go. Oh, and you have lunch with Vivian today, don't forget!"

The morning passed in a breeze, and I left around eleven-thirty to meet my friend. She had chosen one of the McGill restaurants and being there made me a little smug knowing that Bill had likely just discovered the missing painting. When I got there, the hostess seemed a little somber, but I figured it was just something personal. The restaurant also seemed quieter, the usual buzz of chatter reduced to whispers and murmurs.

Vivian waved me over to the table she had gotten us and greeted me with a kiss on each cheek. She was dressed impeccably, of course, but there were some worry lines on her face. "You alright, Viv?" I asked.

"Oh I'm fine," she replied, waving off my question. "Just so shocked by the news. I heard the hostesses chatting when I arrived, it's so sad."

"What's so sad? What news?" Surely tales of my theft hadn't reached all the way to the staff at one of McGill's restaurants? I'd been sure they would have only just noticed it and would want to keep the break-in under wraps. After all, reputation was everything in their circles, and they had so much to lose.

"That one of the owners was murdered last night..."

167

FRAMED

My heart stopped. I couldn't breathe. It wasn't possible—there was no way that it could be Bill, not on the same night that I had robbed them.

Vivian continued, oblivious to my reaction, "It's so terrible, I hope that they don't end up having to close down. I do love the food here." Of course, she would be more concerned about the inconvenience to her life, not that someone was dead. One of Ralph's parents. Oh, poor Ralph! Our next session was going to be brutal.

"It's the McGills that own this place, right? Which one of them died?" Please say it was Mrs. McGill. She was supposed to be returning from a spa trip today according to Ralph, maybe she never made it home.

"Yes, I think that's their name. It was the husband. Bob? Brad? It definitely starts with a B."

"What happened?" Maybe it was a shooting at the restaurant he worked at last night. The timing would be inconvenient but surely it wouldn't get connected to my theft.

"I'm not sure, the staff may have more information. But let's not let that ruin our lunch! How are you, dear? You're looking a little pale. Oh, I know! Now that the weather is getting better, do you want to join me for yoga in the park? They meet in the mornings around ten, and I'd just love to have another friend in the group. Exercise is so boring unless you can gossip while you do it," she said, chuckling.

My mind was going a hundred miles an hour. It was a miracle that my fear wasn't written all over my face. Or maybe it was but Vivian was too polite to say anything.

ELLIE HOHENSTEIN

"You know, Viv, that's such a nice thought but I have sessions most mornings during the week so I probably can't do that. I appreciate the invitation though. I do probably need to get some more sun, but I've been under the weather these last few days. In fact, I thought I was over it but I'm starting to feel a little sick. I'm so sorry, can we possibly reschedule our lunch?" I had to get out of there. I needed to talk to Jess and see what we could find out.

"Poor dear, that must be it." She patted my hand understandingly. "Are you sure? Maybe you just need something light to eat?" She started to wave the waiter over, but I jumped up to stop her.

"No, no. I'm sure I can't handle any food right now. The smells are getting to me already. I'm so sorry, I've got to go." I tried not to rush out the door. Outside, I looked back through the window as I passed, waving to Vivian. For a moment, it seemed she had a strange expression, torn somewhere between anger and victory? But it was replaced with a genuine smile in a flash, so I must have imagined it.

As soon as I was out of sight of the restaurant I tried calling Jess. She usually had her phone on silent during her lunch, something about taking time each day to disconnect, and she didn't answer. I hurried back to the office, hoping she would be there. We needed more information on what the heck happened last night.

Every second seemed like an eternity, and it felt like I was having a panic attack. The elevator was closing in on me on the way up to my office, my breathing was shallow.

FRAMED

I burst through the doorway and was relieved to see Jess sitting at her desk.

"He's dead!" I exclaimed as I slammed the door closed behind me and collapsed against it. I hadn't even looked to see if anyone else was here, but thankfully the waiting room was empty.

"What? Who's dead?" Jess asked, confused.

"McGill." I struggled to catch my breath as I spoke, spiraling down into an anxiety attack. "I don't know how... or when... or why... But somehow... he's dead."

Jess frowned, and turned her computer back on. She was much calmer than I would have expected, but maybe she realized that I was completely freaking out and I needed one of us to be stable right now.

"I haven't set up my alert for the McGill job yet, I figured I had until at least this afternoon before the police would have anything at all in their system. Let me see what I can find. Go ahead and turn on the news in your office and see if they are saying anything."

She walked over to me and helped me to my desk. Once I was seated, head in my hands as I tried to get a grip on myself, she brought me a glass of water. "Drink this, it will help. And do your counting thing."

I started counting to ten out of order, a trick I had picked up to help my patients when they had anxiety attacks. The distraction of counting the numbers out of sequence, of remembering which ones you had said and which ones were left, was a great way to get the mind to calm down and the body to relax.

My breathing began to get steadier, and my head started to clear. I drained the glass of water and turned on both of my televisions to different news channels. One of them showed a background of the McGill estate, so they must have a reporter live on the scene. I turned up the volume to allow Jess to hear as well.

"—coming to you live from the McGill estate, where earlier this morning the body of Bill McGill, proprietor of many prominent restaurants throughout the city, was found dead in his home. The cause of death is not yet known, but sources say the police are treating this as a homicide. In addition to the death, reports also indicate that at least one piece from the family's valuable art collection is missing, leading us to believe that this might be a robbery-gone-wrong.

"The family has declined to comment at this time, and the police are wrapping up their work on the site as we speak. We will continue to monitor the situation and provide updates throughout the investigation of this gruesome event. Our thoughts and prayers are with the McGill family during this tragic time."

The screen cut away, back to the anchors in the studio. Overall I didn't learn anything new, other than it looked like my heist was getting the credit for the murder too. I was fairly sure I hadn't left any evidence, but a murder investigation would be a lot more thorough than a simple theft, even one for a piece of this caliber.

I walked back out to the lobby to see what Jess had found. We had time to research before my next appointment, since I had planned on taking a long lunch with Vivian. "Not much on the news except they blame me. I should be safe as long as my normal precautions held. At least we know the alarm didn't send some silent

FRAMED

signal to the security company, since they would probably be talking about it being tripped. Anything in the police databases yet?"

"They've created a file, let me see here... Okay it says he was found in the office, no cause of death listed yet. They noted the picture being stolen, but they don't have the details on what the painting was, probably having to catalog the whole dang house to figure out exactly what's missing. No information on any evidence collected yet either. If they are still at the scene then they probably have to get it all back to the station before they put anything in the computer, so it will be a little while."

"No news is good news, right? You'll let me know if anything changes that could impact us?"

"Absolutely," she confirmed.

I took a deep breath. Everything would work out alright. I just needed to keep an eye on the investigation. I had plans in place in case it was ever looking like I would be caught, but there was no real need to panic just yet.

The rest of the afternoon sped by. My sessions proved to be a good distraction now that I had calmed down a bit. Still, I kept one ear out toward the lobby even though I knew Jess would interrupt if something important was discovered. I wasn't sure how I was supposed to get through the night, though, much less the weekend, without her right there to provide any new insights about the investigation. I would need to make sure that Jess had the alerts forwarded to me somehow before we left tonight.

I called Jake after seeing my last patient. Jess had already gone home and I was alone in my office. It was a

172

little earlier than I usually called him, not quite five yet, but I was hoping he would pick up. He answered on the second ring.

"You know," he said instead of a greeting, "if it weren't for these phone calls, I'd think you were avoiding me. Am I ever going to get to see your beautiful face again?"

I laughed, his teasing lifting my spirits already. "How about tonight? Or do you already have plans?"

"Tonight is perfect. Are you still at the office? I can swing by and pick you up for an early dinner?"

I had skipped lunch, and now that my anxiety had eased a little I was starving. "Yes, that would be wonderful. How soon can you be here?"

"Fifteen minutes, maybe? Is that enough time to wrap up whatever you're working on?"

"Yep, I'll meet you out front." I shut down my computer, locked everything up for the weekend, and headed down to wait on the same bench I had used last time. It was a beautiful afternoon, not a cloud in the sky. The weather was finally warming up, and I wanted to eat outside and take advantage of the warmth as much as possible. I would be sure to ask Jake if we could go somewhere with patio seating.

He pulled up almost exactly fifteen minutes later, and jumped out to open my door for me. I loved his chivalry, and knowing he had a rough upbringing made it even more impressive. Dressed in a simple T-shirt and jeans, much like the day I first met him, his eyes lit up as he took me in. He greeted me with a kiss, enough emotion put into it to show me how much he missed me but not so much that anyone around us might feel uncomfortable. Still, it

FRAMED

warmed me up inside and I forgot for a moment why I had waited so long to see him. Surely these kisses would have been worth blowing off a stakeout or two.

"Food?" he asked as he broke our kiss. He didn't step away yet, keeping his arms around me as if he couldn't stand to let go.

"Food," I agreed.

"Where to?" he asked once we were both buckled in the car.

"Somewhere we can sit outside and enjoy this beautiful weather."

"I know just the place," he said with an easy grin. As he drove, he reached across the console to hold my hand. He ran his thumb over the back of it, the touch both soothing and igniting something inside of me.

Jake drove us to the edge of town, a more rural area. We pulled up at a small building, the sign reading "Sunshine Grill". Despite the early hour, the parking lot was packed with cars and trucks. Picnic tables filled the space in front, and I noticed as we approached that there was a window built in where customers were lining up to place orders.

There was no inside seating, just the tables out front. Looking around, a handful of people were eating in the beds of their trucks or had the tailgate of their SUV popped open and were sitting inside the trunk area.

It definitely wasn't what I expected for dinner, and I was certainly overdressed, but it was also exactly what I needed tonight. There was a sense of small-town camaraderie around, everyone chatting and visiting with people from other tables and groups.

ELLIE HOHENSTEIN

We approached the window and the young girl working the counter beamed when she saw Jake. "Jakey! How've you been? We haven't seen you out here for a few weeks."

He laughed and smiled. "I know, I know. It's been pretty busy lately, and I haven't had a chance to make it out this way. But my friend wanted to enjoy this beautiful weather and I knew there was no place better. Seems like everyone had the same idea as me, though."

He turned to me, "There's no better burger or hot dog in the city than right here. It's a small menu, but everything on it is damn near as good as it can possibly get."

"Well, with that glowing recommendation, I guess I'll have a burger and a dog."

He placed our order and got us each a milkshake to drink. There were a couple free rocking chairs open to the side of the building, and we rocked and chatted while waiting for our food to be ready. A few tables opened up, so we snagged one as soon as our order number was called.

"Oh my goodness," I said as I took my first bite of burger. "This might be the best burger I've ever eaten." It was thick and juicy, covered in cheese, and seasoned to perfection. He had also ordered us onion rings and fries, and I'd probably need to eat salads for the next week to balance out all the fried food I was eating, but it was absolutely worth it.

"I told you," he chuckled. "I've been coming out here for probably ten years now. The cashier used to visit the shelter when she was younger, then she got moved out here to a new foster family. I'd known the owner for a

FRAMED

while so I helped her get the job. It worked out great, and gave her the sense of home she had been searching for. This is the kind of place where everyone knows everyone else, and their family too."

"It almost feels like a different world. I can't imagine growing up in a place like this," I admitted.

"I know what you mean. This is the type of life I wished for as a kid, but it never really worked out that way. Maybe one day, though. In the right place. With the right person." He smiled up at me and I smiled right back, imagining that life with him for a moment.

But of course, having that life meant staying out of jail. This open space, this freedom, reminded me of just how precious it all was, and how close I might be to losing it. My smile dropped a bit at the thought.

"You alright?" he asked, sounding concerned.

"Yeah, just some hard stuff going on right now with work. I'm under a bit of stress with an unknown situation."

"I know what you mean, we've got kind-of a big deal going on at the office, but I'm just glad to get away from it for a while. That's what weekends are for, right? To have a life of our own and disconnect from the stresses of work."

If only. My weekends weren't usually relaxing, but maybe I needed to take a little more time for myself. Now that I had someone in my life, I could do with some little getaways.

"You're right," I agreed. We finished our meal and visited with some of the other people who recognized Jake. Each one of them told me how great a guy he was,

176

and mentioned how glad they were that he found someone. He took it all in stride, always pushing it back that he was the lucky one to have met me.

After dinner, he took me to a mini golf course down the road. String lights lined the pathways, creating a romantic glow against the sunset. This was not a sport I had much experience with, and he completely trounced me. I might have set a record for the worst score. Fortunately, the rules of the course set a maximum number of strokes that could count for each hole.

Jake tried to "help" me with my stance a number of times, coming up behind me and reaching around and placing his hands on mine, positioning them properly on the club. I was aware of every spot where his body touched mine, heat building within me each time he came close.

After two rounds I finally threw in the towel, not able to take the humiliating defeat any longer.

"Where to now? Are you tired, or would you like to get a drink?" he asked, letting me take the reins from here.

"Hmm..." I knew exactly what I wanted, but wasn't sure if he would think I was being too forward. Every touch he had given me so far tonight had me about to combust from wanting him. Every kiss, every smile, every time he so much as looked in my direction with his sexy, smoldering gaze, had led me towards exactly how I wanted this night to end.

I pulled in close against him, wrapping my arms around his neck. I gently pulled him down for a kiss, pressing my body against his in all the right places. "Can the drink be at your place?"

FRAMED

"Absolutely," he growled out huskily. He pulled me in for another kiss, hands cupping my face to his firmly. When he released me, he grabbed my hand and led me quickly to the car. I laughed as he dragged me along, glad he was as eager as I was to take our relationship to the next stage.

The anticipation built as we drove the half-hour route back into the city. He kissed me at every red light, not letting my desire fade on the journey. His building had a parking deck exclusive to residents, and once we pulled up, he drew me in close for another hot kiss before letting me out of the car. He came around and got my door for me, holding my hand as we walked inside to the elevator.

His apartment was near the top floor, offering a beautiful view of the city lights. One wall was entirely windows, and a table with two chairs was sat next to it, a perfect spot to watch the city wake up while drinking morning coffee. He took my purse from me, putting it away in the bedroom since there was no closet by the door to hang it in. He closed the door behind him—maybe he didn't want to seem presumptuous.

"Wine or beer?" he asked as he came back out and headed to the kitchen.

"Whatever you've got is fine by me," I replied. He grabbed two bottles out of the refrigerator, popped the lids off, then handed one over to me. Lightly taking my hand, he led me to the couch, then pulled me down beside him.

"You're absolutely incredible, Alexis," he said, reaching up to lightly hold my cheek. "I'm so lucky that I met you." The sincerity in his voice filled my heart, and I leaned into his touch. I was beyond words at this point, needing to show him how much he meant to me, how much I cared.

I closed the distance between us, capturing him in a passionate kiss. He kissed me back like I was a last gulp of air before drowning. His tongue gently touched my lips, requesting entry, and I opened fully for him. His hands ran up and down my back, pulling me in closer to him with each pass. Flush against him, I still needed more.

I swung one leg over him and straddled his lap, lining up my core with his. His hands toyed with the bottom of my shirt, dipping under and grazing the skin beneath. I could feel his desire for me growing under me as I ground back and forth, running my hands over his sculpted chest.

Beers forgotten on the table, he stood, wrapping my legs around his waist as he carried me towards the bedroom. Rather than open the door, he pinned me roughly against it.

Using the door to help support my weight, he used one hand to tilt my head back, giving him access to my neck. He worked his mouth along my jaw, nipping and kissing as he went. His hips held me in place, lightly grinding his arousal against me, while he used his other hand to caress my skin gently under my shirt. I moaned at all the sensations, losing myself in his touch.

He pulled my top up and over my head, only parting his mouth from my skin for long enough to get the shirt past, then he returned with a renewed vigor, devouring my lips. I went to return the favor, reaching for the hem of his tee, when he grabbed my hands and pinned them against the door.

FRAMED

After a few moments losing ourselves in the kisses, he suddenly dropped his hands back down to my legs, and opened the door behind me. He lowered me gently to the bed, looking me over with a steamy gaze. Our love-making was gentle, exploratory, but as I fell asleep in his arms, I knew this was the start of something magical.

Chapter 14

Jake

The shrill ringtone jerked me out of what might have been the best sleep of my life. I grabbed my phone, rushing to ensure it didn't wake Alexis. I silenced the ringer and glanced at the clock. Two-forty-five in the morning. I settled back in next to her, determined to salvage the night, but the phone rang again.

Someone better have died. Nothing short of a murder was going to get me out of my apartment tonight.

I checked the caller ID, and it showed Ryan's name and picture. That meant it was at least work related. I hit the button to answer, but stayed silent while I grabbed a pair of sweatpants off the floor, slipped them on, and walked out of the room.

"What?" I demanded roughly as I pulled my door shut.

"Jake! Sorry for the late hour, or well, early hour, but I just had to tell you. I did it! I got us a link between the

FRAMED

robbery cases." His voice was ecstatic, the happiest I might have ever heard. Shit, with news like that I couldn't even be mad at him for calling.

"That's incredible. How? Who? What?" I was stammering, blown away and not sure where to even start.

"It's thanks to you, actually. I mentioned to Mrs. McGill about the therapist you knew for her son, in case he needed someone to talk to about the loss of his dad, and she said he was already seeing a doctor. The best in town, of course, and she named a few other friends who had their kids seeing the doctor too.

"Get this, three of the friends she mentioned were victims that had been robbed before. Our cold cases." A therapist in common? How did we not know about this before? We had explicitly asked the victims to name anyone close to the family that might have been involved, and not a single one mentioned they had their kid in therapy.

Ryan went on, "I called a few of the other victims as well, and literally every single one of them had their kid in therapy. The same doctor! She specializes in troubled kids, and moved to town just a few months before the first cold case."

"That's fantastic! Who was it? What's her name?" I asked.

"Dr. Lee. I'm texting you a picture now. Best of all, it looks like she has long, dark hair. I'm betting we get a DNA match to the strand we found in the McGill house if we can get her to turn over a sample. We might even have enough evidence to get a warrant for it."

ELLIE HOHENSTEIN

Wait a minute... Lee? A female therapist with long, dark hair, who specializes in troubled kids?

I turned to face my door, slightly shaking my head.

There's no way, it couldn't be Alexis. I *knew* her. We had talked about all kinds of things in the last week and none of them had been "I like to steal shiny things from rich people". She was well off financially, but she wasn't rolling in money like someone who had stolen millions of dollars of antiquities. It just couldn't be her, right?

But tonight she had mentioned that something had happened and she needed a distraction from it... and the passion she shared with me could have come from the adrenaline and fear of being caught for murder. She had no idea I was a cop, I'd taken great pains to hide that up until this point. I had planned to tell her soon, especially after tonight.

I needed to know.

I switched my phone to my messages, and saw Alexis's beautiful, perfect face staring back at me.

"I'm too amped up to sleep, can I come over? I've spent the last few hours pulling out all the old files so I could be ready to go before I called you. We can work on a game plan so we can start making moves tomorrow."

"No!" I yelped quickly, clamping my hand over my mouth as I realized how loud I'd gotten. I softened my voice, hoping Ryan wouldn't pick up on my panic. "Are you at the station, or at your place? I can come to you. Just... give me an hour or so."

He was at his apartment, but we agreed to meet at the station so we would have all the resources and files. I hung

FRAMED

up the phone and turned to stare again at my door, unsure of how to proceed.

I was confused, mad, frustrated, hurt, heartbroken. Honestly, I had no idea how to process what I was feeling right now. Alexis was in that room, in my bed, asleep. Do I wake her up? Ask her to leave? Leave her here without me? This woman might have killed someone, and I just slept with her. I'm getting fired for sure.

I had to end this now, take her in. Hopefully the whole thing was a misunderstanding, but once I accused her of murder the relationship would be over. This woman had felt like the best thing that had ever happened to me, possibly ruining me for future relationships, and now I was going to lose her.

I took a deep breath and opened the door to walk back into my room. Alexis was half awake, still naked, and turned to look at me with a lazy smile on her face. "Come back to bed," she said with a slight yawn.

The look on my face must have given away my mood, because when I stepped into the moonlight streaming in through the window, she propped herself up, thankfully pulling the sheet with her to keep her chest covered—I wasn't sure if I could get through this if her body was on display.

"What's wrong, Jake?" The look of concern on her face seemed genuine, but did I really know her at all?

"Can you explain to me," I began slowly, "why we have a string of unsolved thefts in this town dating back years, and you seem to be our only link?" *Please, deny it. Please have no idea what I'm talking about.*

184

ELLIE HOHENSTEIN

If the look on her face hadn't told me everything I needed to know, her next words did. "You're a cop?"

"And you're a thief and a murderer."

She got out of bed, turning her back toward me while she hunted for her clothes and pulled them on. "No, Jake, I swear. I can explain." She turned to face me, now fully dressed. "I never killed anyone."

"Oh really? Because I'm betting the body of Bill McGill down in our morgue would beg to differ!" I was starting to raise my voice. I wondered where the lies stopped. Had anything she told me been true? Did she know I was the cop who had been tracking her for the last few years, and did she target me for it? Was our whole relationship just a ploy to see how far she could push it and not get caught?

"I don't know how that happened. I haven't even seen Bill in weeks, not since the last time I tried to get a conference with him about his son. I would never kill anyone, Jake. You know me. You know I couldn't be capable of that."

"Know you? I clearly don't know you. How am I supposed to believe anything you've told me?" I started pacing. I couldn't even look at her, each glance filled me with rage and humiliation. I had to have her gone so I could think clearly. "I need time to think about this, Alexis. You need to leave. I've got to go down to the station and figure out what the hell is going on."

She grabbed her purse and keys from my dresser and walked toward my bedroom door. She paused and turned back to me, sincerity and devastation all over her face. "I swear to you, Jake. I haven't lied to you. I'm not a killer. When you're ready to listen, come find me." I nodded

FRAMED

gruffly, refusing to meet her eyes, and she headed to leave my apartment.

"Oh, and Alexis," I stopped her just as she had reached my front door. "Don't leave town." She nodded, then opened the door and walked out. I was a fool, I should have just taken her to the station. If she ran, I'd never hear the end of it for letting her get away. I'd have to resign from the humiliation, if they even let me keep my badge.

But I wanted to believe her. I wanted her to be innocent. She said she didn't do it, didn't I owe it to her, and to myself, to be sure before I took her in?

I went to take a shower, wanting to wash off the scent of her before going to see Ryan, as if he would be able to tell what I had done and who it was with when he saw me.

As the water ran down my body, I couldn't help but remember how Alexis's fingers had done the same, just a few hours earlier. Fingers that had enough skill to pick locks, poach sculptures, and lift paintings off the wall. Fingers that may have been coated in blood just twenty-four hours ago. No, she said she was innocent. I needed to try and believe her until we proved otherwise.

Wait... she said she didn't kill anyone, not that she wasn't the thief. She hadn't seen McGill, but she didn't say she didn't rob him. His son was a patient, what kind of trouble did he have that needed to be addressed by a therapist? Were her targets exclusively clients?

Could she be using the kids to get information on how to break in, making them unwitting accomplices? I was horrified. How could she claim to care about troubled children when she was abusing their trust in her like that?

186

I needed more information. I dried off and dressed, heading towards the station to see everything Ryan had discovered.

When I arrived at the station, it was mostly empty. There were a small number of night-shift officers, but they spent most of their shifts out in their patrol cars. Only a handful remained in the building in case someone needed to speak with an officer immediately, and there were a few desk workers who processed the criminals that got brought in after-hours. Upstairs, all the offices were dark with the exception of mine, as well as the conference room where Ryan had set up.

I walked in to see pictures displaying all the items stolen over the last five years that we had assumed were committed by the same person. By Alexis. He also had pulled the files for each case with headshots of the victim's family members. There was a corkboard in the room that he had pinned a handful of photographs to, under a label of 'Confirmed Patients.'

"You've been busy," I said as I took in the room and all he had done. "Do you even sleep?"

He laughed. "Not right now, I'm way too excited. Check this out: Those files up there," he indicated to the corkboard, "are mostly the ones that Mrs. McGill told me about. I checked bank records to confirm that they had been paying Dr. Lee, and that's what I'm looking for in the rest of these files.

"It's hard, they all seem to be paying her in different ways. Some have an automatic payment system hooked up to send a recurring amount to the bank account for her office, others have an accountant manage the payments

FRAMED

and mask it in a huge transaction to the accounting firm. Some of them are even writing personal checks or getting money orders and paying during their appointments."

"So, we comb through bank statements until morning when we can call and ask the rest of the victims, or get a patient list from the doctor. Got it." Paperwork I could handle, even in my current state. Ryan had graciously made a fresh pot of coffee in this floor's break area. I grabbed a mug and settled in to start on some of the older cases.

We had made it through roughly twenty of the case files by the time the sun came up. The evidence was hard to refute. Almost every single victim had a child that was a patient at Alexis's practice around the time of the theft. There would be no issues getting a warrant for a hair sample to compare to the one that was in evidence.

I looked over at Ryan, trying to decide how much of my personal involvement with this woman I should reveal while needing a sounding board for my doubts. I had no doubt that she had stolen all these items, but the murder of Bill McGill was the piece I was struggling with.

"Alright, so say this woman, this therapist who focuses on helping children, took all these things. Robbed her clients. Why? There's no shot she needs the money— according to these bank statements she's being paid a fortune to treat the kids.

"And the reviews on her website are phenomenal." We had taken a short break and looked at her online presence. "Why would she risk it all to steal this stuff? And how does someone go from helping kids work through issues to murdering a patient's father in their home? I just have

188

a hard time believing she would be able to cope with the guilt of this."

"If someone can justify living their life stealing, especially when they don't need the money, then I'm sure they can justify anything. You'd be surprised at what people can be capable of," Ryan said darkly. I didn't know much about his past, but I did know that he had faced some injustices that led him to becoming an officer. In his mind, the law was black and white.

"When do you think we can bring her in for questioning?" Ryan asked. He seemed restless, despite being up all night.

"It's the weekend, so we probably won't be able to get ahold of her short of going to her home. I'm not sure we're ready to do that yet." Ryan's scowl told me he didn't agree, that he was ready to wrap this up. I tried to rein him in. "We don't want to tip her off too soon. Let's see what information we can gather before Monday. I'm going to go to the gym and try to get my blood pumping, then I'll start asking around about the painting with my informants." I wouldn't actually be going to the gym, but he didn't need to know that.

"Yes, sir. I'll get the paperwork started to request a warrant for the doctor's bank records, both from her practice and her personal accounts. Anything else I should try to get?"

I'd normally say cell phone records, but I didn't want it to reveal that she'd been at my place last night, or that we had been talking. "That's a good place to start regarding her. But in the meantime, I want to know all of McGill's movements for the last two weeks. We have a

FRAMED

good idea that Dr. Lee is behind these other thefts, but let's be sure she's actually behind this one before we stop looking for murder suspects. We could risk the killer getting away if it's not her."

I headed out the door, greeting the weekend detectives and officers as they started filtering into the station to begin their shifts. I grabbed my gym bag from my office on my way out so it would look like I was off to exercise, but my real destination would be a lot harder to handle.

I was ready to hear Alexis's side of the story.

I had done a quick search for her phone's location and saw that she was at her apartment. I plugged the address into my GPS and headed over. I didn't call her to let her know I was coming; I didn't want to give her the chance to dodge my visit.

She answered the door quickly, cracking it to block my view of the interior. She stuck her head out to look around the hallway, and seemed relieved to see I was alone.

"I'm ready to listen, if you've got time." I said. She opened the door and stepped back to let me in.

We settled down in her living room. She had changed her clothes to something more casual—loungewear for the weekend. I enjoyed seeing her like this, more relaxed. I just wished the circumstances were different.

"I really should be arresting you right now. Just being here could put us both at risk, maybe even compromise the whole investigation. Maybe I'm a fool, but I wanted to give you a chance to explain your side, off the record." I'd thought about wearing a wire, but couldn't bring myself to be as duplicitous as she may have been.

190

Alexis took a deep breath and didn't waste any time diving into her story. "I didn't lie to you about anything."

My hope rose a bit at her first statement. The lies were the part I was most upset about, being fooled so completely by her and having all the things we had in common be untrue.

She continued. "My parents died when I was young and since my aunt didn't want to take me in, I went into foster care. I was angry, confused, and there weren't exactly resources available to help me work through those issues. The kids who had been in the home longer would pick on me because I was new, and generally made me feel worse about being an orphan.

"I learned how to fight so I could defend myself against them, which of course immediately got me bounced to a new home after they made it look like I had started the fights. I finally landed with the Parker's. They had a rigorous set of rules, and instead of asking for the children to be removed from the home if they caused trouble, they would just lock us away. I had to learn how to pick the lock just to be able to go to the bathroom.

"The other kids would find ways to pick on me outside of the house. I started to walk rather than ride the bus with them. I usually missed breakfast because I left so early, and I didn't have any money to get something to eat on my way. Then I missed dinner too because it was served before I could make it home.

"So, at thirteen years old, I was basically having to choose between starving to death or getting beaten up regularly. I started to steal. At first, I just grabbed snacks from convenience stores on the way to or from school. I

FRAMED

looked pitiful enough, I suppose, that when I got caught the workers didn't have the heart to call the police or my foster parents. I kind-of wished they had, looking back. It likely would have gotten me moved to a different home.

"But I knew my luck would run out, so I got better and better at it. I would start taking more, then began selling the items to the other kids at school. After a while I had enough to afford taking the public buses home. I was starting to fill back out now that I could make it in time for dinner, plus all the extra food I was stealing. The downside to that was that when I got caught, I didn't look as pitiful anymore.

"Stealing went from being a necessity to more of a job or hobby. My only hobby, if I'm totally honest. And I got very, very good at it. But the guilt I felt at taking from the innocent was strong. They were just trying to make a living too, and they didn't deserve what I was doing to them. So, I started targeting businesses with criminal operations: drug dealers, money laundering, even something as small as negligence. The stakes got higher, but so did my payouts.

"By the time I was nearing graduation, I decided to go to college and make a better life for myself so I could stop stealing. I pulled bigger and bigger jobs, and figured out how to set up a fake scholarship fund to make it look like I was getting the money legitimately. Then I needed to go to medical school. The excuses I gave myself were endless. I've finally owned who I am—a thief, and damn proud of the work I do."

She looked up at me nervously.

ELLIE HOHENSTEIN

"You know, I could arrest you for almost everything you just told me. You just confessed to being a career criminal to the head detective of the local police department."

"No, I finally opened up about who I really am to my boyfriend, baring my soul. You trusted me with your past, and now I've given you mine."

Boyfriend? Alexis wanted to be that serious with me? Damn, I wanted that so badly. But I couldn't imagine how that would ever work. I was a cop and she was a thief— possibly a murderer. And I really needed to get clarity on that piece before anything else.

"Tell me about the McGill job," I demanded.

She sighed. "I don't know what happened. I had my reasons for targeting Mr. McGill, but I can't tell you what they are." I figured it had to do with their son and his therapy, and I respected her commitment to not betraying the child's confidence. "I staked them out for a week. Every night while we were on the phone talking, I was watching either the staff or a McGill family member, learning their habits and routines.

"Thursday evening, I headed out to the house. Mrs. McGill was out of town until Friday morning, so the timing was perfect. I waited for the staff to leave, then for Ralph and his nanny to go to bed..."

I was instantly alert. Was that a lie? Mrs. McGill had said Ralph wasn't there that night.

"Well, actually I only noticed the nanny go to bed, Ralph's light stayed off the whole evening, so I'm guessing he wasn't home."

193

FRAMED

I let out the breath I'd unintentionally been holding. Okay, not a lie, just a variation from her original plan that she didn't know about until that night.

"I entered the house through the back door, picking the lock. The office was closest to that exit. The painting was bolted to the wall opposite the desk. I had brought some small tools, and I was able to get it down. I carried it back out the door, and through the woods. I was gone before ten. Mr. McGill never gets home from work before eleven, so I had plenty of time."

If that was the case, someone else killed McGill. Someone else that either had access to the house, or had broken in after Alexis did.

"How did you leave the office, were the doors open or closed?"

"Closed. They were closed when I got there, so they were closed when I left. That's one of my rules. I touch nothing but the item I came for, and leave everything exactly the way it was. It's part of why I don't get caught."

But I had finally caught her. Or at least Ryan had. He was going to be bragging about this one for years.

"And what about the hairs we found in the office. The ones that look like a perfect match to yours."

"WHAT?" she jumped up, truly shocked for the first time tonight. "What hairs? What are you talking about? I didn't leave any hair, it's impossible."

"Why is it impossible?" Was I about to get one of her trade secrets? It was always impressive that we had never found any hair at the scenes of the thefts. Mine were certainly always randomly falling out.

194

"I keep my hair completely covered, wrapped up to ensure that nothing can fall out. I've tested it dozens of times, it's foolproof. Shit, I've even tested in high wind conditions."

"Well we found hairs, and they're trying to get a DNA match, so if your DNA is in the system—"

"It's not," she said, interrupting me.

I continued, "Then they will have it in a few days. If not, well we probably still have enough to get a warrant to make you turn over a sample."

She collapsed back onto the couch, lost in thought. After a few moments, she asked quietly, "How did he die?"

"I can't tell you. If you didn't do it, then you're better off not knowing. You don't want to slip up and say something that you aren't supposed to know."

She nodded. "So does that mean you believe me? That I didn't kill him?"

She had been open and honest with me, there was no real reason to hold back now. If I wanted to take her in, I'd have enough to put her away for the rest of her life, murder or not.

"I believe you," I told her. "And that means that there's a murderer on the street. They might have even known you would be there that night, and used you as a patsy."

Just then, there was a knock on the door. I jumped up and checked my phone, looking to see if Ryan had called me to tell me he had decided to confront Alexis anyway rather than following my instructions to wait until Monday. There were no missed calls, but I also had no signal, which was odd.

FRAMED

Alexis went and checked through the peephole, and said quietly that it was just someone in a delivery uniform with a box. I stepped to the side, out of sight just in case, and nodded for her to open the door. My hand hovered over my service weapon, at the ready.

"I've got a package here for Alexis Lee?" the guy said.

"That's me, thank you." Alexis responded, taking the box from him. She signed the device he held out to confirm receipt of the package, and closed the door.

"I'm not expecting any packages," she said, confused, before opening it up and reaching inside carefully. She pulled out an award, which looked to be solid gold. "It's really heavy. There's an engraving here on the bottom, 'Best Restaurant in Willow Springs'... Wait a minute, is that blood on this?"

I came closer to take a look. The award looked familiar. I had seen others just like it lining the shelves at the McGill house.

"Alexis," I said slowly, "I'm fairly certain you're holding the weapon that killed Bill McGill."

She dropped the trophy in shock.

"You're being framed."

Chapter 15

Alexis

Jake rushed over to my front door, opening it wide to try catch a glimpse of the person who had delivered the package.

"They're gone," he said as he closed the door back behind him. "Did you see the name or a logo of the delivery company? We should be able to get details on who sent that to you."

A murder weapon. Someone had sent me a murder weapon. My fingerprints were on a freaking *murder weapon*.

"It was a brown uniform, but I didn't notice a logo." I checked the box for any kind of shipping label, anything that would give more details of how this package came to be at my doorstep. There was nothing, no labels, no return address, and my address was handwritten on the outside of the box.

FRAMED

"I'll see if we can get the cameras for the building. Maybe we can establish facial recognition or something from them." He came back over and must have noticed that I was still staring at the box, devastation on my face. He gently rubbed my arm. "Lex, look at me." I did. "It will be alright. I know you didn't do this. Even if I didn't believe you before, that right there proves it. Someone is trying to pin this on you."

I let out a breath, relaxing into his touch. It would be okay, Jake would make sure of it, and I trusted him. He was my boyfriend, after all. Or... was he? I looked up at him nervously.

"What does this all mean for us?" Please say we're fine, please. I don't know what I would do if this meant I lost him too.

"Lex... I don't know. You're incredible, but honestly I don't see how we get past this. I'm the cop who's been chasing you for *five years*. Hell, my partner's working up a detail on you right now."

I couldn't believe that I hadn't cared enough to look into who had been trying to catch me these last few years. I had assumed that a different officer had been assigned each time, figuring that's part of why they couldn't find my connection between all the cases. My hubris was my downfall, though, in both my thieving and my new relationship.

"I understand," I said. And I did—I knew that he couldn't be a cop and date a criminal, if I even managed to stay out of jail after all this was over. One of us would have to quit. Since his job was, well, his job, it would have to be me, but I wasn't sure I could do it. That I could walk

198

away from this life. Not to mention all the good I had been doing with the donations I made from the proceeds of my heists.

"Look, I'll help you out of this. I'll find the person trying to frame you and prove you're not a murderer. After that, we'll see." That was more than I could have hoped for. Our relationship might be over before it got a real chance, but from this a partnership would be formed, maybe even a friendship. Hopefully one that didn't end up with me behind bars. Cops let some criminals go all the time to build their informant networks, right? I'd take whatever I could get with Jake at this point.

I'd worked with partners before, early in my career when I was trying to find my niche. Even then I had taken precautions, I established my rules. I never told them my real name. My alias was one I still used today with all my contacts. I always initiated contact when looking for a new partner. I didn't trust anyone who tried to seek me out, not knowing if it was an undercover cop or just someone who might try to screw me. And I always did my homework on anyone I chose to work with, researching them as much as I did my targets.

There had, of course, been a few bad partners. The worst was a girl named Pepper, who had almost gotten us caught during a museum break-in. We had targeted a new exhibit of Ancient Greek pottery, for a client who was obsessed with the period. Back then, I was still taking jobs for others, not myself, so my moral code didn't apply. I had needed help with the security system which was proving too intricate for one person to circumvent alone.

FRAMED

I hadn't yet met Jess, who absolutely could have handled it with no issues.

It was Pepper's job to disable the security while I grabbed the vase. Only, she didn't do it right. The main alarm was deactivated, but a silent one was triggered once the vase had been removed from its pedestal. The doors locked and sirens could be heard in the distance when we tried to escape. I threw the vase at the window in my panic, cracking it, then slammed my body against it, breaking through. I ran, and never looked back.

I didn't know what had happened to Pepper, but since everything I told her about me was false, I felt confident she couldn't rat me out. As a precaution, I quit my job and started at a local bar, which turned out to be a much better place for me to gather information to start picking my own targets in a higher-class world. I learned my lesson and had gotten away clean ever since.

But now I had been caught. I had plans in place for this, if I ever needed to cut and run. I had roots here in this community, and while I'd feel horrible for leaving my patients, they would be in the same situation if I went to jail, so I was prepared to disappear if it came down to it.

Jake added an extra complication into that plan. If he helped me clear my name from the murder, I would have to find a way to run without damaging his career or reputation. That is, if it wasn't already damaged.

"What about your partner?" I asked. Jake might be inclined to help me, but would his partner be so understanding? Did Jake have enough sway to get him to look the other way?

200

ELLIE HOHENSTEIN

Jake rubbed his chin, considering. "Convincing Ryan to help might be… difficult. He tends to arrest first and ask questions later. No, I think we need to leave him in the dark until we have something concrete. He probably will need time to gather enough evidence and testimony to justify a warrant, plus Judge Reinhold is on-call for the next two days and he hates working on the weekend, so I think we have a little time to get a jump on things."

They would likely need a hair sample from me before they could officially arrest me, to compare to the hair found at the scene. But based on the bloody award in my house, I was willing to bet that it would somehow be a match. If I was being targeted, I needed to find out "who" and "how". The "why" didn't matter much at this stage, I couldn't think of what I might have done to make someone come after me to this extreme degree.

It was possible that the culprit was someone I had robbed in the past, but they would have had to figure out who I was. If Jake couldn't do it with the resources of the police department behind him, I doubted one of my victims would be able to. Possibly someone I had worked with or sold something to, but I was very careful to keep my alias separate from my real life.

Solving how they pulled this off would be the most likely thing to lead me to who had done this. They had found out that I was targeting the McGill house, and even knew what night I had planned to do it. They had either been listening to me when I talked to Jess about the plan, or had been watching me and waiting for the night I finally pulled the job. Was Bill just a means to an end? Or was he targeted because of me for some reason?

FRAMED

They could have been waiting for McGill in his office when he got home, and attacked. If someone had been at the McGill house at the same time I was, watching my movements, they would have seen my way in and out and knew it was safe. Were they watching McGill, or me? Either way, the thought creeped me out.

"Okay, where should we start?" I asked Jake, curious to see how he would approach this.

"Well, if I could use police resources, I'd say for you to make a list of possible suspects and start looking into them, but I'd need to explain why I needed the information and that would tip off the department that I'm helping you. So maybe let's begin with anyone who knows about your thieving and see what we can find out for ourselves."

"I want your help but let me be clear. I'm not a source to tap to arrest the people I work with. If we do this, they're off limits. If you can't agree that no harm will come to them, then we better split up."

"I can't promise that I won't be the one who arrests them in the future, but I can agree that if I go after them, it will be for something new, not anything that has already happened. For this weekend, anything you tell me or show me will be off the record. None of it will ever make it into a file or report, unless Ryan somehow makes the same connections, and I promise I won't say anything to him about it either. It's not much, but I can't help you if you can't be straight with me."

"That's enough, I guess. I need to change and then we can hit the road. I know exactly who to talk to first."

ELLIE HOHENSTEIN

Jake waited patiently in my living room while I headed into my room to get dressed. I closed the door behind me, grabbed my phone off my nightstand, then snuck into my closet, the furthest place in my room from the door. With the closet door closed, Jake would not be able to hear me talking on my phone even if he had followed down the hallway to listen.

I turned off the signal jammer I'd had running in case Jake was trying to record my confessions or was wearing some kind of transmitter to feed it to a team outside. I dialed Jess's number, letting it ring for two rings, hanging up, then calling again thirty seconds later. This was our code for "emergency", which was essentially the only reason I would have to call so early on a weekend. It also let her know it was really me, and that it was safe for me to talk.

She answered right on the first ring this time. "What's going on? Has there been movement on the case? I didn't get an alert…"

"It's bad, Jess. Really bad. I don't know how I'm going to get out of this one."

"Tell me what's going on, hon. I'm sure it's not that bad."

If she only knew. "Okay, so you remember that guy I've been seeing? Jake?"

"Mr. Perfect, yes how could I forget" she said with a slight chuckle.

"Well, turns out Mr. Perfect is a cop. Not just a cop, but *the* cop. The one who has been investigating all of my cases the last five years."

FRAMED

The silence on the other end was deafening. I'd finally managed to make Jess speechless, a feat I'd never thought would happen.

"Jess, are you still there?"

"Jake? Jacob Griffin? That's who you've been seeing? Are you crazy?" She was practically screaming at me, some combination of shock and anger coming out.

"I didn't know! I never paid much attention to who was looking into the case; it's not like I've ever come close to getting caught before. But Jess, he knows. That's how I found out about his job. His partner put it together that I'm the link between the cases."

"What's Jake going to do about it?"

"I have no idea, and I'm not sure he does either. We were together for the first time right before he found out, and I'm not sure if he's ever been in a situation like this. I certainly haven't. It's totally uncharted territory. And... it gets worse, Jess. They found hair at the crime scene, and I'm willing to bet it will match mine. Then I got a package today with a bloody award from the McGill house. Jake thinks it's the murder weapon. Someone is setting me up for killing Ralph's dad."

"How is that even possible?" she asked. "There's so many things they'd have to put together to figure out who you are, where you'd be, who you were even targeting."

"I don't know but I need your help to find out. I'm willing to bet they've been in my office or my apartment. I need you to do a sweep of both places today while I'm out investigating."

"Sure thing," she agreed quickly. "If they got past my security I'm going to be pissed." She took great pride in her work. If someone outsmarted her she would take it as a personal offense.

"Oh, and Jess? After you get done, run. I don't want you getting caught up in all this."

She scoffed. "Heck no, girl. You're going to need me through this. We've got plans in place for a reason. If we get to the point of no return, I'll go, but I'm with you until then."

She was a great friend. I really couldn't have chosen a better partner for both my business and my heists. We hung up, and I quickly changed into jeans and a nice shirt, slipping on a pair of sandals on my way back to the living room. I was a little worried Jake would wonder what took me so long, but he didn't comment. Maybe he was used to women taking forever to get ready.

"Alright, let's go," I said, and Jake led me down to his car, opening the door for me to get in the front seat. I was glad that his chivalry hadn't died with our relationship, but I couldn't help but be a little sad knowing that I wouldn't get to experience it much longer. At least he wasn't putting me in the back of a police cruiser.

"Where to?" he asked as he started the engine

"Head towards Pine Valley" I replied, mentioning the town where my last drop point had been. It would take about an hour to get there, maybe more depending on traffic, but Jake didn't complain as he set us on the right path.

After a few minutes, I couldn't help but ask, "Why are you doing this? Why help me?"

"I do care about you, Alexis. You don't deserve to go down for a crime you didn't commit. Not to mention

FRAMED

there's a murderer out there that will get away if this is pinned on you."

"Even after I lied to you?" If I were him, I would have been so angry. I'm not sure I could have calmed down enough to even listen to my side of the story, much less help clear my name.

"Yes, even after you lied. I was mad this morning and wanted to put all the blame on you, but I lied too. I never told you I was a cop. I'm sure if I had, you would have run for the hills."

I'd have been gone faster than he could blink if I'd found out before getting to know him, not willing to risk being caught no matter how amazing the guy might be. If he had told me on our second date, or even last night before it all went to hell... well maybe I'd have reconsidered.

I knew why I had held back my job, but most officers I'd interacted with took such pride in their work. I found it strange that he had been reluctant to share. "Why didn't you tell me? Obviously, me coming clean about being a thief wasn't on the table at this stage, if ever, but you didn't tell me about your job, even after I opened up about mine. I mean, we talked for hours over the last week, how did it not come up?"

He had the decency to look a little ashamed at that. "I know. I'd been meaning to bring it up, but people treat me differently once they know. Some of them fawn over us, praising us for how we risk our lives for the greater good. It's nice to be appreciated but can get a bit overwhelming at times.

ELLIE HOHENSTEIN

"Then there's the other end of the spectrum, where people are convinced you're out to get them, that you're looking for the slightest violation as an excuse to slap some cuffs on them and ruin their lives.

"I just wanted you to get to know me for who I really am, not just what I do. Besides, I more-of fell into it, so it's not like being an officer was a calling for me. Hell, I barely even like it outside of figuring out the puzzle each case presents. Remember how I mentioned that someone took me in when I was a teen? That was the police chief. He put a roof over my head, helped me finish high school, then enrolled me in the academy. I wasn't forced into it, but there weren't a lot of other choices either."

I nodded, even though he wasn't looking my way. "I know what you mean about people treating you differently. That's part of why I didn't mention that I was a therapist when we first met. People are worried I'm going to find out their darkest secrets, and they clam up."

He smiled understandingly at me and started to reach for me, to find comfort in our shared struggles, but must have thought better of it because his hand returned to the wheel. It was hard to believe that only twelve hours ago he was tearing my clothes off, and now he could hardly stand to touch me. My heart broke in a whole new way, feeling the absence of his hand acutely.

"Honestly, being a cop only feels like a small part of who I am, something I don't really care about. My time at the shelter, helping those kids, that's what I love, what makes me feel fulfilled. My job is just another way I can be a role model to them, show them that it's possible to get out, like I did. Believe it or not, but a few different

FRAMED

decisions and I might have been a thief right alongside you."

I laughed, struggling to picture him dressed all in black, sneaking through a house to pilfer some treasured possessions. "No way, I can't see it."

"It's true. One of the local gangs tried to get their claws into me as a teen. They got me to do a few break-ins, so I get how you feel about it—there's nothing in the world like the adrenaline rush of doing something you aren't supposed to, knowing you could get caught at any moment, then actually managing to get away with it. I get a little of that rush playing for the other side, chasing the bad guys. But it's definitely not the same."

I laughed, sure he was making it up to make me feel better about him not wanting to hold my hand. But I appreciated his efforts. My thoughts drifted back to what he said about his true calling being helping the kids at the shelter.

"What's going to happen with the shelters if I go to jail for the burglaries?" I asked somberly.

"What do you mean? I'm sure there are other therapists that would volunteer their time."

"I don't mean working with the kids, although that's definitely important. I mean the money." He looked over at me in confusion. I guessed it was too early for him to have had a chance to look into my finances yet.

"I donate money to the shelters in the city every year, maybe a few hundred thousand. It's mostly from my profits at my practice, but there's a bit that I feed into my accounts from the proceeds of selling the art. If they determine that the money was earned illegally, will they make the shelter pay it back to the families I stole from?"

He looked at me in shock. "You donate *hundreds of thousands* of dollars every year? Just to the local shelters?"

"That's all that goes to the local ones, yeah. But if they really dig and find the shell corporations that I use for the rest of the money, it's being distributed to shelters all over the country. I'm not sure of the specific amount per shelter, my accountant would know. I get the report each month of who he donated to and the total spend, but I usually just glance at it to make sure they're all legitimate shelters. Then there's the scholarship funds and such—I just don't want anyone else to suffer for my actions."

Jake was quiet for a while; contemplating, I supposed. He didn't exactly give an answer, but I hoped he would be able to do something. There wasn't enough government funding in a decade to pay back the money I had donated, and being forced to do so would likely bankrupt the shelters.

The kids were the main ones who would end up suffering from them closing. For many of them, the shelter was a home, an escape from a horrible reality—not just a place to hang out with their friends. I had to hope that if things went south for me after all this was over, Jake would find a way to keep protecting those kids.

Chapter 16

Alexis

We arrived in Pine Valley and I had Jake pull into a storage facility just outside of the city limit. I gave a code for him to enter to get us onto the grounds, directing him to one of the climate-controlled buildings.

The place was deserted, as usual, making it a great location for my drop point with my fence. He had two side-by-side units that he had rented for years. I didn't know his real name—like most people in this business he went by an alias, Mr. G. I pulled out my phone and dialed his number through an app that Jess had created which would scramble my signal and delete all traces of the call after it was done. He picked up quickly, but remained silent instead of offering a greeting, which was his normal move.

ELLIE HOHENSTEIN

"I need to meet," I said. "Drop, now." I hung up after the last word, knowing he'd know what I meant and would make it happen. We had been working together for years, and I was one of his best crooks. He made a tidy sum off me every time I pulled a job, and he did what he needed to in order to keep me happy. I figured we had about five minutes, maybe ten, before he would get here.

"Alright, out we go," I told Jake, opening my door as I said it. He frowned, looking around at the empty lot.

"Is he here?" he asked, confused.

"Nope, he will be soon though. So, we have to get into position. If he sees us, we won't get to talk to him."

Mr. G was cautious to an extreme. He didn't trust any of us not to either turn on him or to try and cut him out, so he used storage units in a few different cities as meeting points or drop spots. His two units here had a hole cut in the wall dividing them that allowed us to talk or pass small objects through. It was blocked from his side any time he was not in the unit, and had a curtain in place to stop anyone from looking through the hole and identifying him.

Since I had a key to the customer unit, I unlocked the door and let us inside, closing it behind me. The lights had come on automatically, revealing the empty unit. Mr. G would take whatever we dropped off and move it to a more secure location as soon as we were out of range.

"Why did you close the door? Is he not coming in?" Jake seemed thrown off by this whole situation, this world new and confusing to him.

I laughed. "Hell no. He doesn't see me, and I don't see him. That's the rules, and it suits us both just fine. I go by

211

FRAMED

'Ghost' to him, so make sure not to say my actual name. No one I work with should know who I really am."

"Ghost? That definitely fits. It sure felt like you were a ghost when I was trying to catch you. We were half convinced the whole thing was an insurance scam, but there were a few outliers that weren't insured and made us doubt the theory."

That reminder of who Jake was—what he was—sobered up my mood a bit. I waited the rest of the time in silence until I heard the rustling of the door being opened in the unit next door.

There were three bangs on the side of the wall, to which I replied with two bangs on one end of the unit and two on the other. It was a call-and-response code that was simple enough if you knew it, but anyone who was faking wouldn't think to move to the two ends of the space for their response.

"Who's that with you?" Mr. G asked in his gruff voice. He didn't trust new people, but I was hoping our history would give him confidence that I wouldn't bring someone here to set him up.

"New partner," I said, with a slight British accent. "Worked with me on my last job. Has it moved yet?" My thief persona was very different from my real personality, another security measure to keep people from tracing my work back to me. Short and to the point, I chose my words carefully to avoid anything explicitly incriminating.

"Not yet, got some interest though. Another week, maybe two. Is there a problem?"

Oh boy, was there. "Of a kind. Hold on to it for a bit, if you can. But that's not why I'm here. Someone's after

212

me. Wanted to see if you knew anything, or if you can find out. Quite the predicament that I'm in. Won't be able to visit anymore if I can't get out of it."

Silence for a moment, likely Mr. G inwardly cursing at the potential lost money train. "Haven't heard nothin', but I'll ask around. That it?"

"That's it," I confirmed. I heard the rustle of the door opening and closing again. No goodbyes, that was his style. I sat down against the wall and let out a big sigh. I had been hoping that he would have some information, but I also had no idea how long this frame job had been in progress, so there might not have been any recent chatter. If that was the case, I'd be in a rough spot.

"Is he gone? Why aren't we leaving?" Jake asked. Poor guy, he really had no idea how things worked on my level. He had said he was involved in some street crime when he was younger, but this was a whole different world.

"Go on, try." I said, urging him toward the door. He cautiously approached it, as if it might bite or explode when he got too close. He lifted up the handle to pull the door up, or attempted to anyway. It wouldn't budge.

"Mr. G doesn't trust folks not to chase him down or try and attack him, that's why he always arrives second and leaves first. There's an automatic lock that holds the door in place until he's out of reach."

"That's actually pretty smart," Jake said with a hint of admiration. "It's no wonder this guy doesn't get caught. This is all some real cloak and dagger shit."

I barked out a laugh. "You have no idea. I hate to say it Jake, but on a normal day you'd have no shot at catching someone like me, not on local police resources. The

FRAMED

people I work with have made a career out of dodging federal and international agencies. My biggest folly was probably staying in Willow Springs as long as I did. And I guess stealing from people in my own town consistently. I should have branched out to surrounding areas, but recon is hard to do when they are further away, and it leads to questions on why I travel so often."

A click sounded the disengaging of the automatic lock. I jumped up and strode to the door, pulling it up for Jake to exit. Once we were clear, I closed it back and secured the padlock on the door with my key. "Alright, ready for another road trip?"

"Where to?" he asked with a grin. I think he was having fun with this *cloak and dagger shit*. I can imagine it was interesting to play the bad guy a bit after so many years as a law-man.

We got back into his car, and I directed him to the town of Avens, two hours past Pine Springs. It would be a long drive home tonight, but hopefully we would be returning with some clues as to who was behind this.

Jake headed off without complaint, a slight grin on his face. "You're enjoying this, aren't you?" I asked.

"I always enjoy time with you," he said sincerely, which made my heart melt a bit. I hated to remind myself that it didn't matter, that we couldn't be together. He continued, "This is my favorite part though, the investigating. Every step is like a new puzzle, and this whole experience has been... eye opening? To say the least. You guys are geniuses, taking precautions against methods I've never even thought of.

"And you, this side of you... I don't even know what to think. That British accent? It was flawless. I'd have never known you were American, and I'd be looking in the complete wrong direction if that's all I had to go on. You changed your tone, your speech patterns, everything."

"You'd be surprised how crazy others go with their personas. I once met a guy who wore a fake leg. Like, he had two perfectly good legs, but he built this giant prosthetic leg and put his real one *inside* the fake one, pretending he had lost it in a war or something."

"That's ridiculous! What if he needed to run away, or if someone asked him to take it off?" Jake laughed.

"I don't know, I guess he hobbled away? Someone did ask him to remove it once, and he got all angry and offended and yelled at them for discriminating against his disability, and that they should be more accepting. I only found out it was fake because he got bitten by a spider or something and his leg was swelling up inside the fake one, so he had to take it off."

It felt insanely good to be able to be open with Jake about this part of my life. I had so many stories to tell, and had met some truly interesting people, but I'd never been able to talk about it with someone I was seeing. That was a big part of why my previous relationships had failed—I was never able to truly be myself with them. The weight of other people's secrets made relationships a challenge, but most people could understand doctor-patient confidentiality, since they would expect it themselves. But the weight of *my* secrets was harder to get past.

FRAMED

We chatted amicably throughout the drive, bouncing between music and casual conversation. Jake would occasionally tell a story about a case he worked on and I'd share details about how I pulled off some of the more challenging jobs he was aware of. He always had a decent theory for how I'd committed the theft, but since there was little evidence, he hadn't been able to prove it. When I confirmed any of his suspicions he would say "I knew it!" and bang on the steering wheel. It became something of a game, with him guessing how I might have done a job and me telling the story.

Just before we reached Avens, Jake shifted our conversation to a more serious tone. "You know, I'm envious of you."

I turned to him, confused look on my face. "Envious? Of what?"

"Your freedom."

I scoffed. "Let's hold off on that whole 'freedom' thing until this whole case settles out."

He shook his head. "I don't just mean freedom from jail, but freedom to do what you want in life. You were dealt a bad hand and still managed to make the most of it *and* help others avoid the same things you went through. I know I mentioned that the chief took me in, helped me get into the academy and become an officer, but since the moment I stepped through his door it's felt like I gave away my choices for my future."

I remained silent, shifting into my psychiatrist role. I could tell he needed to get this out, think through everything. He'd had a ton of information dropped on

216

him in the last day, and it had to be taking an emotional toll.

"It was a blessing to have the chief take me in—he saved me from a horrible path that probably would have killed me before long. But it was his choice for me to become a cop, then a detective, and he's basically been setting me up to take over as chief when he retires. It's a great life, but not the one I ever really wanted. But the idea of disappointing him… I can't do it after all he's done for me.

"If I'd had a choice, though, those kids are what I really care about. Whether social work, volunteering, or something, I've always just wanted to help them. So, I'm envious that you get to do that, of the impact you make, and the freedom you have in choosing how you do it."

I reached across and grabbed his hand, needing to comfort him, myself, maybe both of us, as I felt the tears well up behind my eyes. He squeezed my fingers, but let go too quickly, clearly not ready for my touch again after all the lies and secrets.

As we crossed into the Avens city limits, I directed Jake to a coffee shop that my accountant, Derek, owned and spent his Saturdays. He was very well-known in the small town since he was one of the only CPA's around and was the person who filed everyone's taxes. He regularly had visitors in the shop, and not just the criminals he bookkept for.

We walked in and Jake got us coffee while I sat down at a table. Derek didn't know for sure which town I lived in, but he knew it wasn't this one. He could be sure I was here for business.

FRAMED

"Madison! How great to see you!" he boisterously greeted me, using the alias he knew. I'd needed to have an actual name set up on my accounts and I couldn't very well go by "Ghost" to a crowded coffee shop. Derek sat down at my table, shaking my hand as he lowered himself into his chair. He was a large, bald man but jovial in nature—an odd personality for a career in accounting. He had a passion for people and a talent for numbers, which made him a great resource for someone in my position.

"Derek, how are you? It's been ages since we last saw each other." I didn't need to visit him regularly to work with him. When he made payments to various shelters for me, always sending a report with the confirmations and proof of payment to my PO box a few towns over. I visited shelters in that town regularly enough that I was able to stop in to collect the reports without too much hassle and it helped protect my real identity.

He knew my investment strategies and my donation plans, and he found ways to make them happen, earning himself a healthy portion for managing the funds. He and Jess had collaborated to set up my offshore accounts and make them secure, with only he and I able to access them. I didn't keep enough money in the accounts for him to consider screwing me over; he got a much better payday by keeping me as a customer.

"I'm well," he replied. "What can I do for you today? It must be quite sensitive to have warranted a personal visit."

Jake came over with our coffee and sat down, introducing himself as a potential client. We had decided on the plan on our way here, since Derek usually got new clients through referrals. I didn't necessarily need an excuse to be able to ask the questions I had, but explaining Jake's presence was another thing entirely.

"Oh, wonderful! Let me grab an informational packet. One moment, please."

After Derek had disappeared from sight, Jake turned to me. "He has a brochure for his illegal bookkeeping?" he asked incredulously. "That seems like a spectacularly stupid idea."

When Derek returned with the papers in question, Jake was forced to eat his words. The packets outlined standard accounting services, with no implication that anything was less than on the up-and-up. Only close inspection revealed words that didn't follow industry norms and could have double meanings for criminals, but nothing that could be proved definitively in court.

"While I'm here, Derek, I've actually got a few questions for you," I took the opportunity to ask while Jake reviewed the packet. "Someone's been looking for me, and I'm trying to find out who. It's someone who knows about my revenue streams, and I think they might be looking to interrupt them. Have you heard anything from any of your colleagues about that?"

"Hmm," he pondered. "I can't say I have, but I will do everything I can to find out. Your investments are some of the finest I've handled, I'd hate for that to take a bad turn. You let me know if there are any changes we need to make to your accounts."

"I certainly will. Thanks for your diligence, Derek." I turned to Jake and nodded, indicating I had done what I came to do.

FRAMED

"This all looks wonderful, Derek. Thank you. I will review this and be in touch," Jake said. "Oh, and your coffee is spectacular," he added as he took a sip.

Jake waited until we were back in the car to say what I'm sure he had been wondering since the storage unit in Pine Valley. "Why did we drive all the way out here just for five minutes of face time with each of these guys? Surely that all could have been handled with a phone call or an email?"

I shook my head. "No phones and no email. Nothing that can leave any kind of paper trail. That's the rules. It helps ensure that no one gets caught, and even if they do then it protects the rest of us from going down with them. It's inconvenient, sure, but it's worth it."

Jake nodded, but still asked, "At least explain the conversations to me. It felt like everything was in code."

"You should know how incriminating recordings can be. I always assume that the person I'm working with is willing to sell me out to protect himself. So I avoid saying anything outright incriminating. When I mentioned 'revenue streams', I was talking about my heists and the profits from selling the artwork. When I asked Mr. G whether my last job had moved, I was asking if he had sold the painting I stole from the McGill house. He's still got it, so I asked him to hold it a little longer. We might need it as leverage against whoever killed McGill."

He nodded, then shot me a mischievous smile. "Too much cloak and dagger shit."

I laughed as he pulled out of the coffee shop's parking lot, headed for home.

Chapter 17

Jake

Yesterday with Alexis had been... enlightening, to say the least. My head was spinning with all that I had learned about how this level of criminal operated. As a detective in Willow Springs, the majority of my cases ranged from basic gang violence to an occasional mistress being murdered, with the odd white-collar crime sprinkled in. Very few of the perpetrators were career criminals who thought through their moves with such care as the folks I had met.

I considered myself a great detective, solving almost every case that passed my desk—Alexis's robberies being the biggest exception. Now, I couldn't help but wonder if I was actually skilled or if I just needed better opponents. The crimes we got around here were generally very minor, small break-ins, assault, drunk and disorderly conduct, things like that. We only got the occasional murder outside of gang violence, which were generally pretty easy to solve. But the things Alexis exposed me to made me realize just how shallow our crime pool was. I made a mental reminder to ask Alexis if she was a chess player, and if so, then maybe she could teach me. With her meticulously planned heists leaving no evidence, she clearly was a master strategist.

But I also was more conflicted than ever about how to handle the revelation that Alexis was the thief I'd been chasing all these years. There was no question that she was capable, but I hadn't wanted to believe it could be her. I had been falling for Alexis, hard, but seeing this part of her, it was like a piece I didn't even know was missing.

The ease with which she transitioned into her different aliases and personas spoke to a confidence born of experience. They were each different parts of who she was, only she was more comfortable expressing them to the criminal community than in her real life. She had a "take no bullshit" attitude, and she owned every bit of it, which was extremely sexy.

And that led me to another big issue. I wanted this version of Alexis even more than I had wanted her before. We had been talking every night for the last week, and I had learned so much about who she was—her past, and her likes and dislikes—and I had felt closer to her than I had any other woman in my life. But the conversations we had yesterday, the stories she couldn't tell me before, were even more real and honest, and it felt incredible that she chose to share those experiences with me, to trust me with her secrets.

ELLIE HOHENSTEIN

I had told her that we couldn't be together, and I was right. There was no way I could date her while also trying to arrest her, and continuing our relationship would only give her false hope about her possible future. Once we cleared her name of murder, she was still going to jail for the thefts, probably for the rest of her life. I couldn't be a cop and be with someone in jail, not only because I can't imagine how you properly date someone in prison, but also because I'd be the laughingstock of the station if I even considered it.

Then there was the money to consider. Insurance had paid out on most of the stolen items, but would they force the issue to recover the funds if we arrested her? I needed to find out what the normal protocol was, but if the shelters could have to return the donations... I couldn't let that happen. I'd have to find some way to cover the financial transactions to keep the recipients hidden. Fortunately, it was still the weekend. I was sure that it would be another few days before Ryan had access to her bank records. I might have time to intercept them before they could be included in the official report.

Ryan was meeting me at the station, so I'd be able to see what he put together yesterday. I hoped he had been able to come up with other suspects for the murder—that way Alexis and I could have something else to go on. I had asked for all of McGill's movements for the last few weeks, but I wasn't sure what Ryan would have been able to track down in just a day. It was a little easier to get information on the dead, with there being no one to object to us violating their privacy.

223

FRAMED

When I arrived, Ryan was already set up in the conference room. He looked up with the biggest grin on his face as I approached, which in itself had me a little anxious. That was the face of victory, not exactly what I was hoping for.

"Good news, I suppose?" I said, pulling out a chair to sit at the table.

"Oh yeah. I had the chief call in a favor from one of the judges, so I got access to the therapist's financials, both business and personal. I'm still waiting on the warrant for the DNA, but I'm hoping I won't need one. I'm going to go to her office on Monday and try to get a sample willingly."

There was no shot Alexis was going to turn over her DNA now that we knew she was being set up, but I nodded like it was a great idea.

"After all these years without getting caught," I said, "maybe she will be cocky and think we won't have anything to compare it to. Just make sure to phrase it as if we are collecting samples of every member of their staff, direct and indirect, so we're just trying to rule her out as a suspect.

"It's also possible she treated their son at the house, which actually would be a good reason for her hair to be there if they held the sessions in the office. It would offer privacy without the intimacy of the child's bedroom. We should be sure to ask Mrs. McGill about that. Or possibly the staff. I'll make a trip out to the estate later today to conduct some interviews, as well as talk with Alison and her son."

224

Ryan looked a little crestfallen at my mentioning there could be a legitimate reason for her hair to have been in the office. I didn't think it was actually the case since Alexis would have likely mentioned it after she found out about the sample we collected.

I threw him a bone, wanting both to hear what else he had found and also to cheer him back up, "What did you find in the shrink's finances?"

"That I definitely went into the wrong profession," he joked. He slid the folder containing the bank statements across the table to me, and the numbers I saw made my eyes bug out a little. Alexis was *loaded*. Like, *buy your own yacht and private jet* type of loaded. I flipped through the pages, looking for the donations she had mentioned she made to the local shelters. She gave away ten times my annual salary, at least, to each of a handful of youth or women's shelters across the city.

"Where is all this money coming from?" I asked. Alexis had said that she kept most of the profits from her heists in accounts that weren't directly tied to her, but I couldn't imagine that all this had come from just her practice.

"So far, it all looks legitimate. It's hard to trace every incoming transaction and validate if it came from a patient, especially with confidentiality laws, but both the business's statements and her personal ones look like they are on the up-and-up. I can't believe that people are paying that much to have their kids spend an hour a week just to talk to someone. Some of them look like they are only monthly appointments, too."

"And the outgoing transactions? That's a lot of money being sent somewhere."

FRAMED

"Charitable donations, also legitimate. I called some of the shelters, and they gave glowing recommendations for everything that the doctor has done, both financially and with her time. She apparently treats a lot of the at-risk kids for free."

On paper, Alexis was an angel. Hell, in real life she was too, other than all the stealing, of course.

"Again, what could her motive possibly be? She doesn't need the money. She's clearly got more than she knows what to do with, and can't even seem to be able to give it all away. And if she's working so much and volunteering, I doubt she could be having a personal relationship with McGill. So why would she rob him?"

Ryan looked genuinely frustrated. "I don't know. I can't figure it out, either, but my gut is screaming that she took the painting, and all the other items we've had go missing. I need to talk to her and get a look at her client list. Any advice on how to get a judge to overrule confidentiality?"

"Nope, I've never had to deal with this before. It's one thing to be asking a doctor about one of their patients in the interest of seeing if that patient could commit a crime, another thing entirely when trying to do it the other way around." I replied. Now that I knew he was stuck, it was the perfect opportunity to draw his attention away from Alexis. "What about other possible suspects for the murder?"

"Well, there's at least two other possibilities, maybe more. I traced McGill's movements, like you asked, which primarily consisted of time spent at his restaurants. I visited the ones he worked at the most and asked the

226

employees for any suggestions on who might have had a grudge against him. I was thinking about possible business partners, other restaurant owners, outraged customers, anyone who would have been mad enough to have a public confrontation with him.

"That's not the response I got, though. Many of them actually said that his wife would be their first guess. He was apparently a huge flirt, hitting on every attractive woman he saw. Mr. and Mrs. McGill had apparently had it out a few times in the offices when he had gotten a little too friendly with either a customer or an employee. Rumor had it, there had been more than one affair over the years, but no one knew if there was one actively going on.

"So, I looked back a little further and saw regular, large cash withdrawals. The kind you might make when supporting a mistress and hiding it from your wife. The last one was a little over a month ago, and they usually happened around the first of the month, like clockwork. But I didn't see one this month. So, either the affair ended, or he cut her off. Since the second option would more than likely still lead to the first, I'm guessing that one way or another the affair had been called off."

"You're thinking that the two other options are either the wife or the girlfriend, maybe ex-girlfriend by that point. Both would have a solid motive if we could prove it. Did you get a chance to verify about the wife's spa trip? Could she have left the spa, driven back home to kill her husband, then returned without them noticing her absence? It's quite the drive to make, but if she were

FRAMED

hellbent on killing her husband, it might have been worth it."

"I did. The spa is one of those 'retreats' that basically holds you hostage while you're there. You have to turn in your phone, keys, wallet, everything that could be a 'material distraction'. All those things are kept under lock and key in a storage room, it works kind-of like a safety deposit box at the bank. The resort staff has a key and the guest has a key, and you can only access the boxes by inserting both keys at the same time. She would have had to have a staff member go with her to get the keys, and would have been on camera opening up the box. Neither of which purportedly happened."

I shook my head. Rich people did crazy things, and I couldn't imagine going on a vacation and being told I couldn't have contact with the outside world, especially if I had a child back home.

"So that makes it much less likely to be the wife. I'll ask the staff while I'm there about any potential girlfriends. Maybe he was careless enough to bring someone back to the house and they saw something."

I stood up. "Anything else you've found, or are we ready to head back out?"

"No, that's it for now. Are we going out together?" he asked, looking a bit hopeful. I felt terrible, especially since I had promised to guide him on this investigation, but I also couldn't have him working with me directly if I was going to clear Alexis's name.

"No, I need to go talk to my CI network, and you know how they get spooked around other cops."

228

ELLIE HOHENSTEIN

"Didn't you do that yesterday?" he asked. I forgot that I had mentioned that I was going to do that. At the time, I hadn't planned on spending the whole day with Alexis, so I had needed to come up with a believable use of my time.

"Oh, yes, I dropped some seeds yesterday," I said. It wasn't technically a lie considering Alexis and I had asked some questions that we were waiting to hear back on. "I need to check back in to see if anyone has found anything yet."

"What's the best thing for me to do, then?"

I needed to keep him as far away from investigating Alexis as possible. "See what you can find out about either the wife or the potential mistress. If you notice any hotel charges, or restaurants, start flashing McGill's picture around and see if anyone recognizes him and can give a description on who he might have been with."

Ryan nodded. I could tell he was a little frustrated to be chasing down leads that weren't related to Alexis, especially since he was so proud of having made the link between the cases. Once we knew who was framing her, I'd give him the chance to do the diligence on solving the theft.

I called Alexis once I was back in my car, on my way to check in with a few of my informants.

"Any news?" she asked in lieu of a greeting. Her nervousness was coming through loud and clear, so I was guessing that she hadn't yet heard back from the guys we visited yesterday.

"Yes, and no. Ryan's already gotten into your financials, but he hasn't seen anything that's a red flag.

FRAMED

However you disguised your proceeds, it was done well. He's planning to come by your office tomorrow to interview you, and he's going to ask for a sample of hair for the DNA match. I'm sure this goes without saying, but you can't give it to him.

"He's also probably going to ask you to voluntarily turn over your client list. It's his only real move given the struggle he'd have to get around confidentiality to get a warrant."

"I can't do that," she said firmly. "I won't violate my oaths. My patients expect my discretion, and most of them are children with trust issues. I can't contribute to that. It's wrong, not to mention it would ruin my reputation."

"I understand, and I can respect that. The other piece of news is that there's a chance that McGill was having an affair, which would give another suspect for his murder. You wouldn't happen to know anything about that, would you?"

For a moment, there was silence on the other end of the line. Then, "I can't violate my patient's confidentiality."

Was she telling me something without being able to say it? Her clients were mainly children, and we already knew that the McGill kid was seeing her. Was he the patient she was referring to? Did he know something about a possible affair?

An idea sparked, something that might allow us to work around confidentiality and have both Alexis and the kid tell me what we needed to know. "How would you like to come with me to the McGill house later?" I asked.

230

She sounded a little stunned as she replied, "The McGill house? What would we do there?"

"You could show me how you got in, for one. And maybe there is something there that was different than the way you left it, something that might give us a clue about who we're looking for."

She could tell there was more I wasn't saying. "And how would we explain who I am and why I needed to be there? You can't exactly introduce me as the person who stole the painting."

I laughed. "I mean, I could, but it probably wouldn't go over too well. No, I was thinking that we just introduce you as who you really are. A psychiatrist who I thought might be able to help the kid with losing his dad. I mentioned that I knew someone, so while me bringing you by might be a bit of an overstep, it wouldn't be that farfetched."

She pondered a moment. She didn't know that I already knew she was treating the son, and she respected her oaths enough not to correct me or reveal it. "Alright," she said, finally.

"And," I continued, "maybe the kid will be comfortable enough to let me hear some of what he tells you. That way you wouldn't have to break any confidentiality agreements to pass on the information to me."

"I see. That's actually a really good plan. Where and when should I meet you?" I could hear the smile in her voice.

We agreed to meet in a few hours, which gave me plenty of time to hit the streets to check if there was any

FRAMED

information circulating about McGill's death or the stolen painting. My informants were pretty useful, they knew most of the criminals in town—lawbreakers of all varieties—and were willing to talk about it in exchange for me turning a blind eye to some of their smaller crimes. They knew not to step too far out of line, that I wasn't going to be responsible for anyone getting hurt, so they kept to low-level shoplifting or spraying graffiti for the most part.

The first two CI's didn't have anything to contribute, but promised to ask around and keep an ear out for related chatter. We knew where the painting was, but it was possible that the murderer was trying to get their hands on it to further the efforts of setting Alexis up.

It was only when I met with a third informant that things started to get interesting.

Viktor was a former member of the Russian mob in California, but had fled from his family, finding protection in the obscurity of our small town across the country. He worked as a matchmaker of sorts, pairing criminals with jobs that suited their styles and talents for a small cut of the profits. His association with me was well hidden, for his protection and for his business. If anyone knew he was a snitch he would never get another job.

Our relationship was mutually beneficial, where he gave me information on jobs that he was not part of or about people who screwed him over, and I got a lot of dangerous criminals off the street. It stopped him from killing people as well. He always had his ear to the ground, listening for any signs that his family had tracked him down, so he was aware of just about every criminal player

232

ELLIE HOHENSTEIN

in town. He had given me a few tips on Alexis's jobs, but never had more information than the alias she used at the time.

I always met him at the bar that he ran, where I could pretend to be just another patron and he could pass information through casual conversation, rather than trying to sneak around dark alleyways. The name of the place was written in Russian above the door, which I believed simply translated to "bar". It was a popular local hangout for the seedy types, as well as a few locals of the neighborhood. It was a small dive, dark and dingy, and was usually empty before lunchtime.

The two patrons at the bar turned my way as I walked in. I sat at the far end, believing enough distance lay between me and the next guest that I wouldn't be overheard if speaking low. Viktor ambled over and poured a shot of vodka for each of us. We toasted, then downed the drink, the clear liquid burning its way down my throat.

"Good to see you, Viktor," I said with a laid-back grin.

"Jake! It's been too long, my friend." His thick accent made me smile, there weren't many of his countrymen in our town, so hearing it was a rarity. If I ever got a call reporting someone with a Russian accent, he would be my prime suspect.

"It has," I agreed, dropping my tone lower as he leaned in. "I'm hoping you can help me find someone. Did you hear about Bill McGill's murder the other day?"

"Da, I was only surprised it took so long."

"Took so long? What do you mean?" I asked, finally feeling like I'd be getting a lead.

FRAMED

"There were rumors that someone wanted him dead, somewhere around a year ago maybe. I heard someone accept the job, but then nothing. No body. I figure person either change their mind, or maybe payment fell through. You have a suspect, yes?"

I struggled with how much to say. "Yes... and no. We have someone that we're looking at, but I've been thinking we're going in the wrong direction. You said that his death might have been a hit?"

"It's been so long, who can say for sure? But there *was* a hit on him at some point. If you need, I can ask around for some more details on who took it and what happened?"

I smiled. "Absolutely. Let me know what you find, yeah?" Finally, things were starting to go our way. Between Viktor and Alexis's fence and accountant, I felt sure we would get something to point us in the right direction. Viktor nodded, then headed back down the bar to tend to other patrons. I threw some bills on the bar for the shot and for the info, then strolled back out the door.

I couldn't wait to tell Alexis what I had discovered. If McGill had been killed in a hit, it could change everything. No longer were we investigating a random murder, or even a simple frame job. We were looking for an assassin.

Chapter 18

Jake

I picked Alexis up outside of her building. I had done my normal routine of getting out to open the door for her, but it was a real struggle not to kiss her in greeting. Being with her was so effortless, we just clicked. It would be ages before I'd be able to find someone I belonged with like this, if I ever did.

Once we had gotten settled back in the privacy of my car, I dropped the bomb I'd been bursting to tell her.

"McGill's death was a hit."

Her jaw dropped and her eyes practically bulged out of her head. "Wh-what?" It might have been the first time I'd ever seen her at a loss for words. I grinned at the sight, relishing in my success of finding a piece of crucial information.

"Well, it most likely was, at least. I talked to some of my informants and one guy said that he had heard about

FRAMED

a hit being placed on McGill about a year ago. Someone had agreed to take the job, then silence. I'm not sure why they waited so long to do it, and it's still technically possible that his death was unrelated, but I feel in my gut that this is the right path. It just makes sense. Other than where you come in, of course."

She nodded, and I could practically see the wheels turning in her head. "Did the guy know who the hitman was? A name or at least an alias?"

"Not yet, but I'd give it a day, maybe two, and we should have a lead on that. In the meantime, are you ready to go see what McGill's kid has to say?"

We stopped at a drive-thru for lunch, and a short while later we were turning into the McGill estate. After getting out of the car, Alexis smoothed down her outfit and I watched as she switched her composure to the professional doctor, just another facet of her incredible personality.

She fit the bill with her appearance, dressed in slacks and a soft blue shirt. Since she would be going in under the guise of talking to the McGill kid about how he was coping with his father's death, she explained that she had chosen her outfit with care, blue being a calming color and also tied to sadness. I knew a bit of how people related to colors, body language, cadence and tone of speech, she really had a firm handle on all the psychology stuff, her education blowing my learned habits out of the water.

In all honesty, the poor boy could genuinely use someone to talk to, and Alexis would be one of the best people for the job. Not only did they already have a relationship since he was her patient, she had also lost her parents suddenly at a young age.

"Are you ready for this?" I asked as we approached the front door.

"Of course. I just hope we learn something useful." It really felt like we were getting close to making a real breakthrough on the case, and this would be another step in the right direction.

The housekeeper answered the door shortly after I rang the bell. "Can I help you?" the woman asked. She had been at the house when we were first here to investigate the murder scene, but she had likely met so many officers that night that she might not have remembered me. She was older, maybe mid-sixties, with gray bleeding through into her brown hair at the roots and laugh lines on her face.

"Hi, ma'am. I'm Detective Griffin with the Willow Springs Police Department. I'm the lead on the murder investigation of Mr. McGill. I was hoping to be able to come in and take another look at the scene, as well as ask the staff members a few follow up questions, if that would be alright?"

"Oh, of course! Please come in." She stepped out of the way to allow Alexis and me to enter.

"Thank you so much. This is Dr. Alexis Lee," I said, indicating to her. "She is the city's leading psychiatrist for children, and I was thinking it might be beneficial to have her speak with Mr. McGill's son, if that's alright with Mrs. McGill?"

The housekeeper looked positively gleeful. "Oh Dr. Lee! It's so great to finally meet you. Ralph goes on and

FRAMED

on about you, he will be thrilled you are here. Mrs. McGill was planning to give you a call tomorrow to set up a session, but if you're here now that's even better."

Alexis smiled politely. "I'm glad this was able to work out. Detective Griffin had mentioned that his case had a young boy who might be struggling, but I had no idea we would end up here. I was so sad to hear about Ralph's father, I just hope I can help him on his journey to processing the loss."

"Oh, bless you," the housekeeper said, laying her hand across her heart with a sigh. "I'll go get Ralph and let him know you're here."

"Actually," I interrupted, "I was hoping Dr. Lee would join me in the office first to help me reason through what the killer's thought process and state of mind might be, if that would be alright?"

"Of course. Just come find me when you're done, I'll just be cleaning up the kitchen from the lunch mess."

I led Alexis to the office and closed the doors behind us. From the looks of things, not much had been changed. A rug covered up the spot where McGill's head had bled on the carpet, so I moved it out of the way so Alexis could see all the details. It was clear that the cleaning staff had put in serious work trying to get the stain out, but they weren't quite able to accomplish it. The carpet would most likely need to be replaced.

"Okay," she said. "Walk me through the scene." I did a quick recap, pointing out how the body was positioned, where key pieces of evidence were found, and so on. The wall where the painting had hung was unchanged, with only the mounting hardware indicating anything had been there.

"So how did you manage to take the painting?" I was dying to know how she worked, how she pulled off some of the most incredible heists I had ever seen. She smiled coyly, knowing how excited I was for this moment.

"Alright... I guess I should take you through it. So, I got into place just after dark, hiding up in a tree far enough into the woods that I couldn't be easily seen, but close enough that I could watch the house. Once the nanny went to sleep, I made my way through the trees and emerged into where I had moved a camera to ensure a blind spot—"

"But none of the cameras were tampered with," I cut in. "We went back days and didn't find anything."

"Oh honey," she said, shaking her head. "You forget I work the long game. I repositioned the camera over a week ago, figuring your team wouldn't go back that far. And even if you had, it was done using miniscule movements over the course of hours. You'd have to be watching at super-speed to even notice it. So, I had a clear path to the house, and picking the simple lock on the back door was a cakewalk. No one but the nanny was home, and her room's upstairs and across the house, so as long as I didn't make any big noises, I knew I was golden.

"The office doors were closed, but not locked, so no big issue there. The painting was mounted to the wall, but I was able to unscrew it with the small assortment of tools I carry. I didn't need the mounting kit, so I left it. Then it was a simple job to get back out the way I came in."

FRAMED

"What about the alarm? And how did you carry the painting? It's huge, and from what information Ryan gathered, the frame was solid gold. It had to weigh a ton."

"I trained," she said simply, shrugging like it was no big deal. I couldn't help picturing her pacing around her apartment or through the woods at night carrying a giant picture as practice. I was thoroughly impressed with how she could take such a huge job and make it sound so effortless. "And the alarm company uses satellite signals to keep its connection, which are unreliable at best. They were basically begging to be robbed."

I shook my head with a smile. "Alright, back to the murder. McGill's head was smashed in, having been hit multiple times with that lovely award that was mailed to you. The working theory at the department is that he came home, found you stealing the painting, and you panicked and beat him to death.

"If you were standing here," I continued, positioning myself at the middle of the wall where the painting had hung to illustrate the narrative as I spoke, "then you would have easily been able to grab the award off the bookcase over there and attack when he walked towards the desk. You hit him once, knocking him to the ground unconscious, then proceeded to beat him to make sure he wouldn't wake up. The patterns on the wall showed where blood had been slung from the multiple hits. Then you proceeded to finish taking the painting down and ran for it."

"But why would he have turned his back on someone who broke into his house? What could he have been going for in the desk?" she questioned, mirroring the same concerns I had with the theory.

"We searched the desk but didn't find any kind of weapon, so he wasn't going after something to defend himself. And even if he were, I would think he would have wanted to keep a thief in his sights so they wouldn't bolt out the door and get away.

"Now, you and I are pretty sure this was a hit. Which makes even less sense for him to turn his back on a hitman, unless it was a mad dash for a weapon. And how would they have even gotten in here in the first place, unless they followed your path in and out? No one was visible on the camera feeds when we checked."

"It would have to be someone sleight, I only moved the camera enough to give myself a very small path to the house. Anyone much bigger than me would have had a hard time avoiding the camera. I even had to walk sideways while carrying the picture to be sure I wasn't visible."

We both pondered for a few moments, then said together, "It was a woman."

She picked up the train of thought first. "A female killer... it was the perfect choice for a man like McGill. He would never have suspected it, and he probably wouldn't have considered a woman to be a threat, especially a beautiful one."

"So, she committed the murder to look like a robbery-gone-wrong, but was also careful enough to not leave any evidence herself. She must have been experienced to be able to pull off that level of detail, but why target you? If

FRAMED

this is the same person who took the job a year ago, why wait until now to kill him?"

Those were questions we didn't have the answers to yet. We left the office for the kitchen, checking in with the housekeeper to see if we could go ahead and speak with the kid. She looked a little bit confused when I said "we", perhaps unsure if it was acceptable to allow me to speak with him during his session with Alexis. Still, she went to let him know we were here.

"Alexis!" the child said as he came bounding down the stairs. He barreled into her with a hug, which she lightly returned, gently patting his back. "I'm so glad you're here. Why are you here? Mom said she was going to call you tomorrow to schedule me an appointment."

"Hi Ralph, I'm glad to be here too. My friend here asked me to come by with him," she said, gesturing to me. "In case you needed someone to talk to. Is your mom here?"

"No, she had to go to work at one of the restaurants... She hasn't been here much since she found Dad."

Hearing that really pissed me off. This child was clearly feeling lonely and neglected. He was experiencing the trauma of suddenly losing his father, and his mom couldn't even spend the few days immediately after to console him, let him know he still had her. I could understand that the restaurants might be busy, more than usual with the buzz that the murder would have generated, but her child should come first. The restaurants had managers and staff, while Ralph only had her.

"I'm sorry, sweetie," Alexis said, looking at Ralph sympathetically. "Well then, I'll leave the decision up to

242

you. This is Detective Griffin. He's trying to figure out what happened to your dad. Do you mind if he sits with us while we talk? He might learn something that could help him, and he might have some questions for you if you're comfortable with that."

Ralph looked over at me, and I'd never felt so judged by a child. "He doesn't look like a cop," he said to Alexis. I couldn't help but laugh. I was dressed casually in jeans and a polo shirt, but I didn't think it looked bad.

"And what's a cop supposed to look like?" I asked with a smile.

"You're supposed to have a gun and a badge. Maybe two guns in those fancy straps that go on your back? And a hat. Detectives always have a hat, like Sherlock Holmes."

The kid clearly watched too many movies. I reached into my back pocket, pulling out my wallet with my badge in it.

"What about the gun?" he challenged.

I bent down low, my face level with his. "Who says I'm not wearing one?" I said mischievously. His eyes widened, looking me all over, no doubt trying to figure out where I could be hiding my weapon.

"Alright," he relented. "He can sit with us. Let's go to the living room."

We followed him over to the couches. Ralph sat on the larger one leaving Alexis and I to share the loveseat. It was a tight fit, and her body was pressed up against mine. I couldn't help but remember our night together—just two days ago but it felt like a lifetime. Even with us sitting so close, it felt like there was an unsurpassable distance between us. I wanted more than anything to be able to

FRAMED

cross that line, to be able to be with her, I just couldn't see a way to make it work.

Alexis leaned back in her seat, a casual position that pushed her legs even more against mine. I followed suit and relaxed into the chair, and it took a conscious effort to not put my arm around her shoulders.

"So, Ralph, how are you doing? I imagine what happened on Friday was quite a shock," Alexis said, starting the session.

"It was, I'm not exactly sure what to think right now. We didn't have a close relationship. Honestly, I don't really feel like I knew my dad well. But he was still my dad, you know? I'll never get the chance to fix that, to get to know him. I'll never even get to decide if I *want* to get to know him better. He didn't seem like a very nice person."

"Why do you say that?" Alexis asked, much more calmly than I would have. She phrased it more like prompting him to work through why he felt that way, rather than trying to get information out of him. Between how she was with him and what I saw at the shelter the other day, I could already tell that she was an all-star shrink.

"Well, he and my mom didn't seem to get along. They fought a lot when they were home and never seemed to work at the same restaurant on the same day. I don't know if they really liked each other much. And he was always really rude to Mom's family. Then there was the whole thing in the office the other week, with the other woman. I've been thinking about it a lot, and I don't think it was the first time. He's always been overly touchy with Mom's

244

ELLIE HOHENSTEIN

friends when they come to the house. He even does it in front of Mom, which just seems mean."

I took the opportunity to jump in. "Ralph, do you think you could tell me about the woman you saw? We would like to talk to her to see if she can help us figure out what happened."

"Oh, yeah, I guess that makes sense. She had blonde hair, short, maybe to her shoulders? And she looked fancy. She wore really nice clothes, like my mom wears when she goes out. She was tall, almost as tall as Dad, and I think in really good shape. She looked a bit familiar; I think she had been here before, maybe one of my mom's friends? I can't remember any more."

"That's alright, Ralph. You did great, buddy." I thanked him and let Alexis get back to the session. I didn't need anything more from the kid, so I left the room to give them some privacy. I needed to find the housekeeper so I could question the staff members.

I didn't have to go far to find her. She had been keeping an eye on us from the next room over. She tried to appear busy as I approached, like she hadn't been spying, but I wasn't offended. If anything, I appreciated the commitment she had to Ralph and the family.

"Do you have a minute, ma'am? I'd like to ask a few questions, if you're available."

"Of course, Detective. What can I do for you?"

"Ralph mentioned that Mr. Schwartz had a... female visitor a few weeks ago. It would really help our investigation if I could speak to her. Could you provide me with any details about her or the nature of their relationship that might help me identify her?"

245

FRAMED

She looked a little nervous, seemingly torn between her loyalty to the family she served and wanting to help get justice. "Bill was… oh, what's a nice way to say this… a dog."

I barked out a laugh in shock, taken aback by her attitude towards him.

"Over the years he's had more than his share of female company." She continued. "It's a miracle Alison hasn't divorced him, but I suppose with all the restaurants it would be quite messy. The latest was a young blonde woman, maybe late twenties or early thirties?

"I think he found her at some charity event, a socialite for sure. He was always giving her new clothes, or bags, or hats—anything really that he could get away with, without leaving a paper trail. Alison could never prove that he was blowing their money on his whores, not for a lack of trying though."

"So, Mrs. Schwartz knew about the affairs?"

"Good lord, the whole city knew. He was the world's biggest flirt, and I don't think he met a single woman that he didn't hit on. He wasn't like that when they first got married, but the restaurant business wasn't good for them, or their marriage. I think being surrounded by all the young women working for them was just too much temptation for Bill."

"It sounds like you've known them for a long time," I observed.

"Oh yes, I used to work for Alison's parents back when she was a teenager. She's like a daughter to me, the poor dear. She deserved so much more than this from her life."

246

ELLIE HOHENSTEIN

I thanked the housekeeper for her time, then spoke with a few of the other staff members. By the time I was wrapping up, Alexis had finished her session with Ralph, and they were having cookies in the kitchen.

Watching her interact with kids was incredible. I could tell how much she cared about all the children she met with. She took such a genuine interest in their lives, asking them questions and remembering personal details. It had been like this at the shelter too, where she knew so many of them by name and they all loved her. This woman was amazing.

I cleared my throat to get their attention after a few moments of leaning in the doorway. "Cookies? Without me?" I joked. Alexis held one out to me, which I took with a smile. We chatted a few more minutes with Ralph, then excused ourselves to leave, Alexis promising to see him again soon.

"So is Alison a suspect?" Alexis asked once we were back in the car.

"No, she has an alibi for that night, she was up at the spa a few hours away. I figured that's part of why you chose that specific night to break in?"

"No, just a lucky coincidence. I didn't want to deal with the weekend, but I still wanted enough time to investigate their habits. It wasn't because she was out of town, that bit just made my job even easier. Although if she had come back a day earlier, I probably would have pushed it back, not wanting to risk the unknown of her routine and potentially getting caught in the act," Alexis replied.

"Why did you choose that particular piece? Why the McGills at all?" That had been bugging me this whole

FRAMED

time. I still didn't know how Alexis picked her targets, though she had told me about a few of the other jobs she had done.

"I'm surprised it took you this long to ask," she laughed. "Well, I've always considered myself a bit of a Robin Hood type. I've noticed over the years that the rich never seem to face justice. There is always someone they can pay off, or excuses they can make, and then they go about their lives like nothing ever happened. And it doesn't sit right with me.

"They don't see how what they do matters, especially to the kids growing up watching them. So, when my patients tell me about being abused, mistreated, neglected, and so on, it breaks my heart for them, especially since the kids usually don't do anything to deserve that treatment— most of them aren't even doing anything outside of normal kid stuff and yet their parents call them 'troubled'. I get them justice, in my own little way. They took something vital from these children, the love and respect of their parents, so I take something that they consider vital."

The picture was becoming clearer. Every job she pulled was one of the most precious items to the victims. Most recently, the Schwartz job where she stole the bust that was the pride and joy of their collection. I doubted the parents always made the connection back to what they did to their kids, but they definitely felt some of the hurt that I'm sure they passed on to their children.

"And why was the painting the thing to take from McGill?"

248

Her expression hardened. "Ralph saw the affair. He struggled with that secret. The painting I took was called *The Secret*, and Bill had it prominently displayed in his office, where he could look at it all day. It had its own wall, for crying out loud. And it was such a subtle jab at his wife, rubbing it in her face, that I knew it was the piece as soon as I saw it."

We arrived back at her place and she invited me up for a drink to run through everything we knew so far. She grabbed us a couple of beers from her refrigerator and we settled onto opposite ends of her couch. It had been a long day. Hell, it had been a long weekend, and my mind was buzzing with the information overload.

"Alright, so we're waiting to hear back from Mr. G. and Derek from my end, and a few folks from your informant network?" Alexis asked. She had changed into comfier clothes and had her feet tucked up under her as she leaned against the armrest. Her hair was pulled back, and I couldn't help but think of how perfect it would be to spend every evening like this, with her.

"Yep," I said. "I'm hoping to hear something about who might have contracted the hit and who took the job, but I'm not sure how long it will take. I've been trying to send Ryan to chase down other leads, keeping him away from looking into you, but I don't know how much longer I can hold him off."

"That's alright, I'll deal with whatever comes. Confidentiality should protect me from most of his questions, and I've got enough respect in this town that he will be hard-pressed to get a judge on his side." Her confidence was admirable, but I was still worried about the DNA evidence placing her at the scene of a murder.

"And what do you plan to do with the murder weapon?" I asked. If Ryan raided her place and found it, it would be a slam-dunk trial and Alexis wouldn't stand a chance. After seeing her with Ralph today, I couldn't imagine how badly it would break him for Alexis to be simply accused of murdering his father, much less convicted.

"It's in a safe place for now. And I cleaned all my prints off it just in case it gets found. There should be nothing that can point back to me, at least not from that."

I nodded, trying to think of anything else we could do to make progress while we were waiting to hear back.

Her phone rang, stopped, then a few minutes later it rang then stopped again. She stood and went down the hallway towards her bedroom, returning a minute later with another cell phone. My brows furrowed in confusion, unclear as to why she would need to use a different phone than the one she was contacted on originally.

"It's a secure line," she said, answering my silent question. "It's Mr. G. I'll be right back."

She went back to her bedroom, this time closing the door behind her. I was surprised that she was taking the call in private—she had been so open the last two days about her past, the jobs she had worked, the people she had met. But I was still a cop, and while I had promised not to go after any of her friends while we were investigating, there might be something I overheard that she worried would compel me to act. I understood her reluctance for me to hear, even if I didn't like it.

ELLIE HOHENSTEIN

It turned out not to matter since my phone also rang a few minutes later.

A thick Russian accent greeted me as I answered. "Jake, my friend! I have good news for you. I asked around about that job on Bill McGill. A down payment was made to the contractor a year ago when they first took the job, but the rest was held with an intermediary service. Not me, of course, but a friend of a friend. He confirmed that he was given authorization to release the remaining funds on Friday night.

"Now, I don't have the name of who posted the hit, but the woman who carried it out goes by 'Ripper'. He described her as tall, thin, with short blonde hair."

That matched the description of the woman McGill was seeing. So the woman seduced him, then killed him. But how did Alexis fit into this?

Just as I was pondering, I heard the bedroom door open and Alexis walked out into the living room with a big smile on her face.

"That's fantastic, thanks so much Viktor. I owe you one." I said, intending on finishing the call.

"Jake, one last thing. This woman, I hear she's leaving town soon, if she's not gone already. You don't have long. That's the way with these professionals, no sticking around after the job is done to appreciate a place like this."

I hung up, walking back towards the couch where Alexis was waiting.

"Ripper!" we said at the same time.

"Wait, how did you get that name?" I asked.

"Mr. G. said that someone going by the alias 'Ripper' was asking around trying to find me, somewhere around a

251

year and a half ago. He wasn't sure who had pointed them in my direction, but he thinks that they made the connections and found me here. How did you get it?"

"That was Viktor, one of my contacts. He runs a bar downtown. The hit was filled by someone going by that alias. From the description, it sounds like our mistress. If she was looking for you first, then this must have been the plan all along. She got close to McGill and waited until she had the chance for you to get involved."

There were still so many unanswered questions, but this was huge. I couldn't contain my excitement, and I grabbed Alexis by the waist, picked her up, and twirled her around. She squealed with laughter as I spun her.

"We're so freaking close, I can taste it!" I said. I lowered her back down to the ground gently.

As I did, her body dragged slowly against mine. I became incredibly aware of how close we were, how her body was pressed against me. I had been fighting my attraction to her since I had found out who she really was, but everything I learned about her just made me want her more.

Her shirt caught on my belt on her way down, exposing her stomach, and my fingers brushed against her soft skin.

My control snapped.

I pressed my lips against hers, walking her back toward the wall behind her. She returned my kiss eagerly, wrapping her arms around my neck. I'd think about what a terrible idea this was later... tomorrow... never. It felt like we had danced around this moment all day. Now that it was here, the only thing that mattered was the feeling of her body against mine.

She opened her mouth for me and groaned when I teased her bottom lip with my tongue. The sound drove me wild. I pushed my hips into hers, showing her my growing desire for her. My hands moved across her body, caressing her breasts gently through her shirt, moving down her backside to grab her ass. I picked her up and her legs immediately latched around me.

As I led her down the hallway toward the open door to her bedroom, I knew that this woman was worth it, no matter what I had to do to make us work. I would never be able to let her go.

Chapter 19

Alexis

I wriggled carefully out of bed the next morning, determined not to wake Jake up. Last night had been incredible, but it left me totally confused about where we stood. He had said that we wouldn't be able to be together, then proceeded to completely own my body in the greatest of ways. I had never been with anyone who brought me such complete pleasure, and I wasn't sure how I would ever move on once this was over.

I showered quickly, wanting to get to the office early to talk through everything I had learned with Jess. Now that I had an alias to go on, she would hopefully be able to help me dig up some additional information on this "Ripper" person. It was clear that framing me had been their main goal, and Ralph's dad just happened to be the way to accomplish it, but they had taken the job a year ago. How had they known then that I would end up

ELLIE HOHENSTEIN

targeting the McGill family for a heist? Were they prepared to wait the years it might have taken if Ralph hadn't discovered the affair?

Jake came into the bathroom as I was brushing my teeth. He pinned me against the counter from behind with his hips, and kissed my neck as he whispered, "Good Morning". His breath against my skin paired with the morning glory I felt pushing into my backside sent shivers down my spine, and I was instantly ready for a repeat of last night. I turned to wrap my arms around him, and he picked me up to sit me on the counter, kissing me unhurriedly.

I whimpered my displeasure when he pulled away, which only caused him to chuckle. "Do you mind if I take a quick shower?" he asked, dousing the heat that had grown within me at his touch.

"No, that's fine..." I said with disappointment.

He turned on the shower and climbed in once it heated up, which didn't take long since I had just gotten out. "You don't have any clean clothes to change into," I realized. "Are you going to just put your clothes from yesterday back on?" I didn't have any men's clothing here, and I knew for sure that his muscular frame wouldn't fit into any of the larger lounge clothes I had.

"I've got a bag of gym clothes in my car and a nicer shirt and slacks in my office at the station. I'll be fine. No one will be surprised if I come in wearing my sweats."

"That's smart. Do you want me to run down and get them for you?"

He opened the shower door and stared at me with a look much hotter than the water cascading down him.

FRAMED

"What I *want* is for you to get back in here, with me. But then I might never make it to work, and I bet you have some patients depending on you being there today. If you don't mind, it would be great if you could grab them, but I understand if you don't have time."

I was glad he had a bit of self-control because, after hearing his words, I was ready to jump back in and waste the whole day rolling around in bed with him. But he was right, my patients relied on me and I couldn't play hooky, as much as I wanted to.

"I don't mind. I'll get dressed then run down and get it for you." I scooped up his jeans from the floor and fished his keys out of his pocket, then quickly dressed and headed down to grab his bag. He was out of the shower by the time I got back, thanking me with a kiss as he grabbed his clothes.

I tried to focus on finishing preparing for my day, but the beads of moisture running down the planes of his muscles was incredibly distracting. I wasn't able to do my makeup until he had left the room, for fear of making a mess of my face.

Once we were both dressed and ready to go, he offered to drive me to my office. I usually didn't mind the walk, and I had my own car if I really wanted to get there quicker, but accepting the ride meant both more time with Jake and getting to my office faster, so I agreed. He held my hand as he drove, which he pointedly hadn't done yesterday. Once we arrived at my building, he got out of the car to open my door, then gave me a heated kiss goodbye. I wasn't sure what had changed with him, but I was optimistic that it meant we might be able to have a

ELLIE HOHENSTEIN

chance at being together after this was all over, or at least that he wanted to try.

When I walked into my office Jess was standing at her desk, grinning widely at me. "Ooh girl, that was one steamy goodbye kiss! I could feel that heat from here."

I laughed. This was part of why I loved Jess. She was ridiculous, but always meant well. "Were you watching me, you creep?"

"Uh, duh," she replied. "I always have the building's front camera feed displayed so I know when our clients are on their way up. I don't usually pay that close of attention at this hour, but dang! It was hard to miss two people getting hot and heavy on the sidewalk. Imagine my shock when I saw it was you. And was that Jake? The detective?"

I nodded sheepishly. "He's been helping me figure out what the heck is going on with this McGill thing."

"How's that going to work when he decides to arrest you?" she asked. It was a fair question; one I had been wondering myself. I was waiting for the other shoe to drop.

"I have no idea. I'm not sure he does either. One minute he's all 'we can't possibly be together, it could never work' then the next he's practically throwing me down on my bed. At this point, I'm just rolling with it at this point until we know who's trying to frame me."

She sat back down at her desk, then leaned forward with her head on her hands, intrigued. "Threw you on your bed? Oh, girl, tell me more."

We gossiped a little longer as I recounted my night in excruciating detail. Jake would probably kill me if he knew how much I told her, but she also kept asking questions, not letting me move on until she knew it all. Finally, when I had entertained her curiosity enough, we were able to move on to the important things, like who was trying to get me thrown in jail.

"Ripper?" she asked, scrunching her nose. "And it's a woman? That's a terrible alias. It's so masculine and sounds gross."

"Well, clearly this woman is deranged if she's targeting me for something I don't even know about, but whatever. Can you see if you can get some info or maybe a picture? Maybe that will spark something in my memory."

My morning sessions passed quickly, but about an hour before lunch I got a text from Jake telling me that his partner, Ryan, was on his way to my office to interview me. Vivian and I had scheduled a make-up lunch today since I had to leave so abruptly on Friday, so I sent her a text letting her know I might be late.

Ryan arrived a short while later. Jess tried to stonewall him to get him to leave and come back at a later date, preferably never if we could hurry and catch the real killer, but he was insistent that he would only take a few moments of my time. I came out into the lobby to greet him.

"Dr. Lee, it's nice to meet you. I'm Detective Ryan Mason, with the Willow Springs Police Department. Would you have a few moments to speak with me?"

"Of course, Detective. Can I ask what this is regarding?" Jake insisted I play dumb, not even giving away that I even knew Bill was dead. If pushed on why I didn't reveal it, I could always fall back on confidentiality.

258

ELLIE HOHENSTEIN

"I'm not sure if you're aware, ma'am, but the father of one of your patients, Mr. Bill McGill, was found dead in his home Friday morning. We are trying to figure out what happened."

"Oh, that's terrible," I said. "I didn't know Mr. McGill well, the nanny usually dropped his son off, but I'm happy to help you in any way I can. Please, follow me. We can chat in my office."

I led him to my office, which I had already taken a few minutes to clear of any patient files or signs of our investigation into Mr. McGill's death. I sat behind my desk, and he pulled one of the chairs over from the table in the corner and sat across from me. It was a power play from both of us, me sitting in a spot that was inconvenient for him to mirror, putting the desk between us with no seating readily available, and him disrupting the normal configuration of my office without asking. I smiled to myself at his efforts, feeling not remotely phased.

Ryan started off the interview strong. "I understand that you've been treating Ralph McGill for a number of years now. Can you tell me what exactly you're treating him for?"

"I'm afraid that's covered under doctor-patient confidentiality, which will be the answer to most of my questions regarding Ralph. I *can* tell you that I have no reason to believe him to be a danger to himself or others, if that's where you're going with this." I already knew there was no chance that Ralph was a suspect, but I wanted to make sure that Ryan knew up front that I wouldn't have much to offer.

FRAMED

"Did Ralph ever mention his father in his sessions?" he tried again.

"Doctor-patient confidentiality, Detective. I'm not at liberty to say." It was an effort not to smile. Jake would have known better than to try these questions, but I supposed everyone had to learn in their own way.

"Alright, let's try this… Did you feel a close bond with Ralph? You had been treating him for quite some time, watching him grow up. Would you say you cared for him?"

I narrowed my eyes a bit. "I *care* for all my patients, Detective. That's part of what makes me a good psychiatrist. But I also don't let my feelings towards my patients impact my life outside of this office. I'd never get a good night's sleep if I took my patient's problems home with me."

"Of course, I meant no disrespect, ma'am. I can't imagine the struggle you must face, hearing children tell you about poor home lives and not being able to do anything about it." I could see him watching my face carefully, looking for a reaction. I tried not to flinch, but whatever he saw in my expression must have been what he was looking for. He smiled briefly, then got down to why he really came here.

"We were able to recover some evidence at the scene of Mr. McGill's death, and we are approaching all staff members, both directly on the payroll and outside contractors who regularly service the family, to ask for a voluntary sample of hair, so we might be able to exclude any DNA evidence that is not pertinent. Would you be willing to provide a sample?"

260

ELLIE HOHENSTEIN

That was a smart play, acting like they were approaching anyone who might have been in the home recently and phrasing it as an exclusionary collection. If I hadn't known that I was being set up, I would have likely fallen for that trick and provided a sample, confident in my track record of not leaving any evidence.

"I'm sorry, but I've never been in the McGill house, so I can't imagine that you'd need a sample from me."

"I can always come back with a warrant, if you're not willing to provide one voluntarily, Dr. Lee." Ryan warned.

I openly laughed, dismissing the notion. "If you can get a judge to grant you that warrant, I'd be happy to provide a sample. Is that all, Detective? I have lunch plans."

Ryan left, frustrated, but promised to return with his warrant. I doubted he would be able to get one just off the McGill case, but if they had connected me to all the robberies I'd committed then I supposed it was possible. I needed to find out who "Ripper" was, and fast.

I met Vivian at the same restaurant that we had been to on Friday, and I was excited to get to actually try the food this time. Now that we were making progress on the case, I felt like I could breathe a bit easier.

Surprisingly, I beat Vivian there, so I had the hostess seat me at a table on the patio outside. It wasn't long before I saw her hurrying down the street towards the restaurant, carting a handful of shopping bags. I laughed and waved to her as she passed by on her way to the door, cutting through the restaurant to access the patio. She burst through the doorway, dropping into the chair opposite me with a huff.

FRAMED

"Are you alright?" I asked with a chuckle. She was breathing a little heavy, as if she had run the whole way here. I looked down at her shoes, tall high-heels, and was impressed with the feat.

"Oh my... I just... need a minute... to catch my breath. Phew. When you said you were running late I figured I'd go shopping. You know, there's this cute little boutique down the way that just opened up, and I've been dying to see what they have. I was trying on some absolutely adorable dresses when I saw your text that you were on the way. There was this perfect little black dress, but there was only one in my size left, so I had to get it—and of course if I was buying one then I might as well buy a few—but the *line*! I swear it felt like an hour. I rushed all the way here so I didn't end up keeping you waiting."

"Not a problem, I only just got here. I wasn't sure how late I would be, and it ended up taking less time than I expected," I told her, waving off her concerns.

"What had you held up? Your sessions always tend to end on a fairly consistent schedule, you must be a master at bringing things to a natural close! I was surprised when you said you were going to be late."

"A detective came by asking about something involving the family of one of my patients."

"A detective? What happened? Are you in some kind of trouble?" Vivian asked. Her concern seemed genuine, but her inquisitiveness was a little strange.

I waved off her questions. "They wanted to know about some things that the child might have talked about, but confidentiality stopped me from being able to give too

262

much information. I was able to hold him off for now, but I think he will be back."

"Well, I'm glad he didn't hold you off too long," she said with a smile.

The waiter came by and we ordered our food and drinks. We chatted, catching up about some of the things we'd been up to since our last complete lunch. I gossiped a little bit about Jake and the dates we had been on before everything had blown up in our faces, and she revealed she had been secretly seeing someone, but it had recently ended.

As we finished our meal, her spirits seemed to fall. "What's wrong?" I asked.

"Oh, I didn't want to burden our meal with this—I wanted one last good time." She took a big breath, steeling herself for her next words. "I'm leaving town, Lex. I've got to go back to my family. I've got a relative that's very sick, and with things not working out with my guy, the timing just feels right. I leave tomorrow, so I'm really glad we were able to fit this lunch in today."

I was shocked. Vivian had been a close friend for the last year, and our lunches had been a bright spot each week. It was guaranteed fun and gossip, plus she always picked places with incredible food.

"That's terrible, I'm so sorry to hear that. Do you have any idea when you'll be back?" I asked, hoping she wouldn't be leaving permanently. I wouldn't mind going up to New York to visit her, but her presence here in this community would be sorely missed.

"I'm not coming back, Lex. At least, not that I know of. It was so hard to leave my family the first time, I'm not sure I'll be able to do it again. But you can come visit me! Oh, the weather is perfect up there in the spring and summer! And I can show you the city!"

I'd definitely be planning a trip up there; her excitement was contagious and I was already looking forward to it. Maybe if I planned it early enough, I would be able to take a week away from my patients. Assuming I didn't end up in jail, at least.

We gave each other a huge, tear-filled hug before we left, saying goodbye with promises to keep in touch.

On my walk back to the office my phone buzzed from a blocked number. It only had one word, "Ripper", and an attachment. I opened the picture and saw a woman around my age staring back at me. She had copper-colored hair, blue eyes, and a soft face, but her expression was hard, closed off. She wore no make-up, and had freckles sprinkled along her nose and cheeks. She looked familiar to me, but I couldn't quite place her.

I showed the picture to Jess when I got back in, hoping she would be able to help me place the girl. Jess had an amazing memory and had been a friend since college, so if anyone besides me could identify someone from my past, it would be Jess. She stared at the photo for a few moments, then it seemed like a lightbulb had lit in her mind as she started typing away on her computer.

"Ah-ha!" she exclaimed in victory. "You were right, she *is* familiar, but not from here." She turned the screen towards me, showing the same girl, but about fifteen years younger. "Pepper Collins. You partnered with her on a job shortly before we met. Museum heist, I think?"

264

I remembered. It had been the last time I had almost been caught, and I had just about sworn off partners after the experience. I lost the artifact and the job that night. I might have escaped the police, but I had to cut all ties to that alias. "But that was so long ago, why would she be coming after me? What did I do to her? And how did you even recognize her if that was before you and I met?"

"I researched all your old jobs before we teamed up, duh. You didn't know then how to cover your tracks against someone like me, and I needed to know you were on the level before I agreed to work with you. I almost didn't, after reading about Pepper."

"What do you mean? What happened to her?" I had gotten away, and assumed she had too. I made a point to disappear as best as I could without interrupting my college program, and, assuming she had done the same, I never really checked back in on her.

Jess looked at me like I was an idiot. "She went to jail, Alexis. You got away but she got caught. She took the fall for the destruction of the vase you guys were supposed to steal. At first I thought you had set her up, or didn't care that she had gone to jail because of you. Then I saw that she tried to rat you out, but you had effectively disappeared, so I figured she was probably the one who couldn't be trusted."

"She tried to rat me out?" I exclaimed. "That little bitch, she was the reason we were getting caught in the first place. She couldn't even disable the security right. Why would she try to set me up for murder, though?"

"Wait, you got confirmation that she's Ripper?" Jess asked. I realized I hadn't told her what the text had said

FRAMED

along with the picture. "I thought you said that Jake's contact described her as having short, blonde hair?"

"He did. I assume she dyed it as a disguise in case I recognized her, but I haven't seen..." my heart dropped into my stomach as I realized that I *had* seen her. A lot, actually.

"Jess, can you take that photo and show me what she would look like today, but with short, blonde hair? And make her look rich, bougie, with full make-up to hide the freckles."

She did as I asked, then gasped at the result. I grabbed my phone to call Jake. We needed to move, now, before it was too late.

Chapter 20

Jake

We were racing against the clock trying to make sure we caught Ripper—Pepper—before she had a chance to skip town. Alexis had Jess cancel all her afternoon appointments, and I picked her up on the way, Viktor's warning about her imminent departure ringing in my ears.

We got to the apartment building, hurrying up to the top floor where Pepper lived. I made sure my service weapon was easily accessible—this woman was a killer after all. Jess had handed Alexis a small gun that she kept hidden in the office, insisting that she needed to be able to protect herself if the situation called for it. Alexis hid in the hallway to the side, firearm at the ready, while I knocked on the door. A woman answered, tall with shoulder-length blonde hair. One hand rested on the door, but the other was out of my line of sight.

FRAMED

"Vivian Bellefonte?" I asked.

"Yes, may I help you?"

"I'm Detective Jake Griffin with the Willow Springs PD, I'm going to need you to come with me."

The next part seemed to go in slow motion. Vivian's other hand emerged, holding a dagger. I sprang backwards to dodge her attack, and as her momentum drove her forward, Alexis jumped in to knock the blade out of Vivian's hand, then struck her on the head with the butt of the gun. Vivian crumpled to the ground, and I hastened forward to kick the knife out of reach, my gun trained on her the whole time.

I pulled out my handcuffs and tossed them over to Alexis, who grabbed Vivian's arms and secured them behind her back.

"Nice to see you, Pepper," Alexis said smugly.

We led Pepper back down to my car, putting her in the back while Alexis and I spoke outside. I had put up a gate between the front and back seats and turned the child locks on; Pepper wouldn't be able to get out or hurt us while we were driving.

"I don't have the evidence we need to arrest her yet. Everything is circumstantial." I said, considering our next move.

"Oh, don't worry, I've got a place we can take her." Alexis looked pissed. Wrathful. I had never seen her like this, so out of control, and I was a little worried that she wouldn't be able to restrain herself from hurting Pepper before we took her in.

"You good?" I asked. "What's the deal with you two? You mentioned her the other day, something about a job

268

gone wrong, but that doesn't explain all this" I motioned toward her, trying to indicate her ire.

"She was my friend... Vivian, I mean. I had no idea who she was, but I considered her one of my closest friends for the last *year*. It's been over a decade, and our interactions back then were so brief, but I don't know how I didn't see it, how she fooled me. I'm livid at her, but I'm mad at myself too."

I rubbed her arms up and down before pulling her in for a hug. "We'll figure it out baby, don't worry."

She relaxed in my hold, returning the hug and composing herself before we got in the car. I gave her a kiss on the head and opened the door for her.

Alexis directed me to the edge of the city where a small, run down building sat empty. There weren't any other structures in sight, and we had gone down back roads off back roads to get there. Without her directions, I'd be well and truly lost. No one would be stumbling upon us, that was for sure.

She pulled Pepper roughly out of the car, escorting her inside the building.

Despite the appearance of the exterior, the building was actually in good condition. The inside appeared to have been remodeled in the last few years. It had a full kitchen stocked with dry-storage food and bottled water, and a bed set up in one of the rooms, complete with luxurious-looking bedding and a full walk-in closet. Through another door I could see a tiled bathroom with a shower.

"This is my doomsday shelter, in case things were looking bad and I needed to run," Alexis explained,

FRAMED

responding to my confused expression. "It's not in my name, and no one would be able to find this place by chance when looking for me."

"It's perfect," I said. We would be able to stay here with Pepper until we knew what to do with her, and we would be able to be in relative comfort.

Alexis dug through one of the drawers in the kitchen and pulled out a pack of metal zip-ties, then led Pepper over to the radiator and attached the handcuffs to it. She wouldn't be able to go anywhere, and was forced to sit on the floor while Alexis and I sat on the couch.

"Pepper Collins," I started. "We know you killed Bill McGill. We know you tried to frame Alexis for it. What we don't know is why?"

"Why? *Why?*" Pepper exclaimed, yanking her arms against her ties. "You ruined my life, Alexis! You left me at that museum, only concerned for yourself. I went to *prison* because of you. Do you know who else is in prison? Murderers. Arsonists. Rapists. Bad people. The things I had to do there to survive, there's no coming back from that.

"Then, once I got out, I couldn't get any honest work, and no other thief would work with me since I was out of practice. No one would hire me for illegal jobs because I tried to flip on you to save myself. So, I had to remake myself, and use the skills I learned in prison to change fields.

"And you were just gone. No signs, not even a whisper of who or where you were. I searched for years. Then I heard about 'Ghost', with the description of her. I just knew it was you. I asked around to try and find you, but

270

no one would turn over your real name. I traced the items you stole back to the towns your fence works out of, and I staked him out until I saw you and could follow you back to Willow Springs. From there, I just needed to figure out how to bring you down."

"Wow, I really thought I was going to have to work harder to get all that," I said to Alexis. She laughed a bit, but I could see tears in her eyes. Vivian's betrayal was hitting her hard.

"You've been holding that back for a year, haven't you?" she asked Pepper. "Well, I have to give you credit. You had me. How did you know that I was going to go after McGill back when you took the hit?"

"I *made* you go after him. I made sure his son saw us together, which I knew would lead him to breaking up with me, and I knew the brat would talk about it in his sessions. Then you started talking about it at lunch and I dropped the hint about 'getting justice' or whatever, and you jumped right on it.

"I listened to you and your assistant talk on and on about what to steal, when and how, thanks to the bug I planted in your office. You might as well have drawn me a map right to the perfect setup. I followed your route into the house and got Bill right as he got home." She looked smug. "I've been doing this long enough to know I didn't leave anything you could tie back to me. All you've got on me is that I was dating him."

She was right, we needed more in order to arrest her for the murder and clear Alexis's name. I motioned for Alexis to follow me into the kitchen so we could discuss what to do.

FRAMED

"We need to get her to confess and flip on whoever hired her. That's the only real way to clear your name. We don't have anything to physically tie her to the murder, but we have your hair from the office to at least place you at the scene. I'm sure if Ryan can get you connected to all the heists then the robbery-gone-wrong theory will be strong enough to stick. Pepper's staged scene was perfect. Do you have any ideas on where to go from here?"

She thought for a moment, then her eyes lit up as she smiled mischievously.

"You said the theory is robbery-gone-wrong, right? But what if I wasn't the one who stole everything in the first place?"

"You want to set up Pepper for the robbery?"

"Why not? She tried to set me up. Plus, the murder is the serious crime here, and she actually committed it. We know she's guilty, we just need to tweak the evidence to prove it."

"You asked Mr. G. not to sell the painting just for this, didn't you? Did you know you'd need it to set up the killer?"

She shrugged. "I thought it might come in handy, just in case."

I couldn't help but kiss her. "Always thinking ten steps ahead. I love it." It should bother me that we would be manipulating evidence, but my job had been one of the furthest things from my mind since I met Alexis. All that mattered was her, and keeping her out of jail.

She called Mr. G. to arrange for the painting to be moved to Pepper's apartment. It turned out that the murder weapon had been stored here as well, so we would

ELLIE HOHENSTEIN

be able to put that in her apartment as well. Alexis meticulously wiped the award down, then she tossed it at Pepper. When it got close, Pepper's reflexes kicked in and she caught the award before it could hit her. She instantly dropped it, realizing too late that she had touched the metal without gloves on, leaving her fingerprints on the evidence. I grabbed a tissue and plucked the award off the ground, using the paper to protect it from my prints.

"If the painting is in her apartment, then that should be enough to connect her to the robbery. Add in the murder weapon and it will be a slam dunk that she killed him. But we still need to explain why your hair was in the room. Baby, do you trust me?" I asked. I had a plan, but it was risky.

She stared at me, hopefully seeing the sincerity of my desire to help her, to save her. After what seemed like an eternity she finally nodded.

"I'm going to need a sample of your hair to give to the lab techs down at the station."

Whatever she'd thought I would ask for, it hadn't been that.

"What? You can't be serious. It will be a match to the hair they found! They will arrest me before we even get a chance to point them toward Pepper." She looked angry.

"I promise I will take care of it. This is what we need to do for this to all play out right. If you let me, I can get you out of not only the murder, but the whole string of burglaries." I'd be throwing my career away, but if I was honest with myself, I'd been ready to do that from the moment I found out who she really was. This woman was

FRAMED

it for me, the one. And I would do anything I needed to in order to keep her.

She looked at me warily. "Alright, I trust you." She plucked out a few of her hairs and I fished out a plastic bag from the kitchen to put them in while I laid out the details of my plan.

I was a little nervous about leaving her alone with Pepper, but Alexis assured me she would call someone here to make sure Pepper couldn't escape until I was ready to bring her in. Pepper seemed to have lost her fight after her monologue about how she had pulled off the frame-job, but I didn't want to take any chances.

I gave Alexis a kiss, pouring my whole soul into it, trying to convey how much she meant to me in case my plan didn't work. She was putting the ultimate faith in me—I held her future in my hands, and I wouldn't disappoint her.

I sped back toward town to put everything in motion. I'd sent Ryan a text asking him to meet me at the lab with an evidence bag.

"How did you get that sample?" he demanded, having approached my car the moment I arrived. "She adamantly refused when I tried."

"Sometimes it just takes a bit of charm," I replied, winking at him. I dropped the hairs in the bag and signed off on the label to preserve the chain of custody. "I watched her pull them out myself, they're the real deal. Let's get these inside and see if they are a match to the ones we found at the McGill's house. If they are, you can make the arrest. You're the one that cracked it, after all."

That seemed to satisfy him, and we made our way into the building together. We handed off the sample to the lab techs who said it would take about an hour for them to get the results. That was perfect for me to get the next step going.

"I'm going to follow up with my CI's to see if there is any chatter about the painting yet," I told Ryan.

"Okay, sounds good. I'll stay here and call you when the results are in. Hopefully we will get a match and then we will be able to search the doctor's office and home. With any luck, the painting will be there, but in case she has already fenced it, hopefully someone knows something." He sat down in the lobby, nodding as I walked out the door.

I was actually planning to visit a CI this time. One of my guys was about to get the easiest payday of his life.

He was a contact who actually spent time alongside the upper circles, generally working as a waiter during the parties. Since the guests generally didn't pay much attention to the staff, he was able to overhear a lot of information, which he sold to me whenever I needed. I drove out to his apartment building and grabbed the folder I had prepared.

"Detective Griffin!" he greeted as he opened his door. "What can I do for you today?"

"Alan, I'm about to ask a huge favor of you," I told him. "I've got a report here, already filled out, and I just need someone to sign it so that I can make it look legitimate." This was crossing a serious line for me, and involving someone else meant I'd never be able to go

FRAMED

back. I just hoped he would go along with it. "I'll give you ten times your normal fee if you do this for me."

His eyes grew big. He was the perfect guy for this type of report on what might have happened to the painting, and Pepper's deception combined with Vivian's status made the false report plausible.

"Alright, Jake. I'll do it. But don't you forget it, yeah?" I nodded and thanked him, holding out the folder for him to sign. He briefly read through the report to make sure it all looked believable, and I gave him a copy once he had signed it, so he would have all the details in case someone questioned him later.

Ryan called while I was walking back down to my car.

"Jake! It matched! I'm heading to the station to fill out the paperwork and get a team together to arrest the doctor. I'm going to send some officers to her office to start collecting information, but I'm heading to her apartment since it's after five."

"Sounds great, congrats buddy! I'll wrap up here soon, and meet you at the station later tonight. We can do the interrogation, then it's drinks on me to celebrate!"

I called Alexis right after. "Hey baby, you need to get back to your place ASAP. Ryan's on his way to arrest you."

"Already here, and everything is in place. Did you get someone to sign off on the tip sheet?"

"Yep, I'm going to kill another hour to make sure Ryan is on the way then I'll send a team to Pepper's apartment and go back to the safehouse and get her. Are you ready for this?"

"No, but I guess I have to be. This is definitely closer than I've ever planned to be in getting arrested. Thank you

276

ELLIE HOHENSTEIN

for doing this for me, it means everything," she said. It sounded like she was on the verge of tears.

"Anything for you baby. Chin up, we're almost at the finish line and then it's going to be happily ever after, I promise."

Ryan texted me about an hour later saying he was on his way to her place, which meant I was in the clear to go to the station and turn in my tip sheet. I needed Alexis to be in custody for this part of the plan, so it wouldn't look like she could be involved.

I gave the report in directly to the chief, who skimmed it quickly then looked at me like I had two heads. "Vivian Bellefonte? You're sure about this?" he asked.

"Yes, sir. My informant was positive. She was having an affair with McGill, and he ended it after his son caught them together. My informant said he overheard her planning to get revenge, bragging about taking something from him to make a statement. She definitely has the painting and likely killed McGill when he interrupted her."

"You know Ryan is already bringing in a suspect, with DNA evidence. Are you saying they were in it together?"

"No, sir," I said adamantly. "There's no evidence to support more than one person being there, but the doctor treats the kid. I'd be willing to wager that she just did a session at the house and that's how her hair ended up at the scene. Probably a coincidence."

The chief considered for a few moments. Finally, he nodded. "Alright, Jake. I'll call the judge to get an emergency warrant. If this report is true, then Bellefonte is going to be gone by tomorrow, so we need to move tonight. I'm trusting you, don't let this blow back on me."

FRAMED

"I'll get the team together. Thanks, Chief." I left his office and went downstairs to gather a few uniformed officers. The warrant was faxed over a few minutes later, and we were off to Vivian's apartment.

Unsurprisingly, no one answered when we arrived, but the warrant enabled us to legally break in and search the place. I let one of the officers check the closet where Alexis had hidden the weapon and the painting. "Detective! Come look!" the officer cried out.

I glanced in the closet, seeing the painting against the far wall, originally hidden behind a row of dresses. The award that had been used to kill McGill was in a large plastic bag, which made collecting the evidence convenient. "Fantastic! Document everything. I'll call in to the chief and see if we can get a location on her cell phone so we can bring her in."

The analyst at the station identified Pepper's location as at the safehouse, where we had purposefully kept her phone on. When I arrived, I saw a girl waiting there with long, deep-red hair. She greeted me as I walked up.

"Ah, Detective Perfect. So nice to finally meet you. I'm Jess."

I recognized the name as Alexis's assistant. I had no idea that she was involved in all the heists though. I bet Alexis had purposefully left out any details about Jess to protect her.

"Of course! Great to put a face to the name. Thanks for helping out. Is Pepper ready to go?"

"Yes, please get that lunatic out of here. Oh, and before I forget, here's that other piece Lex asked me to take care of." She handed me a small slip of paper with a

278

long string of numbers written on it, and the name of a bank in the Caribbean. The account where all the proceeds went each time Alexis pulled a job.

"Alright, Pepper. Let's get this show on the road."

Pepper was quiet as I drove her to the station and didn't resist when officers escorted her through to one of the interrogation rooms. Overall, she looked defeated. All this careful planning to have everything fall apart at the end, and mostly due to her own hubris. She could have left sooner, but she'd stuck around to watch Alexis's life crumble.

Instead of formally questioning her right away, I decided to let her stew. I gave the account number to our analysts to pull the transaction records and account details so we could prove that the money from the heists had been going into that account. Once I had received some of the pictures from whatever else the team at Pepper's apartment managed to find, Ryan and I would go talk to her.

I walked into the viewing room of the other interrogation room to watch Ryan speaking to Alexis. She looked angry. I'd imagine being accused of murder when she was innocent would piss anyone off, and she did a good show of selling it. Ryan was trying to get her to admit that she broke in and stole the painting, but all his evidence was circumstantial. He was trying to use intimidation to force the confession, but didn't have the proof to back it up. That was probably Ryan's biggest weakness, talking to people. He didn't have the communication skills to adapt his approach to each person. With someone like Alexis, you needed to trick

FRAMED

them into admitting something—playing the person, not the game. He would never get a confession the way he was going at her.

I pushed the button on the intercom, sending my voice through the speaker built in under the glass. "Detective Mason, a word?"

He started and turned toward me, recognizing my voice.

"One moment, please, Dr. Lee."

He stormed into the viewing room. "I thought you told me never to interrupt someone else's interrogation?" he demanded angrily.

"Ordinarily, no. But you're never going to get anywhere with her, so I thought I'd save you the time. We have to let her go, she didn't do it."

"Wh-What?" he sputtered at me. "How do you know?"

"I got a tip from one of my CIs. I led a raid on Vivian Bellefonte's apartment. She's a socialite who was having an affair with McGill. We found the painting and the murder weapon."

"But what about the hair from the office? It was a perfect match to Dr. Lee. That can't be a coincidence, she told me she had never been in their house before."

I pretended to ponder for a few moments. I knew Ryan would cling to the one piece of evidence we had, unwilling to hear the truth. "Let's ask her."

I entered the interrogation room. "Good evening, Dr. Lee. Good to see you again. I'm Detective Griffin, in case you've forgotten. Would you mind coming with me for a few moments?"

ELLIE HOHENSTEIN

"I'm not sure what this is about, but fine. If it gets me out of this room, I'll go almost anywhere." She played the role of not knowing me very well.

We walked into the viewing room next door where Pepper waited. "Do you recognize this woman, Dr. Lee?"

"That's Vivian Bellefonte. She's one of my dear friends."

My phone rang. It was the officer at Pepper's apartment. Perfect timing. "Pardon me for one moment... Hello?" I said, answering the phone.

"Detective Griffin, we've found something strange. It looks like Miss Bellefonte had bags packed, ready to flee. But we found another ID that has her picture, but with a different hair color and name. Pepper Collins. Looks real. My guess is that this woman was just posing as Vivian, but I have no idea why. We also found a brush with long dark hairs, like those found at the McGill house."

"Thank you, I'll get the team started on that." I hung up and turned back to Alexis. "Does the name Pepper Collins mean anything to you?"

"Um... It sounds like the name of someone I met in college... I'd need to see a picture to be sure though."

I held up the image of Pepper's ID that the officer had just sent me.

"But, that's Vivian?" Ryan said, looking between the picture and the window to the interrogation room.

"Dr. Lee, is there any reason that Pepper would want to set you up for the murder of Bill McGill?"

"Not any sane reason, but when we knew each other, Pepper definitely had some psychological problems. We had a huge falling out. Are you saying she killed him?"

FRAMED

I nodded. "Yes, it looks that way. I'm sorry to say this, Doctor, but I think Ms. Collins deceived the entire town and set you up to take the fall for her crime. We found DNA evidence to place you at the scene, but the murder weapon was discovered at her house."

"DNA Evidence? What kind?" Alexis asked, acting confused.

"It appeared to be a strand of your hair. You had told Detective Mason that you had never been in the McGill family's home, but since the strands you turned over to me matched those found near Mr. McGill's body, we of course found it suspicious."

"I'm not sure how my hair got there, but I assure you I've never been their home." Alexis crossed her arms defiantly.

"Based on the brush our officers found in Ms. Collins's apartment, I'm afraid you were the victim of a break-in and a con. You're free to go."

Ryan sulked in the background, but Alexis just stared at Pepper, anguish on her face—her expression almost identical to when she had first found out about Vivian's deception. I had Ryan escort her out of the station, before joining me in our office.

With her real name, Ryan and I were able to trace the incoming payment for the hit, both the down payment a year ago and the remainder of the funds over the weekend.

As soon as we laid the proof down on the table in the interrogation room, Pepper confessed to killing Bill McGill. To top it all off, the account Jess had given me had been altered to look like Pepper's, and had

ELLIE HOHENSTEIN

transactions dating back the last five years, linking her to all the heists.

I asked my last question in the interrogation to clear Alexis of all suspicion. "So, over the last few years, you tried to ruin Alexis's business by stealing from her clients. Your accounts prove you fenced the items taken. When that didn't work, you took the hit on Bill. You set it up to start dating him, then killed him after it ended. Then, you left Alexis's hair at the scene to frame her. Is that right?"

Pepper glared at me, livid but clearly knowing there was no way out of this. She had already refused to flip on who hired her for the murder, saying that it would damage her reputation too much and wasn't worth the reduced sentence. The same held true for the thefts; even if she tried to claim Alexis had committed those, it would look like she was grasping at straws and ratting someone out again.

"Yes," she finally said. We had all we needed.

Chapter 21

Jake

All that was left was to figure out who ordered the hit. Pepper refused to give us any details, not saying anything past her simple confession. Ryan and I were pouring through her phone records. We saw a lot of calls to Bill McGill, and to the restaurants he owned. There were plenty of calls to Alexis as well—Pepper had really committed to her role of pretending to be her friend.

"What's this number here?" Ryan said, looking at the page that contained the calls from around a week ago. "It's got a different area code that seems familiar, can you look it up?"

I did as requested. "It's a spa a few towns over. Is it the one that that Alison McGill was staying at?"

"Oh yeah, I called them before to confirm her alibi. I knew I recognized it. Why would Pepper be calling there?"

ELLIE HOHENSTEIN

"She was playing the role of a socialite, so it could have been her making an appointment, but the timing definitely feels strange. Let's reach out and see what they have to say."

Ryan called them and put it on speakerphone so we could both hear.

"Hi there, this is Detective Ryan Mason with the Willow Springs Police Department. I'm working on an investigation and I was hoping you could confirm if someone has a reservation scheduled at your resort."

"Oh, of course Detective Mason, I remember you called just a few days ago. What's the name you are looking for? I'll see if I can find it."

"I'm not positive which name she might have used, but let's start with Pepper Collins."

"Hmm... no, I don't see anything under that name. Is there another name you'd like me to look up?"

"Try Vivian Bellefonte."

"Nothing for her either. I'm sorry I couldn't be more help, Detective.

"That's alright, thank you for checking."

He went to hang up but the receptionist stopped him.

"Oh, Detective! I almost forgot. You mentioned that I should reach out if I remembered anything unusual about Mrs. McGill's stay, and I was planning to call you later. I talked to the night receptionist, and she said that somewhere around the beginning of Mrs. McGill's stay, a message was delivered that was very strange. All it said was 'Thursday' and the only name we got was 'R'. After it was delivered, Mrs. McGill extended her stay from just a weekend visit to a full week. Since the reservation was

FRAMED

modified, I didn't see the original check out date, so I had no idea that she hadn't always intended on staying the full week."

Ryan and I grinned at each other. This was the break we needed.

We called Alison McGill to the station under the guise of updating her about her husband's murder investigation. When she arrived, we led her to an interrogation room rather than meeting with her in one of the conference rooms in the front of the building. I always loved the reaction of folks when they realized they weren't here for the reasons we said, but it was too late for them to escape. Alison did come prepared, though. Her attorney joined her a few moments after we met her in the lobby.

Pepper might have refused her chance to reveal who'd hired her, but Alison didn't need to know she had kept quiet. We were allowed to lie to get a confession – it wasn't advised since it could show the suspect that we didn't have the evidence needed if they called us out on it. With Pepper in custody, there would be no one to refute it so I felt like we would be safe. But Alison was smart, and she was a patient woman, if waiting a year for her husband to be murdered was anything to judge by.

I let Ryan take the lead again. I needed to make it up to him for coming in and stealing the show. After all, I had promised him we'd work closely together so I could teach him how to handle this type of investigation. And the truth was he had cracked the whole case, even if I had made it look like hadn't.

286

He decided to get straight to the point with his interrogation. "Why did you have your husband killed, Mrs. McGill?"

The shock on her face was genuine, but not because she didn't do it. She just never expected us to figure it out. Half the people who came in this room seemed to think they were a criminal mastermind, incapable of being caught, but I now knew they had no idea how to operate on a level like Alexis did.

"What are you talking about? I didn't kill my husband, I wasn't even there," Alison sputtered in mock outrage.

"Alright, we can try it your way. Why did you extend your trip from a weekend plan to a full week?"

"I... I needed a getaway. Once I got there, I decided I wasn't ready to come home so I extended my trip by a few days."

"I see," Ryan said. "And it had nothing to do with the message you received from the hitman known as Ripper telling you what day your husband would be killed on?"

Her face visibly paled. She started glancing at the door, a subtle tell that she was looking for an escape, a way out of being caught.

"I never received such a message. I don't know who Ripper is, and she certainly never contacted me."

Ryan looked up at me, having caught her mistake just like I had. He nodded for me to step in for my favorite part of the interrogations. He really was such a good partner.

"She? I don't believe Detective Mason ever mentioned that Ripper was a woman. In fact, I think he said 'hitman' and not 'hitwoman', so how do you know that Ripper is a

FRAMED

she?" I bent down near her face. "Ripper flipped on you, Alison. We know you hired her to kill your husband, we know you placed the job a year ago, giving her part of the money then and the rest after you came home and saw it was done."

"Don't say another word, Alison," her attorney advised. She clamped her mouth shut, determined not to make a sound. I'd need to rile her up, really piss her off, to get her to confess.

I started walking around the room. Alison kept her stare straight ahead, face schooled into a mask of indifference, but she could still see me in the mirror across the room, and I kept my eyes on her reflection.

"You were so patient, weren't you, Alison? Your husband had a taste for attractive women—even friends of yours, from what we've heard. He would flaunt them in front of you, make you the talk of the town. A fool."

I could see cracks in her expression forming, so I continued to press. "You made a plan. You'd get rid of him once and for all, and you hired someone to take him out and keep your hands clean. You paid a middleman, and Ripper got a nice down-payment for the role she would need to play. Her cover as Vivian Bellefonte was flawless, a perfect trap for your dog of a husband. You knew it was only a matter of time before he was out of your hair for good.

"But months and months passed; months while you knew he was there with her, sleeping with her, giving her gifts, taking her to dinner, all of the things he never did for you. Maybe she fell for him, couldn't stand to kill the man who now held her heart. After all, why else take a full

ELLIE HOHENSTEIN

year to carry out the job? Would it have even ended if your son hadn't caught them?

"Then she finally made her move, finally gave you the heads up that it was going down so you could make sure to be gone. No suspicion would fall on you. It was the perfect plan."

Alison was close to breaking. I could see a twitch near her eye as she strained to keep quiet.

I had circled back around beside her, and got down low in her face again.

"You didn't know she had her own plans, did you? She had her own enemy to take out, and she was sloppy about it. We caught her in just a few days. She was supposed to be gone, but her hubris in wanting to face her foe one last time was her downfall. And she couldn't wait to take a deal to flip on you. Sang your name just as soon as she got in this room. Easiest interrogation we've ever had, wouldn't you say, Ryan?" I laughed to rub it in.

It worked. Alison exploded. "That bitch!"

Her lawyer tried to interject, to stop her from incriminating herself, but Alison spoke over him. "She swore she would never flip on me, that no one would even look twice at me for his death. I had to watch her with him for *months!* She swore it wasn't real, all part of the job to make it look convincing. That she needed to set someone else up to keep me out of suspicion." She burst into tears, head in her hands.

"Why not just divorce him? Why kill him, Mrs. McGill?" Ryan asked, taking back over.

"Divorce? So he could get half of my restaurants? I devoted my life to our businesses, and they would all have

289

FRAMED

failed without my hard work. But he took all the credit. He was the face of everything, and made sure I knew it. I couldn't let him have them, not when I had worked so hard and he had already taken so much from me."

We had what we needed. A pair of officers came in and led Mrs. McGill down to processing. I wasn't sure what would happen to Ralph with his father dead and his mother going to jail, but I hoped he had some family members that would take him in. Possibly the nanny could be granted custodianship if she wanted, that way his life could be fairly uninterrupted. It didn't sound like he spent much time with his parents anyway.

I crashed hard in my bed that night. The last few days had been exhausting and an overload of information. Alexis had texted me after she left the station saying she needed some time alone to unwind and process all that had happened. I understood, but I couldn't help feeling like my bed was too big, too cold, without her in it. I hoped I'd never have to go another night without her beside me.

The next morning at the station, the chief called me into his office as I walked by.

"Incredible job, Jake. Truly your best work yet. I don't know how you cracked this one, but it's going to feel damn good to put all those burglaries in the 'closed' column. Plus, a high-profile murder by an actual contract killer? I don't think our town has seen anything like this."

I shook my head, having officially made my decision last night, but really I'd known this was coming since my first night with Alexis.

290

ELLIE HOHENSTEIN

"Actually, Chief, I want you to take my name off everything. Make Ryan the sole investigator. He's the one who actually cracked it, anyway. Without his connection to the psychiatrist, we would never have gotten this far. Ripper would have fled, and a killer would still be on the streets."

"Why would I take you off? Even if you wanted Ryan to be listed as the primary detective, you were still involved." He looked incredibly confused. I wasn't after fame by any means, but I'd never been one to give up credit before either.

"I'm leaving, Chief, quitting the force. This is my official resignation notice." I pulled a letter out of my jacket pocket and set it down on the desk.

The chief was shocked. "I don't understand, Jake. You're an incredible cop. I figured you'd be my replacement in a few years when I retire. Why on earth do you want to give this up?"

The chief was like a father to me. He had rescued me from the streets when I was just an angry kid, taken me in and gave me a life. I hated to disappoint him, but I knew this was the right move.

"I'm sorry. I just found something I want more." I could hear the smile in my voice, the love I had for Alexis shining through. I'd never sounded like that before, and I think the chief understood.

"Well, Jake, I hate to see you go. But if that's what you want, then alright. You know if you ever need me, all you have to do is call."

"Thanks, Chief."

FRAMED

We shook hands and he pulled me in for a hug, patting me hard on the back. I wasn't sure what my future held, but all I needed to know was that it would have Alexis in it.

Chapter 22

Alexis

I still couldn't believe that Vivian—no, Pepper—had hunted me down after all these years. She was such a minor person in my memory, and I'd never realized how major of a role I had played in her life. I had been just a kid, getting started on my first few serious heists, and she was one of a handful of people I had tried to partner with. I didn't even know she had gotten caught.

Her persona had been perfectly crafted. I hadn't suspected even for a moment that she wasn't exactly who she said she was. She was my closest friend, apart from Jess. I didn't have many people that I considered a true friend rather than just an acquaintance, and I had truly valued our relationship. I couldn't imagine her dedication to taking me down, how she spent so much time with me and never once let her true feelings slip.

FRAMED

It also made me start to question my ability as a psychiatrist. I had thought I was so incredibly good at reading people, the emotions they tried so hard to hide and the underlying reasons that drove people's actions. But I had missed what was right in front of me. I couldn't help but replay all the interactions we had through the last year in my mind, searching for clues I may have missed.

They weren't there. She was flawless in her recreation. I never had looked up Vivian Bellefonte before, wanting to have one relationship in my life that was pure and easy. I had never allowed Jess to look her up either. *There's no possible way that she's anything other than what she appears to be*, I had told Jess assuredly. *Just let me have my friend and let her keep her secrets.* Well, she certainly had...

But I looked her up now. There really was a Vivian Bellefonte, and if I hadn't known it was someone else, I would have thought I was looking at my friend in the pictures I found. Pepper had chosen someone with a similar facial structure and had used make-up to cover any physical traits that she hadn't shared with Vivian—like her freckles. All her accounts were set up with back-up addresses to Vivian's house in New York, she even set her cell phone up with a New York area code, pulling out all the stops in case Jess or I investigated.

Forget stealing art, Pepper should have made a living out of stealing identities.

While I might not be behind bars, ultimately Pepper had still been successful in ruining the life I had created here. Thanks to Jess, we had successfully pinned all the heists I'd pulled in the last five years on her, but I wouldn't be able to keep the same pattern now that Ryan had made the connection between my patients and the targets. With Pepper locked away, any more thefts would have him coming straight to me. This town was burned, and I'd either need to quit stealing or start over somewhere else.

As much as I'd like to say I could walk away from the game, I wasn't sure how I would fill the hole I'd have in my life if I gave it up. Having Jake would go a long way to making up for it, but I couldn't stand to bring him down with me if I slipped up.

He was a cop, and I was a criminal. It could never truly work. My eyes were puffy from the night before. I'd realized what I needed to do to protect us both after coming home. He was a good cop, and I couldn't take that away from him. But I wasn't sure if I would ever find another man who understood me so well. Our pasts had shaped us both into who we were today, and had things gone differently we could have been perfect together. Our time investigating had brought us so close, forged such a bond, that it felt like I was leaving a piece of me behind. But, for his sake and mine, I'd have to let him go.

I started packing away all my files. I'd spent the morning calling each of my patients and referring them to other psychiatrists in the area. I knew that some of them would be set back from the change, but I hoped they would recover quickly.

There were a few patients who decided they were ready to discontinue therapy altogether and weren't interested in starting over with someone new. I agreed with most of them but was doubtful about others. I made sure to give them all my recommendations for who they should see if they felt they needed to go back, but that was all I could

FRAMED

do. I could lead a horse to water, but I couldn't make it drink.

I'd compiled transition reports for all the clients that were moving to a different doctor and had them packed up by the door to hand-deliver to each provider. I didn't trust sending confidential information through any public mail system, and I knew my patients appreciated my attention to their confidentiality.

Jess had been working on her computer all morning, transferring her activities to external hard drives and wiping all traces from her computer. She would set everything back up once we got the new office established, but she didn't trust who might get their hands on her equipment in the meantime. When she found out that Pepper had planted a bug on her computer, she had been livid and almost threw the whole thing out.

I had given Jess the option to take her own path if she wanted. My almost getting caught had been a stern dose of reality for me, and I didn't want her to come under investigation by association. But Jess was confident in both her ability to protect herself and the assurance that I'd be a lot more cautious in the future. She was ready to go wherever I did.

I was incredibly lucky to have a partner and friend like her. I'd be leaning on her more than ever in a new town, especially while still mourning the loss of what Jake and I could have been.

We had hired a moving company to come and get all the furniture, but they would wait until after we had removed all the sensitive information from the office. I hadn't decided where we would go just yet, so all the couches and chairs were going to stay in storage until I found a new space. It would take time to establish a new client base in a new city, so I wasn't likely to need it all soon, anyway.

It was taking everything in me not to reach out to Jake. I had decided a clean break would be best, and I needed to be in the right frame of mind when I spoke with him. I needed to be the cool, confident woman he had first met, and not leave any room for him to try and convince me to stay. I knew what I was doing was the best thing for him, even if he might not see it right away.

Almost like I had wished him into being, the door to the office opened up and Jake walked inside. He looked around in confusion at the boxes stacked by the door and the paintings leaning against the walls.

"What's going on?" Jake asked tentatively.

I sighed, knowing how hard this would be. Jess looked at me to see if I wanted her to stay, to which I gave a small shake of my head. She moved into the back rooms to continue packing and give us our privacy. Once Jake had gone, Jess and I would probably need to stop for the day and either go drinking or drown my sorrows in a tub of ice cream.

"We're leaving, Jake. I'm sorry, but I can't stay here after all that has happened."

"What do you mean?" Jake asked, furrowing his brow. "Pepper is gone, she's going to be locked away for a long time. She won't be able to get to you again. We made sure of it."

I had already played all the potential arguments out in my head, and knew he would try and convince me that I

FRAMED

didn't need to keep stealing, that I could earn enough of a living and still do good at the shelters with just what I made from my sessions. I had never really told him how important my night work was to me.

"It's not just her. It's everything, Jake. I would be living under a microscope with that partner of yours if I stayed. The next time any art was stolen his first stop would be here to see if the victim was a client. You and I both know that there were some holes in what we pulled together to implicate Pepper. From what you told me, Ryan is good enough to find them. And then it won't just be the one theft that's going to fall down on me, but it will be all the ones she's going away for too.

"Then it's going to come out about what we did, and you'll lose your job—or worse. I just can't do that. And I know what you're going to say… I could still do good just by treating patients and donating my time to the shelters. But Jake, it's just not enough for me. I need to do more, and I need to do what I'm good at."

Jake let me finish my speech without interruption, but his stance relaxed as I spoke. He crossed his arms casually, with that annoying, adorable smirk, like he was so much smarter, and I had missed something right in front of me.

"I know all that. I know we've only been seeing each other a short while, but in case I wasn't clear before, I'm all in. I understand how important the stealing is to you, about the rush you get, how it makes you feel alive. Crime's a hard habit to give up.

"But Alexis… you're incredible. You can do anything you put your mind to. And the fact that you could probably have bought a private island many times over by

ELLIE HOHENSTEIN

now, but instead you chose to give away so much, is one of the many reasons why I love you. You aren't just someone who does good, you *are* good. Even if you don't think so.

"You think you're leaving without me to protect me, to keep me from losing my job? I got news for you, baby: I can't lose something I don't have. I turned in my notice first thing this morning."

He took confident steps toward me. My jaw had dropped—this was the last thing I had expected him to say. He was throwing away his career? For me?

"What? Why would you do that?" I exclaimed, tears starting to well in my eyes.

"I told you, I'm all in. You and me, we can do this. We can go anywhere in the world, it's all ours for the taking. You want to steal the Mona Lisa? Let's do it. Loot a tomb in Egypt? I'm there. Smuggle some statues from the MET? I've been working out; I'll get the feet. We can live high *and* do more good than I've ever dreamed possible.

"Everything I've done, all the time I spent at the shelters and the youth center, the mentorship programs, it could never touch the benefit of all you gave. They need volunteers, but they need money more than anything else. This city is going to hurt without you, but people will step up to make up for the time. No one could legally match everything you gave.

"I want in on that, but more importantly, I can't imagine going back to my life here without you. You bring out the best version of me, even if it's not the strictly legal one, and I can't get enough of you. So no, you aren't

FRAMED

leaving me behind. Wherever you go, I'm right there with you."

Tears were freely falling from me now. I rushed over to him with my arms open wide. He caught me and swung me around, dipping me low. His lips were on mine like he needed them to breathe. Like he felt how he almost lost me, and with his kisses alone, he could talk me out of leaving him behind.

"I love you, Alexis. Now and forever," he whispered to me, green eyes locked on my blue ones.

"I love you too, Jake," I replied and kissed him again. And I did. I loved this man with everything in me. With all the air in my lungs, every beat of my heart, every thought in my mind. It was an all-consuming love and I'd never stood a chance.

I'd never thought I could feel this way, that I'd be with someone that I could be so open with, talk to about anything, and have them understand completely when I had to keep some things from them. Someone who could be a partner not just in my hobbies, or my business, but a partner in every part of my life.

"Woohoo, this calls for a celebration!" Jess said, coming back in and totally ruining the moment. She was clinking champagne flutes together and carrying a bottle. "I had gotten this for us to say a final 'farewell' to this place, but I think this is *much* better!"

Jake and I laughed, each accepting a glass. Jess popped the cork and champagne fizzed out. She poured all three of us a glass and raised up her own. "To Jake and Alexis! Crime's new power couple!"

300

"Cheers," we said in unison. Jake wrapped his arm around me as we drank. I leaned into his hold, happier than I had ever been before.

"Alright, now it looks like you were packing. Think you could use some extra muscles?" Jake said with an easy grin, falling back into his cocky swagger.

"Yes!" Jess and I both exclaimed.

The three of us set to work, chatting and laughing while we packed up my office. The mood, and the prospect of the future, was considerably brighter, and the rest of the day flew by in a blink. Before I knew it, we had everything loaded into the trailer I had rented, and we were locking the doors for the last time.

***

I tore the tape off the roll and sealed up the last box in my apartment. Jake had arranged a sublet for his place and the stuff he kept had been boxed up and brought up to my place to be handled by the moving company once we got a place. My realtor already had my apartment listed for sale, and there were a handful of offers already, sight-unseen.

It had been both exhilarating and heartbreaking going through all our belongings and deciding which of mine along with those of Jake's would be going with us. Everything I had was carefully selected to make me feel at home, but it wouldn't just be my home anymore, it would be his too. We had kept a few pieces of furniture, but ultimately decided to pick out new stuff together once we found where we were going. I'd never had to share my space, and the idea was a little daunting.

FRAMED

But my excitement about this next chapter, or maybe the lingering oxytocin from our *many* packing breaks, had kept me going as we prepared to leave my home of the last five years.

Jake grabbed the box and headed for the door. I took one last look around to make sure I had everything I needed while we were on the road. Satisfied that I did, I turned and followed to the awaiting truck. No turning back.

Jake put the box in the small trailer hitched to the truck and locked the door up tight. He climbed into the driver's seat, then faced me with a grin.

"Where to?" I asked, returning the smile.

"Wherever you are, I'm all in, baby."

Epilogue

Ryan

You know how you have those things in your life that just don't sit right, things you can't let go no matter how hard you try to convince yourself to move on? When everyone around you is telling you that you're crazy, and to just forget about it? If not, then you're lucky. It might just be the most frustrating feeling in the world.

Pepper Collins might be a murderer, and may well be an art thief, but I just couldn't accept that she had pulled off all the robberies our town had experienced in the last few years. This case haunted my dreams, invaded my thoughts, and simply wouldn't let me go.

The evidence was all there; she had even confessed, to a certain degree. She hadn't detailed out that she had committed all those specific thefts, but she admitted she was guilty of framing Alexis, my former partner's new

FRAMED

girlfriend. She even had some justification for why she would want to set Alexis up, something about conflicts when they were younger.

I'd talked to Pepper at least ten times now, trying to nail down exactly what it was that bothered me about her confession. She generally refused to cooperate, but I'd picked up bits and pieces through our conversations. It was more what she didn't say that convinced me I'd finally nailed it. She seemed to have no idea *how* the robberies were done. She recognized all the stolen items, and knew when they were taken, but she didn't have the finer details. And that left me with possibly an even more daunting question. If Pepper hadn't stolen those pieces, who had?

Since Pepper had already been convicted, I had no resources to open the investigations back up. We didn't want to risk causing doubt and potentially put a murderer back on the street, especially since the killing appeared so tightly wound in with the last robbery.

I also couldn't deny that no prominent artworks had been stolen in the ten months since we had brought Pepper in. Based on the previous trends, there should have been at least two thefts by now. But it had been silent. At the very least, it seemed the perpetrator was off the streets—either arrested, deceased, or moved away.

In my spare time I looked deeper into anyone who had been brought in within six months of the last robbery. I checked obituaries for anyone who might have had the means or motive to pull it off, and I had my own crime board and files displayed in my apartment. Almost every waking hour I wasn't working was devoted to this. It was reaching the point of obsession.

304

There was one other possibility, nagging at the back of my mind. Alexis and Jake had left town shortly after we booked Pepper. Jake had resigned his position as the head detective, which took me by total surprise.

Jake was a rock-star; he closed almost every case he was given, seemed to know about things before they even happened, and had a charm that put everyone at ease. He was impressively adaptable to any situation, and his mind worked like no other cop I had partnered with. The future had been his to claim, and he probably could have become chief whenever our current one retired, which would probably be sometime in the next five years. He must have really been in love to have walked away from that.

I'd had dinner with the couple before they left. Alexis had said she didn't feel safe here anymore, that her reputation with her client base—the upper-class community in town—had been ruined between being stalked by Pepper and being under suspicion for the thefts. She didn't have much choice but to start over somewhere else, though they weren't sure yet where they would land.

I'd expected to have seen something come across about Jake when he applied to the police department in whatever town they settled in, but there had only been silence on that front as well. I was disappointed, Jake had been a mentor to me, and I valued that relationship, but apparently it hadn't been as meaningful to him.

But while Alexis's reasons made sense, I felt unsettled about the timing. I hadn't been able to find any record of Alexis setting up an office anywhere new, and none of the other psychiatrists in the area had heard from her in a few months either. She had been responsive to them initially as they reached out about clients she had transitioned, but silence since then. It was like both she and Jake had dropped off the face of the earth.

My phone rang, shaking me out of my daze. The caller ID showed it was the reception desk. "Detective Mason, there's someone here to see you."

"Who is it? Did they say what this is regarding?" I asked, confused. I didn't have any family in town and rarely got visitors, especially ones that didn't call first.

"She didn't say, but she's here from the FBI. I've validated her credentials," the secretary replied nervously.

The FBI? I couldn't imagine who would be coming to see me from the Bureau. I might have made a name for myself within the Willow Springs department, and I had gone on record as the lead investigator on the Pepper Collins case, bringing me a small amount of notoriety within the higher social circles, but nothing I could think of that would have gotten my name up to a federal level.

"Alright, can you please escort her up to my office?" I knew this agent would have clearance to see anything that I was working on, and I might need access to my files if her visit was regarding one of my current investigations.

A few minutes later, a woman stepped through my doorway and knocked. "Detective Mason? I'm Donna Hartley from the D.C. Art Crimes division of the FBI. We've been working on a case and think you might be able to help."

I stood up to welcome the agent. "Please, come in, Ms. Hartley. How can I be of service?"

306

ELLIE HOHENSTEIN

She walked across my office, pulling out a file as she approached, and passed it to me. "We've been stumped by a string of art thefts working their way down the coastline. I noticed that you recently closed a high-profile art theft and murder case, and wondered if you might have some insights. These robberies fit almost perfectly into the ones you closed: little evidence, no forced entry, high-dollar targets, and usually home invasions of one-percenters rather than museums or auction houses."

This was it. It was almost too good to be true. All the work I had done in the last few months might not be in vain after all, and this was a chance to get noticed by the Bureau. It could really jump-start my career!

I grinned at the agent and sat back down in my chair. "When do we start?"

About the Author

Ellie Hohenstein has just released *Framed,* her debut novel. She has been an avid reader since childhood and has always dreamed of finding time to pursue her passion for writing.

A North Carolina native, Ellie enjoys her "quiet" country lifestyle (as quiet as it can be with three kids and three dogs), spending summer weekends at the lake, and curling up each night with a nice book.

Visit www.EllieHohensteinBooks.com to keep up with the latest news and releases from Ellie!

Printed in the USA
CPSIA information can be obtained
at www.ICGtesting.com
LVHW051827301023
762209LV00036B/653/J